DUST

Children of the Republic: Book 1

Jason T. Hutt

This is a work of fiction. The characters, incidents, and dialogues are products of the author's imagination and are not to be construed as real. Any resemblance to actual events or persons, living or dead, is entirely coincidental.

Second Edition
Published by Hutt Publishing

ISBN: 0615593364
ISBN-13: 978-0615593364

For my father, who left my life far too soon.

Contents

ACKNOWLEDGMENTS

Thanks to my wife, Melinda, for supporting me throughout the writing of this novel and pushing me to pursue this goal. Thanks to Clint Balmain and Bill Frank for providing feedback on the initial drafts. Finally, thank you to Corey Davis for his dedication and attention to detail in developing the excellent cover art.

CHAPTER 1

Nick Papagous sat in the unlit home office of his father, looking through his father's files, when he heard a noise coming from the hallway. His head jerked up suddenly and he sat perfectly still for a moment, waiting for the door to fly open. The young man's gaze was drawn to a family portrait on the wall, illuminated by the light of two moons shining through the window. In that painting, he saw himself as he was ten years ago, smiling with his father's hand on his shoulder.

Nick grimaced and looked back at the computer screen built into the top of the desk. He tapped a folder labeled 'Progress Reports' and copied it to a small data crystal inserted in a notch on the desk. It was an archaic method of data storage, he knew. It had taken him several months to track down a working crystal, but he wanted the files stored somewhere safe, somewhere offline.

In an instant, the files were copied. Then, Nick selected his father's mail archives and made a copy of those. He shutdown the system and glanced at the curved face of the paper-thin computer he wore on his wrist. The taxi would be arriving in ten minutes.

He grabbed his bag and stood up. He could feel the pounding of his heart. After a moment, he crept out of the room. He looked back and forth down the hallway; no one was there. He stepped into his bedroom and took one last look around. Trophies and picture frames littered his desk; clothes were strewn around his room. He grabbed a shirt from the bottom of a pile of clothes at the foot of his bed.

He'd love to bring more, but nothing else would fit in his bag.

He closed the door to his room and silently made his way down the stairs. He looked out the front window just as the taxi descended onto the front lawn. He smiled nervously. He touched his thumb to the pad to the right of the door and it quickly slid open.

Nick had one foot through the entryway when his mother called out from the darkness behind him.

"Where will you go?" She asked softly, her arms folded across her chest. Nick could barely make out her silhouette in the shadows of the hallway.

"I don't know," he said.

"Your father won't be back for a few days. You could wait-"

Nick shook his head and said, "No, not this time. I have to go."

He heard her sniffle and he hesitated briefly.

"I love you, mom," he said, "But I can't live with him. Not anymore."

"Be careful."

Nick nodded and stepped through the door. It slid shut behind him and he hesitated to take the next step. He exhaled slowly and walked to the taxi. Within moments, he was away.

After three days, Nick was sitting at a table in a music-themed chain restaurant just off the main concourse of *Nexus Station,* one of eight city-sized space stations that served as hubs to the many worlds of the Republic. His mother would never have been caught dead in a place like this, he thought. Nick chewed the last rubbery bite of his bland steak when an alert popped up on his wrist computer.

Account Balance: $0.00

Nick gulped down the final bite of his meal. It seemed to lodge in his throat. Seconds later, another message popped-up.

I know.

As he read the short note from his father, the world beyond Nick seemed to fade; his hands began to sweat. The server robot rolled up to his table. Nick looked in its direction with wide eyes.

"Can I get you anything else?" The robot asked in a sweet, feminine voice.

Nick stammered, "I…uh…no. I don't need anything."

"Very good, sir."

Another alert popped up on his computer as the check for his meal was delivered by the server. Nick didn't know what to do. The silver robot waited next to his table. Nick brushed crumbs off of his steel-gray pants and pulled slightly at the collar of his shirt.

"Payment, please," the robot said.

"Uh…I'm sorry. I don't know how this happened," Nick whispered, "But I don't have any money right now."

In the blink of an eye, an appendage deployed from the chassis of the robot and hovered over the back of Nick's neck.

"Nicholas Papagous, you have twenty-four hours to remit payment," the robot said in a voice that seemed ten times louder than it needed to be, "If no payment is received in twenty-four hours, you will be fined one hundred dollars. At that point, you will not be allowed to leave *Nexus Station* until the fine and the amount owed has been paid."

The delinquency notice appeared on his wrist computer. Nick let out a heavy sigh as the robot abruptly turned and left. Nick's shoulders slumped as he stood shakily and smoothed some wrinkles in the sleeve of his red satin shirt. He avoided eye contact with any of the other patrons. His cheeks turned as red as his shirt as he quickly made his way to the exit.

When he was safely embedded in the throng of people that filled the concourse, Nick finally felt he was able to breathe again. He leaned against the wall of the corridor as others sped past him. He ignored the aggravated glares of those who had to step around him. Nick had to stop for a moment; he had no idea what to do next. He looked through the chaos around him for anything that might help.

Families were hurriedly rushing through the corridor trying to catch a passenger liner that was soon departing. Long separated relatives embraced and said tearful hellos while forlorn lovers embraced for a final time and shed tears of sorrow. A dog broke free from its leash and started sprinting through the flowing crowd. His owner set off after him at a breakneck pace. Black uniformed security guards kept watch over the entire scene.

Bright colored signs for dozens of businesses lined the corridor. Three dimensional holograms featuring highlights of the latest baseball game floated directly over the crowd. Monitors lined the far wall just above head height and showed a constant spool of the latest news broadcasts. Right above those, tote boards showed the latest arrival and departure statuses for hundreds of different flights and destinations.

A restaurant to his left was exuding a subtle odor of grilled steak and baked beans with bacon. Nick even thought he caught a whiff of apple and maybe cherry pie. A dessert bar across from him created the luscious smell of sweet chocolate with a hint of marshmallow.

Nick blinked heavily as tears threatened to spill from his eyes. He let himself get caught up in the flow of the crowd. He fretfully marched with the current of traffic until he came across a waiting area that was only partially full. Nick sat down heavily on a bench and rested his forehead in his hands.

He scrolled back through the recent messages on his wrist computer. He stopped at the one from his father.

I know.

The slight bulge of the data crystal in the pocket of his pants seemed as if it was growing in size every second. His father would be coming for him; he had no doubt of this. Nick pulled at his collar again; his forehead was covered in sweat.

Nick looked at the message on the screen again. This time his eye caught the tab for local notices. Nick tapped it with his finger and found the help wanted listings. Nick gritted his teeth. In order to get out of this, he was going to have to do something he had never done before.

Nick entered the sterile, nondescript interview room wearing his best wrinkle-free, white faux silk shirt and black pants. The man sitting on the other side of the gray table looked up at Nick with an intense glare. The man was short, stocky, and wearing a suit that must've been at least a hundred years old. Nick noted that the suit was pulling in all the wrong places.

"Kid, if this is some sort of joke," he said, "Just go ahead and turn around. I don't need you to waste my time."

Nick resisted the impulse to slump his shoulders and sigh. His left eye twitched slightly. He blinked to try and focus.

"I promise I'm not here to waste your time," Nick said, offering his hand. The older man hesitated a moment, but stood and shook Nick's hand firmly.

"Max Cabot," the old man said, "You must be Nick."

"That's me."

Max gestured to the seat across from him.

"Tell me, Nick," Max said after he had taken his seat, "Why does a twenty-year-old kid drop out of the University of Delle, where he's on an academic scholarship, in order to come to *Nexus Station* and apply for a job as a freighter co-pilot on the ass-end of space?"

Nick hesitated and said, "I decided it wasn't for me. I want to get out, see the galaxy. I figure before I settle down into my career I should have some fun."

Max frowned and looked Nick in the eye. Nick fidgeted in the seat, inspecting the cuffs of his shirt for any loose threads. Max scratched at the sides of his ill-fitting suit coat.

"Kid," Max said, "You don't sign on for six months on a freighter just to have some fun."

"I know, that's not what I meant. I need some real world experience. Things weren't going too well at U-D."

Nick found it difficult to maintain eye contact with Max; the older man's stare was penetrating.

Max exhaled loudly.

"Do you have any experience with spaceship maintenance?"

Nick shook his head and said, "No, but I was responsible for the boats on our crew team. And I've taken some basic circuits courses. I've also had a couple of programming courses."

"How about Astronavigation?"

"Uh, no."

"Do you have any prior work experience?"

Nick rested his head on his right hand and rubbed his temple. He could see this was going as well as the three previous interviews.

"No," he admitted, "I've never had a job. Never needed one."

"And you're from Valhalla?"

"Yes, that's right," Nick said, "But-"

"Well, Nick," Max said, "I think that will about do it. Thanks for spending the time with me today."

Max started to get up to shake Nick's hand, but Nick protested.

"Please, Mr. Cabot," Nick said, "Just give me a chance."

"I just don't think you'll be a good fit for this operation."

"Look, I know I don't have the right experience, but my mechanical aptitude scores are above average and my learner skills also test out high," Nick protested, trying to keep an even tone.

"And you have no practical experience and no relevant training," Max said, "Given your background, you're not going to be a good fit for living on Dust. The people there are, well, private. They're also a bit more free-spirited than where you're from. People from Valhalla generally aren't a good fit out there."

Nick sat back heavily in his chair, almost pitching it backwards.

"Wait," Nick said, "I just need a chance here. Look, the truth is my father and I have had a bit of a falling out. So, I'm trying to strike out on my own. Yes, I'm from Valhalla. I've already heard how we're regarded as straight-laced and narrow-minded, but I wouldn't be here if I didn't feel like I needed a change. It would have been easy for me to carve out a niche there, to be the person everyone wanted me to be, but that's not an option for me anymore.

"I'm not here to go on a mission for the Church or to get people to see the error of their ways. I'm just trying to live my life. The corner of the galaxy that I happen to be from looks very pretty from the outside, but there are a lot of warts under the surface. I need to get out of this place. So, if you're looking for someone who's willing to try hard and follow directions, then I'm your man. Otherwise, well, I appreciate that you gave me the time."

Nick cast his gaze down at the table, disappointed at letting his desperation show. Nick knew what came next. He knew that now Max would get up and extend his hand, thank him for the time, and send him on his way.

"Dust is pretty far off the beaten path, kid," Max said, "Six months can seem like forever in a place like that."

"The farther away from here the better."

"What's the matter, kid?" Max asked, "Did you get some girl pregnant without a permit?"

Nick was taken aback.

"I would never…"

"Relax, Nick," Max said, "It was just a joke. You know, my last three co-pilots were two drunks and a drug dealer. None of those worked out for me. I could stand to hire someone with a bit better moral compass."

Max extended his hand and said, "Welcome aboard, kid."

"Oh, thank God," Nick said. He gave Max a crooked smile and had to resist the urge to leap up and hug the elder man. Nick felt tension drain from his shoulders as he enthusiastically shook Max's hand.

"I don't have a whole lot of people banging down my door for this job," Max said, "You get one flight out and back to prove you can handle it. Otherwise, I'll drop you back here and we'll go our separate ways."

"Sounds good to me. You won't regret this," Nick said.

Max gave him a long, slow look. Nick braced himself for a change of heart. Max then looked down at his wrist computer, tapped a couple spots on the screen and extended his arm to Nick. Nick wasn't sure what to do.

"Put your thumb on the white spot," Max said, "It's your contract."

"Sorry," Nick said, hurriedly pressing his thumb to the thin screen wrapped around Max's wrist.

Max shook his head. "I must be getting soft. I'd like to get going as soon as we can. How soon can you be ready?"

"I need about an hour," Nick said.

"Very good. Meet me in docking bay twelve."

Nick nodded, eager to be out of here as well. For the last few hours, Nick had felt his father's grip tugging at him. With no money and slim prospects for a job, Nick was effectively trapped. He felt positively giddy now. He was about to escape his father's grip. The only problem was this wasn't a one-way ticket; he would be expected to come back.

I'll deal with that later, Nick thought. Nick got up to leave before he realized he needed one more thing from Max.

"So, any chance I could get a small advance?"

Nick entered the spacious, brightly lit docking bay thirty minutes later. He immediately saw Max waving to him from across the hangar. Nick returned the wave and stepped through the customs scanner. The scanner beeped and Nick saw his personal information appear on the monitor in front of the security guard.

Nick always felt the urge to itch the back of his neck in these situations. He knew he couldn't feel the chip that was implanted there, but it seemed to itch just the same. The security guard nodded for Nick to proceed.

Nick took a step away from the counter when another message arrived on his wrist computer.

I will find you. - Love, Father

The message made the hairs on the back of his neck stand on end. Nick couldn't help but look around, even though he knew there was no way his father would be there. The security guard gave him a funny look which Nick returned with a weak smile. The sooner he got out of here the better. Nick jogged over to Max who stood at the foot of the entry ramp of a bulky, rusted, dark purple-colored behemoth of a freighter.

"Welcome to the *Hannah*, kid," Max said, "She's my pride and joy."

Nick nodded politely and didn't say a thing.

"You're going to hurt my feelings," Max said dryly, wiping his hands on a rag.

"She's, uh, big," Nick said.

"The technical term is she's got a lot of cargo capacity," Max said, "But, yes, she's big. And old. And rusted. And a piece will fall off if I'm not paying attention."

"Maybe you should invest in something newer," Nick said.

"Are you trying to get fired on your first day?"

Nick shook his head. Max laughed and gestured towards Nick's travel bag.

"Is that all you've got?"

"Yep," Nick said, "Traveling light."

"Good," Max said, "Go on up the ramp and take a right. Your quarters are the first on the left."

"Great," Nick said, "What do you need me to do first?"

Max gave him a wry smile.

"You're not allowed to touch anything until you've read every manual I have on file, gone through all the maintenance training programs, and run as many launch and landing simulations as you can stomach. Until then, I don't even want you to set foot in the cockpit. I may have had a momentary lapse of reason in hiring you, but that doesn't mean I'm a complete fool.

"You'll do what I say, when I say. No exceptions. Got that?"

"Yes, sir," Nick said out of habit.

"Good, but drop the sir."

"Yes, Max," Nick said. Max gestured toward the ramp and Nick hurried into the ship, eager to get moving.

CHAPTER 2

Drool threatened to drip from the corner of Nick's mouth as he stared dazedly at the console in front of him. He wiped at the corner of his mouth with his shirt sleeve and groggily looked around his room. There wasn't much to look at. The room was empty save for his travel bag, a couple shirts lying about, and the small bunk opposite the console. He had spent the better part of the last three days seated in this spot, reading manuals, watching training videos, and running through landing and lift-off simulations.

Max was true to his word; Nick had not been allowed to set foot in the cockpit while he was going through all the training materials. The flight out to Dust had been incredibly boring, save for the brief moment of excitement when Nick's stomach nearly revolted after the wormhole jump. Beyond that, he had been seated at the desk studying.

Every now and then, Max or his maintenance robot, Reggie, would pass by and offer a word of encouragement. Once Max had stomped down the corridor, grumbling obscenities about a problem with the toilet. Other than that, the trip was uneventful.

Nick hadn't received any additional messages from his father since they made the jump into the Dust system. For that, Nick was relieved. He felt the data crystal in his pants' pocket. He still wasn't sure what to do with the information it contained. He wasn't even sure he could do any good with it. But his father wanted it back, that Nick knew for sure. His heart beat faster just thinking about that.

Nick was stirred from his reverie by a crackle of the intercom.

"Okay, kid," Max said, "We're approaching Dust. Time to see if you've learned anything."

Nick stood up and stretched. He massaged the sore muscles in his neck. He slipped on a billowy shirt and a pair of stylish, metal boots and headed for the cockpit, his palms sweating slightly. The boots clanged off the deck plating as he marched into the cockpit.

Max sat in the pilot's seat mindlessly chewing a toothpick, which had the faint tang of the recycled garbage it was made from, as he stared vacantly out the window. His arms were folded across his chest; his legs propped up on his console with his black boots resting perilously close to the thruster manual controls.

A million stars littered the view from the cockpit window. Just below the horizon was the reddish, tan planet of Dust. Nick couldn't help but be exhilarated by the view.

"Does that ever get old?" Nick asked.

Max smiled. "Do a couple hundred supply runs and tell me if they lose a little bit of their grandeur."

"No sense of romance for you then."

"Romance died a long time ago. Now, I just gotta pay the bills," Max said.

Nick shook his head and sat down in the co-pilot's seat. His boot banged loudly off the bottom of his console.

"Why the hell do you wear those things?" Max said.

"Because, boss, somebody on this crew has to have a sense of style," Nick responded, "We can't all be old and crotchety."

"You sound like a rusty, old robot lumbering down the hallway."

"You'll get used to it," Nick said.

Max sat up and slowly lowered his boots off the console.

"Welcome to Dust, the last colony humanity ever established. Last stop for warm showers and cold beers."

"I thought Petra was the last colony," Nick said.

"It was up until about six months ago. Colony collapsed due to some kind of outbreak," Max responded.

"Wow."

"Colony life's a hard lot, kid. Probably why the Republic has given up on establishing new ones," Max said, "That and they've lost whatever sense of courage they ever had. If it's not good for the bottom-line, it's not good for the Republic."

Nick shrugged off the comment; he had no desire to discuss politics at the moment. The sun crested the horizon and revealed a barren landscape below with two enormous beige continents and vast green bodies of water. Few clouds littered the sky. A mountain range appeared on the horizon followed by the greenish-blue of the planet's ocean. Nick stood there quietly, taking in every detail.

Max shook his head and said, "Nick, the only things you'll find out here are shattered dreams, shady pasts, and the occasional misguided wanderer, though they usually wise up real quick. So which one are you?"

"Ha," Nick said, "I'll go for misguided wanderer at the moment, though shattered dreams might not be far off, given my father and all that."

Max nodded knowingly. "Just what did your old man do?"

"Don't want to talk about it," Nick said with a shake of his head, "Just mentioning his name makes him feel closer."

Nick had to resist the urge to shiver. His father's last message was rattling around in his mind. He could hear his voice, bating and berating him. Nick needed something else to think about.

"Well, I should be glad you're not out here on some damn-fool adventure. I've seen kids your age out here with some stupid glint in their eye, with some sort of romantic fantasy about adventure in the far corners of the galaxy. There's no magic out here, Nick. Sure, there are a lot of pretty sights, but most of the time, all you're doing is grinding out a living.

"For me, the only journey is from one job to the next, paycheck to paycheck, earning a living, keeping to myself, and staying out of everyone else's way. The sooner you learn that, the better off you'll be."

"Not exactly a slogan for the Central Exploration Office," Nick said, staring idly at some flashing indicator lights on the console.

"It's called reality, kid," Max said with a shake of his head, "Now, let's focus on landing this crate."

"Right," Nick said, looking ahead at the shining star that illuminated the sand-covered planet below. Call him naïve all you want, but Nick refused to believe that this life had to rob you of your sense of wonder. He had seen more of the horrors of life than Max realized, but he didn't feel like going into that.

Max leaned forward again and tapped the console just below the green communications indicator.

"Medium Freighter *Hannah*, this is Dust Spaceport Control, do you copy?" A strong, male voice resonated throughout the cockpit.

"Dust Spaceport Control, this is the *Hannah*," Max replied, "I copy loud and clear. Two minutes until re-entry profile initiates. Please provide pad coordinates."

"Pad coordinates en route," the voice responded, "Please verify receipt."

Another indicator on the console turned blue and Max replied, "Coordinates received. See you on the ground, Control."

"See you on the ground, Max. Welcome back."

Nick listened with one ear as he continued to take in the majestic view.

"I thought the landing sequence was automated?" Nick said.

Max cracked a you-have-so-much-to-learn smile, "It is, kid. Some things are done more out of tradition than necessity. Besides, it gives me something to do."

Nick shook his head.

"Tradition is for those afraid of change, set in their ways."

"Oh, shut up," Max said.

The bulbous bulk of the *Hannah*, a modified Venali Medium-Class freighter, slowly positioned itself for re-entry through the firing of a dozen thrusters spread across its hull. The thruster firings were measured, precise, and completed efficiently at the direction of the massive ship's flight computer. Moments later, the two main thrusters fired and the ship lurched forward on its re-entry trajectory.

Within minutes, the massive ship, shaped like an engorged tick with an elongated head, began glowing from the friction of the atmosphere along the hull. A hair's width protective coating absorbed the heat, used the energy to charge the ship's batteries, and then shunted the excess energy. In the cockpit at the fore of the ship, Max had reassumed his reclined position with his feet propped on the console. His eyes were closed and his fingers laced behind his head, enjoying the ride.

Nick stared intently at the tendrils of flame that obscured the view out the forward windows. He felt beads of sweat sprout on his forehead and trickle down his face. A knot formed in the pit of his stomach and his mouth became parched. His knuckles were white as his fingers dug into the arms of his chair. He forcibly slowed his breathing. Nick blessed himself with the sign of the cross.

Max looked over at him and asked, "You going to be okay?"

"Yeah," Nick said, the word slurred slightly due to the dryness of his mouth, "Just not quite used to this."

"This technology's tried and true, kid," Max said, "Nothing to worry about. Haven't done much space travel, have you?"

Nick shook his head. "My parents got me a couple of suborbital joyrides on Valhalla when I turned 18. Other than that, my first trip on a spaceship was the one out to *Nexus*."

Max shook his head and gave Nick a wry smile. "Remind me why I hired you again?"

"Desperation," Nick said with a sigh, unable to take his eyes off the forward window, "Few people share my sense of adventure or willingness to get in over their heads."

"Right," Max said, "It certainly wasn't for your humility."

The giant, ungainly ship was now gliding through the atmosphere, streaking towards its destination. Max sat up and did a quick scan of the data on his console.

"Everything looks good," Max said, "We're about a minute out."

Nick watched as a giant, ten-petal, gray flower bloomed out of the desert floor. Each petal was a landing pad roughly two-hundred meters in diameter. In the center, a giant sphere covered with an array of satellite dishes rose fifty meters or so above the pads. As they drew closer, Nick could make out giant spikes lining each pad like elongated teeth. The spikes made each pad look like a giant Venus fly trap, just waiting for an unsuspecting ship to land.

"What are those?" Nick asked.

"Lightning towers," Max finally answered, "You'll see them around the settlement. This place gets some nasty electrical storms, local byproduct of the terraforming process."

"Is that normal?"

"Don't know. I just chalk it up to being another part of the local charm of Dust," Max said with a sardonic smile.

Nick surveyed the barren landscape surrounding the spaceport. He could make out a couple of rectangular shapes sticking out from the sandy surface, but nothing else. There were no skyscrapers or factories or even neighborhoods, just miles and miles of sand.

"Well, where's the rest of the colony?" Nick asked.

"This isn't a bustling metropolis, kid. Most of the colony is below the surface. Was the easiest way to protect everything from the sandstorms."

The ship slowly settled in over its assigned pad and hovered. Within moments, it began a slow descent. A quick scan of the area showed that there were only a few other ships on the landing pads.

"This place is a ghost town," Nick commented.

Max couldn't contain a laugh. "This is about as far out on the fringe of humanity as you can get. When the Marshall Conglomerate decided there was no money to be made here and the Republic decided that exploration and colonization were no longer sound uses of taxpayer money, this place withered. Like I said, only reason to come out here is if you're running, hiding, or are up to no good. Dust has plenty of the former and the locals don't really tolerate the latter. Sorry to disappoint, kid."

Nick scowled. The 'kid' moniker was getting old and they'd only been travelling together for four days. He quickly put his annoyance aside, letting it show would just give Max an excuse to dig into him a little more.

He leaned forward on his elbows to watch the freighter descend to the pad. Two pads over, he spotted an old Patton-class military transport. Judging by the amount of rust on the roughly trapezoidal craft, he would be surprised if it could get off the pad let alone reach orbit. Directly across from them was a saucer-shaped light freighter with a bubble cockpit of a make and model that he couldn't quite remember. The saucer looked half as old as the rusted Patton, which probably put it at about a hundred years old.

Finally, right next to the saucer sat a conglomeration of rusted, dented, and ill-fitted parts that looked like it was built from scrap scavenged from a junk yard. Nick didn't bother trying to figure out what it was; it probably had fewer than ten percent of its original components. So much for shiny cruisers on the cutting edge, he thought; though he kept the remark to himself to avoid another round of advice for the 'kid.'

They were about thirty meters above the pad when the clunk of the landing struts lowering echoed throughout the cockpit. Then, with ten meters to go, a red indicator light appeared on the console and the descent stopped.

Max grumbled, "Ah, looks like the hydraulics on strut twelve just went out."

"So, now what? Can Reggie fix that?" Nick asked, feeling a little nervous.

"Normally, he could fix it with his optics closed," Max said, "But the environment on Dust isn't too agreeable with his systems. Still, we'll need his help."

Max touched another spot on the console. "Reggie, meet us at strut twelve and bring the hydraulics bag. Come on, kid, we've got work to do. Can't float above the pad all day."

Just as Max stood, the voice of spaceport control crackled over the speaker, "*Hannah*, we see your descent has stopped. Please advise as to your situation."

Max grimaced and opened the channel to control. "Control, no big deal, just have some balky hydraulics on a landing strut. We should have it taken care of in a few minutes."

"Copy, *Hannah*, let us know if you need any help."

Max didn't bother to reply. He gestured for Nick to follow as he left the cockpit. The two men quickly walked down the long corridor that ran the circumference of the cargo hold. Along the way, Max stopped at an equipment locker and retrieved some goggles and a filtration mask.

"What're those for?" Nick asked.

Max gave him a crooked smile. "You'll see."

A minute later, they turned right into a relatively cramped access corridor that stank of ages old grease, mildew, and rust. They arrived in a cramped two-meter square compartment the center of which was occupied by a half-meter rectangular shaft. Right next to it a matte gray, four-foot tall humanoid robot squatted next to an access panel.

"Watch your ears," Reggie called out in his deep, smooth baritone. Seconds later, Nick's ears popped. An indicator light on the shaft flashed green as the pressure between the outside air and the ship equalized. Reggie set to work opening the panel.

"Hold up, Reggie," Max said, "Get back, I don't need you getting sand in your gears."

Reggie obediently complied and handed a powerwrench to Max. A minute later, Max had the panel removed and the roar of the rushing wind outside filled the small compartment. With the noise came a mini-sandstorm of dust particles. Max drew his shirt up over his mouth and held the filtration mask out to Nick.

"What am I supposed to do with this?" Nick asked.

"You're going to need it to lower the strut," Max replied, "Trust me."

"You have got to be kidding," Nick said.

"Nope," Max said and although he wasn't kidding, Nick could clearly tell he was smiling behind his pulled up shirt.

Nick sighed and said, "Let's get this over with."

"You'll need these, too," Max said as he handed over the goggles, "There's just enough room in there to straddle the strut. There are footholds around the edge about two feet down below this floor. Work your way around clockwise and you'll see the manual override socket. Just insert the powerdriver and drive until the hard stop."

Nick's eyes glazed at the instructions; all he could really do was look at the ground far below them. His palms started to sweat at the thought of stepping out onto the footholds. His mouth went dry. Max grabbed him by the shoulder and thrust his wrist computer into Nick's face. The screen showed an image of the strut and its housing. Max tapped the picture of the housing and it rotated to show the opposite face. Max tapped the image again and it zoomed in on the manual override socket.

"See it?" Max asked, shouting above the din of the rushing wind.

Nick nodded and tapped the screen on his own wrist computer. The same image popped up on his screen. Nick took a look back into the open space and gulped. His voice cracked slightly as he spoke, "Are you sure Reggie can't do this?"

"Can't leave everything to the robots, kid," Max joked, "Or else someday they'll rise up and kill us all."

"Very funny," Nick said, reluctantly taking the powerdriver from Max.

"Don't worry kid, it's only ten meters. If you fall, the worst you'll do is break an ankle."

Nick nodded numbly and seated himself on the walkway with his feet dangling over the opening. He could feel sweat break out on the arches of his feet. Then with grim determination, he forced himself into the compartment. The wind howled and swirling sand scraped across the goggles.

Max watched as Nick nervously worked his way around the strut. Nick tentatively reached out with his left leg, extending it toward one of the footholds. His foot slipped slightly and his face paled. He looked up at Max, whose expression had gone from playful to concerned.

"Sir," Reggie said, "I would be more than happy to retrieve a tether."

"What was that?" Nick yelled.

"Hold on, Nick," Max said, "Reggie, get that tether."

Reggie, Marshall Conglomerate Automaton serial number RGE-874, tromped off down the hallway and returned with a four-foot long, black tether. Max clipped one end to an anchor point on the floor and handed the other end to Nick.

"Clip this to your belt," Max shouted above the roar of the wind.

Nick nodded in reply and attached the clip with shaky hands. While the tether made him feel safer, he still moved cautiously. After a few minutes of trying to find a comfortable position in the cramped space, with his heart racing and sweat pouring down his face, Nick found the socket. He inserted the powerdriver and within thirty seconds, he felt the drive hit the hard stop.

Nick scrambled to the open panel and held out his hand. Max pulled him up with a jerk and deftly unclipped the tether from the floor. Reggie overpressurized the compartment to keep any more sand from flowing in and replaced the panel.

Nick sat with his back to the compartment wall and tore off the goggles and mask.

"I hate this ship already," he said weakly.

"That's the spirit, kid," Max said, smiling, "You're already coming around."

Half an hour later, after Max completed post flight checks and asked Reggie to check into a cockpit fan that had picked up a slight rattle, Nick found himself in the drab Windy City customs office. An old woman with short, silver hair greeted them with a kind smile.

"Good to see you again, Max," she said kindly.

Max nodded in return. "You too, Sylvia."

"Who's the new guy?" She asked, turning her attention to Nick.

"My new co-pilot," Max said, "Sylvia, this is Nick Papagous. Go ahead; tell her where you're from."

"Valhalla," Nick said, nodding politely at the older woman. She smiled at him and approached with a black baton in her right hand. She was shorter than Nick by a good foot or so.

"Valhalla?" Sylvia said with a skeptical look on her face. "I hope this isn't a missionary trip, hon, or you'll get driven off this rock faster than you can say the Lord 's Prayer."

"It's not," Nick responded, "I promise."

She eyed him cautiously for another moment. It was plain to Nick that she was trying to assess how honest he was being. After a long moment sizing him up, she shrugged and went about her business.

"You're a tall one," she said, grabbing him gently by the right elbow, "Mind leaning forward a bit so I can scan your chip?"

Nick gave her a puzzled look.

"There's no full body scanners here, kid," she said, "I'm going to need to scan your bio chip with this."

Nick was slightly surprised; he had never been through this before. He leaned forward and Sylvia passed the black baton emblazoned with the Marshall Conglomerate logo over the back of his neck. The baton beeped and a moment later an image of Nick along with his official Republic record popped up on her wrist computer. Nick could see his marital status, his child permit status, his criminal record, his immunization status, and the rest of his vital statistics listed on the display.

"Single, huh?" Sylvia said with a raised eyebrow, "Well, I hope you haven't come to Dust looking for love. I can count the number of single women here on one hand, myself included."

Nick blushed a bit and laughed. "Not really at the top of my to-do list."

Sylvia looked over Nick's scrawny, lanky frame and smiled at him warmly.

"You're a little young to be out this way, aren't you?"

Nick tried to hide his agitation. "Just trying to step out on my own a bit. Spent most of my life on Valhalla. Thought I'd try to broaden my horizons."

"Oh, son, you couldn't have picked a worse place," Sylvia said.

"So I've been told," Nick responded, nodding at Max.

Max couldn't help but smile. Sylvia gave Nick a sympathetic pat on the shoulder. She then scanned Max's chip. She glanced at something on her wrist computer, putting her arm as far away from her as she could in order to read the information.

"Max, go ahead and file your forms. It'll be a few days before I get clearance to release your cargo. The return path on our data link is down again."

"Again?" Max said, "Think the Republic just needs to replace that relay. Should get the Governor on that."

Sylvia shot Max a look that suggested he was delusional.

"If you can get that lazy slob off of his fat ass, you are more than welcome to push that idea through, sweetheart," Sylvia said.

Max laughed and headed towards an enclosed booth at the end of the room.

"What's that mean?" Nick asked. He suspected he knew the answer, but he wanted to be sure.

"No communications from *Nexus*, for one," Max said.

"No communications from anyone," Sylvia added, "We can send stuff out, but we can't receive anything.

Nick suppressed a smile. Let's see my father find me out here, he thought. This was better than he could possibly have hoped. He had effectively stepped off the map, well beyond his father's reach. Now he just needed to convince Max to let him stay.

"Nick, welcome to Dust," Sylvia said as she gave him a pat on the back, "Don't let Max be too hard on you."

Nick nodded thanks and followed Max into the booth. It was a slightly cramped space with a computer desk and an interactive map on the wall. Max had transferred the appropriate manifest forms from his wrist computer to the customs computer built into the smooth, glass-topped desk.

Nick ignored Max's bureaucratic filings as he studied the map of Dust on the wall. There wasn't much to look at. They had landed in Windy City, the de facto Capitol of the colony. There were only two other settlements on the map, Fracture, a mining town to the west, and Bloom, a farming community that lay just to the North nestled at the foot of the large mountain range that dominated the upper half of the continent. One other marker on the map caught Nick's attention, a quarantine zone on the northeast tip of the continent.

"What happened up there?" Nick asked, tapping on the screen. Nick was disappointed when no additional information appeared.

Max looked up from his forms. "Where?"

Nick tapped the quarantine marker on the map again.

"Freighter accident," Max said, turning his attention back to the screen embedded in the desktop, "Story is it was carrying a load of supplies in, misjudged some winds and piled into the cliffs in that area. Reactor core was exposed and contaminated the area for the next thousand years."

Nick nodded and said, "Surprised they couldn't clean that up quicker."

"The Republic released some kind of microbe that was supposed to clean it up," Max responded, "Didn't work though. Something native to the soil killed off the microbe. At that point, they decided it wasn't worth the money to clean it up."

"That's lousy," Nick said.

"Like I said, if it's bad for the bottom-line, it's bad for the Conglomerate. If it's bad for the Conglomerate, it's bad for the Republic," Max said matter-of-factly. He finished the form and pressed his thumb to the glass to sign the document.

"Let's get out of here," Max said, "With the link down, it'll take Sylvia a couple days to verify the manifest with *Nexus*. Until that happens, we sit tight."

"Great," Nick said, "So what do we do until then?"

"I don't know about you, kid," Max said, "But I'm ready for a cold one."

Nick said, "Look can you stop calling me kid? I really don't feel like having everyone here call me that."

Max hesitated a moment.

"Fair enough, ki…er, Nick. Bet you a beer you'll hear it from everyone else you meet on this trip anyway."

"You're on," Nick said, "And thank you. I'm sorry, it's just been a long day."

"Ha," Max said, "Gotta earn your stripes, Nick. This day's just getting started."

Max led them to a lift and waved goodbye to Sylvia who had sat back down at her desk and started watching something that was just out of their view. She waved back and gave them a nice smile as they got in the lift.

"Subway," Max commanded the lift.

"I thought you said everyone here was running or hiding," Nick said as the doors closed.

"I did," Max said.

"That old woman isn't running from anything," Nick said, "And I don't think she's got too much to hide."

"Not everyone's running from a crime, Nick," Max said, "Sylvia? She's outlived her husband and her son. She's running from bad memories; came here for a clean start."

Nick listened and nodded.

"So what are you running from?" Nick asked.

"Me? I'm too old to run," Max said dryly, "Makes my knees hurt."

The lift reached its destination and the doors opened. The subway station was all but empty. The only other presence was the robot attendant, who unlike most other humanoid models, consisted only of a large optical scanner and speaker on the left wall. The station itself could not have been more than ten meters square with a single car. In that car, which was roughly double the size of the *Hannah's* cockpit, there were no more than ten seats.

"Is this it?" Nick asked.

"Yep, it's a far cry from Valhalla," Max said, stepping up to the scanner and pressing his thumb on its face. A moment later, the robot beeped.

"Welcome back, Captain Maxime Cabot," the synthesized voice said, "Enjoy your stay."

Nick stepped forward and did the same. This time, Nick noticed a hint of excitement in the robot's voice.

"Welcome, first time visitor Nicholas Papagous! If you have any questions, please stop by the Visitors Bureau located in the lobby of the Drifter Hotel. The hotel is the second stop on the subway. Also, be sure to drop by the Dust Museum of History located in the basement of the Governor's Hall, the next to last stop on the route. Enjoy your stay!"

"Well isn't that nice," Max said, "Come on, I'm thirsty."

Nick boarded the car and looked at the destination list; there were only six possible stops. He looked at the open seat, which one day long ago may have been a cream color but was now mildew-tinged and rust brown, and decided to stand. Max didn't hesitate to sit.

"Dry Dock," Max commanded and the doors closed. Seconds later, they were off with a lurch and a loud squeal.

"Lovely," Nick said.

"At least it works," Max said.

"Right."

Max laughed. He seemed to be getting a lot of enjoyment out of Nick's discomfort.

"This place, this Dust, can get under your skin real quick. The grit and grime will get under your fingernails, turn them black. You'll cut and scrub, but you won't get them clean. It'll get in your teeth, grinding with every bite you chew. Hell, even the beer will feel like it comes with a cup of silt in every bottle. But, you'll adapt. Get to the point where you don't even notice; where a smooth glass of water just doesn't feel right. You'll do all right, Nick. You showed that today when you lowered the strut."

Nick nodded somewhat absently, not sure if he really believed Max. This was a far cry from the clear blue skies of home. For the first time since he left, he felt homesick.

"Ever been away from home for this long, Nick?" Max asked.

Nick shook his head. "I went to a month long summer camp once, but that was on Valhalla, and I put in a call to my parents every night."

"I could've guessed," Max said.

"That obvious?"

"I'd venture to say you're not much of a poker player," Max said, "Going to have to toughen up out here. Else this place'll chew you up pretty quick."

At that moment, the subway car came to a slightly stilted stop and the doors whooshed open. Nick followed Max into the station, this one just as small, cramped, dirty, and empty as the departure station. Max took his old, beat-up, gray backpack off his shoulder and pulled out goggles and a mask. Nick gave him a quizzical look.

"Time to go for a walk outside, Nick," Max said, gesturing to a set of stairs to their right, "Never go outside on Dust without your goggles and mask, lest you want a scratched cornea or two and a mouthful of sand. That swirling sand you experienced while working on the strut just gets worse the closer you get to the surface."

"Great," Nick replied. He felt tempted to get back on the subway car and return to the *Hannah*. After a moment's hesitation, Nick donned his goggles and mask and then gave Max a thumbs-up that he was ready. At the bottom of the stairway, Nick noticed a few scattered grains of sand on the steps. By the time they reached the top, there was easily a half inch layer of sand on everything except for the large metal doors that led to the outside. To Nick's surprise, the doors were not automated.

Max hit the switch that retracted a heavy latch, the door then swung toward them. A foot closer to it and Nick would have been knocked down the stairs. Blinding light from the outside filled the dimly lit hallway. The whistling wind drowned out any other sounds. Max put a gloved hand in front of his face and stepped outside. Nick hesitated, watching as the sand swirled around Max.

He had heard of sandstorms, but had never seen one. The sand rotated around Max, seemingly hitting him from all sides. Max gestured for Nick to follow and tried to yell above the wind.

"Don't just stand there! Let's go!"

Nick nodded and hurriedly stepped outside. Grains of sand immediately pelted his skin. He felt the sting of thousands of little needles digging into his cheeks. He made a mental note to bring a scarf next time. No wonder Max wore a beard. Once Nick stepped through the door, Max pulled it closed with a grunt. The thud of the latch closing automatically on the inside of the door could barely be heard above the swirling winds.

Max pointed to the left and trudged on without a word. Nick fell into step behind him, his cheeks and forehead already red with windburn. Nick had never experienced anything close to this. His home, Valhalla, had a perfectly regulated climate. It rained as needed, the temperatures were mild, and no one was ever surprised by the weather. This was crazy. Nick no longer wondered why he didn't see more people at the subway station. No one in their right mind would live in these conditions voluntarily.

After a minute of plodding along, a noise pierced the droning howl of the wind and sand. It took a moment for Nick to register the sound. It wasn't until Max turned around and clutched his arm in an overly firm grasp that he realized he was listening to the wail of a siren. Max put his mouth right next to Nick's ears.

"Storm siren! We have to move!"

Nick nodded his understanding. On cue, the wind reached an almost unbelievable pitch and a wall of sand smacked into him. Nick staggered back a step. Even though he knew Max could not be more than three feet from him, Nick could no longer see him.

Nick panicked.

His first thought was to run, but his second thought was that he didn't know where to go. His feet locked in place. He could no longer see the doors to the subway station. In fact, he couldn't see anywhere to go. After several long moments, he felt Max forcefully grab his wrist and he was dragged along. The sirens continued to wail and the wind grew in strength.

Max pushed Nick against another hard metal door. He could barely see Max throw it open. This time, Nick jumped through the door with no hesitation. He took a lunging step through and slipped on some loose sand. He fell to his knees in an ungraceful heap as he heard the clunk of the door closing. The roar of the wind faded to a whisper and sand gently settled to the ground around him.

Nick ripped off his mask and yelled, "Oh, thank God."

In response, he heard a roar of laughter.

"Little rough out there for you, son," said an old man seated just to the right of the door. Blood immediately rushed to Nick's face. He felt frustration well up inside of him, frustration with being embarrassed, with being overwhelmed by the elements, and most of all, frustration with not being his best.

While still on his knees, he looked down at the floor and composed himself, breathing slowly in and out. The blood drained from his face. He looked up to Max's outstretched hand, offering to help him up. Max's expression was sympathetic.

"No shame, Nick," Max said in a low tone, "Everyone here gets rattled every once in a while by the weather, especially when you're not used to it."

Nick nodded, but brushed away the hand. "Thanks, but I'm all right."

Max shrugged and walked into the dimly lit bar beyond them. "Fine then, let's have a beer."

Nick stood, somewhat shakily at first, and followed Max to the bar. He looked around at the dark, rundown establishment. The entire room and all the furniture with the exception of the bar was a dull gray. Sand covered the first ten feet of floor, then it turned a dull black with light reflecting off long dried stains of Nick didn't know what.

The bar stools were a mismatched set of old spaceship seats. The bar itself seemed to be scavenged from a variety of spaceship parts complete with what looked like the control panel from Max's ship. There wasn't much of a crowd either with easily less than fifteen people in the room. Nick wondered if this was normal or not for this time of day.

He sidled up to Max and took a seat in an old bucket seat that, judging by the scuff marks and unidentifiable stains, must've been scavenged from a hundred-year-old passenger liner. Nick and Max had the bar to themselves with everyone else seated in the darker corners of the room.

A woman stepped from behind a thin red curtain at the other end of the bar and approached them. She was about as old as Max and probably had the plainest looks of any woman Nick had ever met. She had long brown hair, streaked with gray. She wore no makeup and her complexion was pale. Nick shook his head incredulously.

"What's with you, kid?" The bartender asked in a warm, soft tone the belied her looks.

"Thanks, Myra," Max said, "You just won me a beer."

Nick sighed.

"You can explain that in a minute, Max, but your little travel companion hasn't answered my question."

Nick almost flushed again and said, "I'm sorry, ma'am. It's just been a long time since I've seen a place with a flesh and blood bartender, manual doors, and not a server 'bot in sight. I feel like I've gone back in time. Either that or I'm in some kind of museum."

Myra shook her head at him. "Did you happen to notice all the sand outside, boy? If you can supply a gear or a joint that won't get jammed up within a couple hours, you can make a lot of money around here. But, I wouldn't start thinking of us all as primitive hicks. Do that and you're liable to get yourself knocked on your ass a few times before you leave."

"Words to live by," Max said somewhat smugly.

Nick caught a few more distant chuckles from eavesdroppers around the room. Three men got up from their table across the bar from Nick and Max and started to slowly walk toward them. They looked from Nick to Max intensely before returning their hardened gaze back to Nick. Each of the men had the same grizzled, worn features as Max and, in Nick's estimation, outfits that came right from the pages of Freighter Pilot Weekly. What they lacked in style, they made up for with tattered, ripped, and poorly patched clothing. The three men were a sartorial nightmare, though Nick suspected they weren't coming to him for fashion advice.

Nick averted his gaze as the men continued to get closer. He took a sip of his beer and tried to stare a hole through the bottom of the mug. Nick braced himself, ready to defend himself by any means possible. He tried to remember if the stool was bolted to the floor. He tried to move it subtly, but it didn't budge. His heart raced. He tried to look around without moving his head, but saw nothing within reach that he could possibly use to defend himself.

The largest of the men, a big, black man with close-cropped gray hair, put his large booted foot on the stool next to Nick, clenched his fist, and pounded it on the bar. Nick flinched involuntarily. Then Max started laughing.

"Oh, would you guys leave the poor kid alone," Myra called out, "He's half ready to go running out into the storm."

The big man's face broke into a wide, beaming grin and Max let out another round of laughter.

"The name's Charlie Locker," the man said with an outstretched hand. Nick hesitated a moment before extending his hand in return.

"Damn, Charlie," Max said, taking a sip of his beer, "I think you're going to have to buy him a new pair of pants."

Everyone laughed at that; even Nick cracked a smile. Max received pats on the back from all three men as they settled onto stools around them and they all raised their drinks in salute.

"Good to see you again, Max," said Roman Dupree, the oldest and smallest of the three.

"Likewise, Roman," Max said, "Don't think I've seen you on this route in a while."

Roman nodded and scratched at the gray stubble on his chin. "Yeah, it's been about two years, hasn't it?"

Max nodded. "Lost the Medcorp contract?"

"They closed up shop two months ago."

"Lousy bastards didn't even have the courtesy to give him a goodbye kiss," Charlie said.

"At least I didn't get fired by the Conglomerate for gross incompetence," Roman said derisively.

The smile disappeared from Charlie's face.

"Don't bring that crap up, man. They screwed me royally. There's no damn way those food containers got contaminated in my hold."

The other men laughed and the stories rolled on for another hour, maybe two. Nick lost track of time, withdrew from the conversation, and wondered what he was doing. At that moment, he would've given a lot for the cool ocean breeze that blew in from the shore at his parent's beach house on Valhalla. He could envision the sound of the surf pounding the shore, the smell of the salty air, and the cool breeze that would pass through the open windows.

It had been a long time since he enjoyed that house, probably a year since he had last been back there. The last time he had been there was right before he had first stumbled onto his father's files, before he learned what the man he grew up idolizing really did on a day-to-day basis, before he had begun to hate.

"You're being awfully quiet, kid," said Zanth, the oldest of Max's three friends, "What's your story? What the hell are you doing with this crotchety, old bastard?"

Nick hesitated a moment, slow to come out of his reverie. Admitting to Max that he was having family troubles was one thing; admitting it to these guys wasn't something he was ready to do.

"Just looking to cut out on my own a bit. Thought the frontier would be a great place to go."

"Oh, cut the bullshit, kid," Roman said, "This is no frontier. Frontier means there's something to explore. This is more like a dead end street. The frontier closed up shop fifty years ago. Hell, Central Exploration doesn't even maintain a field office out here anymore and the Republic, well, they stopped funding exploration missions when you were in diapers."

"Maybe you guys are just too jaded to see it anymore," Nick said with a smile that he hoped appeared genuine.

Charlie looked at him skeptically and said, "You're full of crap."

Nick didn't respond. He sipped his drink with as neutral an expression as possible.

CHAPTER 3

Nick woke up with what felt like a mouthful of cotton and sand. His mouth was dry but little granules of sand had wedged in his cheeks, tearing into the soft tissue every time he moved his jaw. He stumbled into the small, dimly lit bathroom and rinsed his mouth with a small cup of water.

He looked around the repurposed storage container that he called his hotel room and decided that on Valhalla no place that looked like this would deign to charge you to stay there. Rust streaked the metal walls. One light in the bedroom constantly flickered. The air smelled stale and musty. Better get used to it, he thought.

Nick looked at himself in the mirror. He had what passed for scruff coming in under his chin and parts of his cheeks. The skin around his eyes was puffy; he hadn't slept well on the *Hannah* or in his first night in this room. His formerly rich, golden tan, earned from spending many days in the perfect climate of Valhalla, was starting to pale.

He plopped back down on the slab he called his bed and dug the vial of Vigor pills out of his backpack. He stared at the bottle briefly, running his thumb over the Marshall Conglomerate logo. He momentarily thought of not taking the pills, but decided now was not the time for a moral stand. He took two and within minutes started to feel revitalized.

Nick pulled a loose fitting, synthetic cotton shirt out of his bag and slipped into it. The cut of the shirt was loose; the fabric was cool. At home, he would've blended into the crowd. Here, he knew he'd look like a star among men. Nick didn't care and grabbed his faux leather pants and metal boots. Finally, he slipped the sleeve of the wrist computer over his right forearm. Within seconds, the screen conformed to the shape of his forearm.

Nick then clomped his way down to what passed for the hotel's restaurant. It reminded Nick of his middle school cafeteria. He took a seat at an open table that would allow him to see the news broadcast being projected on the back wall. He tapped the control on his table and turned the volume up to a low level. The news report was at least a month old. Might be too soon to catch the report out here, Nick thought. It was odd to think that he had probably seen this broadcast already, before he had decided to slip away from home in the middle of the night.

The brown-haired, soft-featured female anchor of the Central News Agency was speaking.

"Food riots erupted today on Canis One," she said stoically, "Twenty people were injured in clashes with Republic security forces."

Nick knew this story. He had seen the report before, just a week before he left. It had sparked a debate with his father on why in this day and age people were still scavenging for food.

"That's why population control laws are in place," his father had said.

"But we should be able to synthesize food for any who need it."

"Food is available for those who want to earn it," Henry Papagous responded.

Their conversation devolved from there. His father's point-of-view rankled the moral backbone that had been instilled in Nick since he was a little boy. The Church said you should help those in need, not bleed them dry. Nick had taken that lesson to heart and he could tell that it displeased his father to no end. The Vice President of Research and Development for the Marshall Conglomerate did not give anything away for free; he sold it to whoever could pay the most.

Nick tuned out the memory and concentrated on the breakfast menu projected on the tabletop. He didn't recognize most of the choices. After a few minutes of searching, he gave up and selected something that sounded like a mushroom omelet.

Max slid into the seat opposite him, sipping from a cup of hot coffee. The older man glanced at Nick's outfit and chuckled.

"You look like you just stepped off the runway," Max remarked.

"Good," Nick responded, "This place could use someone to instill a little bit of fashion sense."

"What good's a fancy shirt and shiny pants if the sand outside will tear it to pieces within seconds," Max responded as he scrolled through the menu choices.

"See that's where you're wrong, this stuff is practically indestructible. It's made out of the same fibers that line Republic Security uniforms. I bet it could hold up to a little rough weather."

"Well, you'll have to tell me how comfortable it is when sand gets in between the tight legs of your pants and your skin or when your boots fill up with sand," Max selected something, then looked at the screens on the wall.

The image now showed a recording of the clash between a crowd of angry rioters and the line of Republic Security forces. The rioters had symbolically armed themselves with empty dinner plates of a variety of shapes and sizes. The plates didn't do much good against the stun batons and riot guns the security officers were using.

"Damn fools," Max commented.

"Why's that?" Nick asked, tearing his eyes away from the screen to look at Max. Max had trimmed his graying beard slightly. Nick could see lines etched into Max's forehead that became more pronounced as he talked. He looked weathered and tired.

"It's a fool's errand," Max responded, "What good does it do those poor folks? The Republic will squash them like the little bugs they are."

"Don't believe in sticking up for your rights, letting the government know when they've overstepped?" Nick responded as their food arrived, hand delivered by an old man with a crooked back and an ancient wheeled cart. Whatever was on Nick's plate, it was not a mushroom omelet. In fact, Nick was pretty sure there were no eggs in it at all. After what he was witnessing on the news though, he felt he needed to be grateful for whatever was on the plate in front of him.

"Just a realist, Nick," Max said, "They'd all be better off channeling that effort into finding a better niche for themselves."

Nick frowned; Max's words reminded him of something his father would say. He cast a downward glance and wondered if that's what Max really believed. Nick didn't. After all, that's why he was here. Nick started idly pushing the food around his plate. Eventually, he took a tentative bite and was surprised at how delicious the food was.

"Wow," said Nick, quickly taking a second bite, "This stuff is great."

Max smiled.

"I would have never guessed," Nick said as he shoveled the food into his mouth.

"See, we're not all savages here. Lot better than military-grade nutritional paste, isn't it?" Max asked with a knowing smile, "You could use a little meat on your frame, Nick. I thought that storm yesterday was going to blow you away."

"Very funny," Nick said.

Within minutes, Nick had cleaned his plate.

"That was tremendous," he said, "I still can't believe it. Where do they get this stuff?"

"Chef's secret, I'm sure," Max said.

Nick pressed his thumb to the tabletop to pay and briefly considered ordering another plate. He looked at the time on his wrist computer.

"What's the plan for today?" He asked.

"I'm going to check the job listings and see if there're any suborbital jobs that need to be done. Fracture usually needs something hauled its way."

"Is there a Chapel around here?" Nick asked.

"Second sub-basement in the Governor's hall," Max responded, "Though they may have converted it to storage after years of neglect."

Nick ignored the comment. "I'd like to go by there quickly, if that's okay."

"Sure," Max responded, "Meet me at the ship in an hour."

Thankfully, both the Drifter Hotel and the Governor's Hall were connected directly to the subway. Nick was very happy to not have to be exposed to Dust's harsh elements. There was only one other person on the subway with him, a middle-aged woman whose eyes were red-rimmed with tears and whose face was a picture of sheer exhaustion. She kept her eyes focused on the floor in front of her, avoiding any eye contact with Nick.

He was compelled to ask her if she needed help, but decided against saying anything just as the words were about to pass his lips. Nick did not feel up to providing any comfort to her. When the subway stopped at the Governor's Hall, she immediately got up and hurried off into the building. Nick intentionally moved slowly, letting her get the distance she wanted between them.

Nick passed through the subway station doors and into the lobby of the Governor's Hall. A robot attendant, identical to the obsolete subway station attendant, was available at a kiosk just inside the lobby. Otherwise, the lobby was empty. The woman on the subway had just passed through a set of doors on the left, which led to the local branch of the First Republic Bank. To his right, Nick saw the barred entrance to the now abandoned Central Exploration Agency offices. A layer of dust lay undisturbed around that door.

"Directions to the Chapel, please," Nick requested. A floor plan suddenly appeared on his wrist computer with arrows guiding him in the appropriate direction. Nick stepped forward and entered the lift heading for the second sub-basement.

"Shall I request the presence of the pastor?" His computer asked.

"No," Nick said, wondering just how long it would take to find one.

Nick exited the lift and slowly made his way through the surprisingly long corridors of the underground structure. He passed the Colony Clerk's office, a shipping and distribution center, IT support offices, and another abandoned set of offices that were labeled Department of Tourism. Finally, he arrived at another dust-covered door clearly marked Chapel. Nick opened the door tentatively and was relieved to find the room in decent condition.

The room was dimly lit with a crude stain glass mural depicting a bible scene Nick couldn't quite place dominating the front of the room. The only light was provided by the artificial light behind the mural which bathed the pews of the chapel in a soothing array of yellows, oranges, greens, and blues. Nick walked to the front of the Chapel, kneeled, and blessed himself with the sign of the cross. He then sat in the first pew to his right.

For several moments, Nick sat in complete silence, unmoving. He stared at the mural and tried to quiet his thoughts. He needed guidance. Somewhere else in the galaxy his father was looking for him and looking for the crystal he had in his pocket.

Nick pulled the small data crystal from his pocket and leaned forward in the pew, letting the dim light shine through the crystal. He knew that the information it contained could be very damaging to the Republic, to the Conglomerate, and, most of all, to his father. Knowing what was on the crystal made it uncomfortable to hold in the light of day.

Holding it made him realize he had no idea what to do with it. He had no idea who to send it to, where to post it, or how to get it out to the masses. He knew, based on the information in those files, that as soon as the information was released, it would be discredited as aggressively as possible.

He needed time to sort things out. Here on Dust, he felt safe and he was more than willing to enjoy that feeling a while longer. Max would want to leave in a few days and make their way back to *Nexus*. Nick needed to find a way to stop that from happening.

An hour later, Nick clanged up the entry ramp of the *Hannah* in his metal boots. He found Max sitting in the cockpit, drumming his fingers on the console. The old man was covered in sweat and a thick crease formed in his forehead due to the scowl he wore on his face.

Nick hesitated in the hatchway.

"Kid," Max said, his tone sharp, "If you're not going to be on time, don't bother showing up. People pay me to bring things when they need them and I pay you to make sure we get their things to them on time. Do this again and I dock you a day's pay. Understood?"

"You should have sent me a message," Nick said.

"I shouldn't need to," Max said, "I told you what time to be here."

"You knew where I was though."

"And it was your responsibility to get back here on time," Max said, "Instead, I had to load a dozen sonic augers into the cargo hold myself. Just because I can look up your location on the computer, doesn't mean I should have to. Show a little damn personal responsibility next time."

"Why didn't you just get Reggie to help?" Nick asked.

"Because I would've had to spend another eight hours cleaning the sand out of his joints," Max yelled, "Christ, kid, learn when to shut up."

"Sorry," Nick said. He sat down in the co-pilot's seat and buckled himself in.

"Don't be late again," Max said, "Now, let's get out of here. There's another damn storm coming in. You're lucky we're getting out of here before it hits or else there really would have been hell to pay.

"And while we're en route, change out of those ridiculous pants and boots. You've got some heavy lifting to do once we get to Fracture."

Nick nodded and stared into the distance as a wall of sand quickly approached. He didn't speak for the rest of the trip.

Nick loaded one of the oversized augers onto a small industrial hover sled while Max stepped to the side of the *Hannah's* open cargo hold and leaned against a strut. The blazing midday sun of Dust beat down upon them. Nick wiped at the caked-on layer of sand and sweat that had settled on his cheeks. The only shade here was cast by the shadow of the ship and the other abandoned structures that surrounded the small landing pad.

Two rundown Republic ore refineries flanked the pad, having been abandoned almost a lifetime ago. Any useful parts had long ago been stripped out of the structures with only the skeletal remnants of each refinery remaining. Nick, now dressed in a tan workman's coverall, gestured to one of the dock workers to help him load another auger on the sled. His shoulders ached from the effort and the coveralls were chafing the inside of his thigh; he was ready to be done.

"You go it, Nick?" Max asked.

"Yeah," Nick grunted, "Don't worry about it. Take your break and I'll finish this up."

The mining crew foreman, Jane, walked over to Max. Her long red hair spilled out from her helmet. Little could be made of her face as it was mostly covered in a respirator and goggles. Though the green of her eyes shone through the goggles and made Nick feel like she was looking directly into his soul.

She extended a hand toward Max and he shook it firmly.

"Good to see you, Jane," Max said, adjusting his own respirator slightly. The wind was tolerable today, but there was still a good amount of sand blowing about. Nick loaded another auger while Max and Jane talked.

"Likewise, Max," Jane said, "How are you holding up?"

"Same as always," Max responded. It was the basic, everyday, rote conversation had by two people who crossed paths on a frequent basis. There was no real information passed between the two, just the customary exchange by two people stuck in a never ending grind. It was the kind of conversation Nick had heard his mother and father have a thousand or more times when his father would come home from a long day, exchange pleasantries with his mother, and then disappear into his home office for a few hours.

"How's the wife?" Nick heard Max ask.

"Doing all right. Needs a vacation," Jane said.

"I'm with her on that one."

"How's the ex?" Jane asked.

"I'll let you know the next time I talk to her," Max responded, "How's the mine doing?"

"Busy," Jane said, "Doc Sinclair has asked for a temporary bump in production."

Nick knew Max wasn't really paying attention to him. He maneuvered the sled over to the lift that would carry both he and the sled, with its full load of augers, into the mining shaft. He stopped the cart a couple of inches from being fully on the platform.

Nick commanded the lift to descend. The sled tipped and Nick jumped out of the way. The load of augers crashed heavily into the floor.

"What the hell?" Max asked.

Nick stopped the lift with the lift platform only a few feet below the surface of the landing pad. He looked around and could see that control panels on two of the augers had shattered.

"Damn it, kid," Max said as he crouched at the edge of the lift shaft, "You have got to be more careful."

Nick shrugged and said, "Sorry."

Max shook his head in frustration and wiped sweat from his forehead.

"How many are broken?"

Nick inspected the control panels.

"Three," he said.

"I'll have to dock you for that, Max," Jane said as she came up behind Max.

Max let out a long sigh.

"This is coming out of your paycheck, kid. Now clean it up."

Nick nodded silently and went to work. He raised the lift back up to the platform and reloaded the augers. Half an hour later, he delivered the working units to the miners in the shaft below and then secured the sled back in the *Hannah's* hold.

"This is going to put us behind, Max," Jane said, "Those replacements are sorely needed, especially at the pace we've been going lately."

"I know, Jane," Max said, scratching the back of his head. She pulled up her sleeve to reveal the screen of her wrist computer. She tapped it twice and then Max's computer beeped. Payment had been transferred, minus the cost of the broken augers.

"You take care," Max said. She nodded and they shook hands. Nick stood there for a moment while Max closed the cargo hold doors. The hold and all of its contents were now coated in a fine layer of sand. Max shook his head with an annoyed grimace on his face.

"I'm sorry," Nick said.

"You damn well better be," Max said, "Your carelessness just cost me money. Do a better job, Nick, or you're done here. Got it?"

Nick nodded.

"Clean up all this sand," Max said, "I want this hold spotless."

"Will do, boss," Nick said.

Max stared at him for a moment and then wearily made his way out of the cargo hold. Nick let a small smile crease his lips and then set about finding the vacuum.

Two hours later as Dust's sun began to settle in the east, the door to the Dry Dock was thrown open with a loud clank and in walked Max and Nick from the blustering wind and another late afternoon sandstorm. The two men patted themselves down, trying to remove as much of the grit as possible.

"Why the hell isn't this place connected directly to the subway?" Nick asked.

Max gave him a wry smile.

"Long story. Something about not wanting taxpayer money directed towards setting up a bar. I'd think given where you're from, you'd have figured that one out."

Nick frowned.

"Not sure what that's got to do with anything," he said.

"Where do you think that piece of legislation originated?" Max asked as they settled in at a table near the bar. Charlie, Roman, and Zanth were already waiting for them. Without prompting, Myra brought over another couple mugs of beer. Max gave her a warm smile as he picked up the cold mug.

"Had to be a reason behind it," Nick said.

"You're probably too young to remember the scandal at the Besh colony," Max said.

"Doesn't ring a bell," Nick agreed.

Charlie took a sip of his beer and leaned on to the table. "Bunch of bible beaters from Valhalla got wind of the millions of taxpayer dollars spent on helping establish a resort on Besh."

Max interjected, "Very wealthy bible beaters."

Max put emphasis on the term but Nick refused to be baited.

"Yeah," Charlie continued, "They had the right connections to push through some reform on how taxpayer funds could be used in the establishment of new colonies. They can be used for municipal buildings, living quarters, establishing an industrial base, but absolutely nothing that could be deemed morally objectionable."

Nick sipped his drink, the cool draft feeling especially refreshing after the difficult day.

"Seems a little overzealous," Nick responded. The other men gave him a smile.

Roman raised his glass in toast and said, "Glad to see you've got a decent sense of reason, kid."

"You guys sure have a negative view of the Church," Nick commented, taking another drink of his beer.

"More like the Church has a negative view of us," Roman commented.

"Actually, I'd say the feeling's mutual," Charlie chimed in.

"There've been a few folks come out this way, Nick, that tried to build up their congregation," Max said, "With the past that most of the folks here have, they usually wind up condemning us to the hell we live in."

"I don't see it. You guys are just a bunch of old softies," Nick said, "Charlie, what've you got to hide?"

"Myself mostly," Charlie responded. The other men laughed knowingly.

Roman answered for him. "Charlie here has three of the bitterest ex-wives you'll ever meet. He only stopped at Dust because there was no place farther from Earth he could go."

Charlie nodded and said, "I'll be paying alimony until I die."

"What about you, Roman?" Nick asked.

Roman took a drink and looked down to the floor with a bit of regret.

"I was a stupid kid, got involved with some stupid things." Roman's gaze was distant and the others around the table grew quiet. "Sometimes, kid, you do something bad enough and no one on Earth will hire you; you'll have no way to make a living. Well, that doesn't matter as much out here."

The table grew quiet for a moment and Nick was left to wonder what exactly Roman had done. Roman's deeply-lined face reflected an expression of deep regret. His eyes looked momentarily hollow and glassy.

"You guys should've seen this kid, yesterday," Max said, breaking the silence, "Nearly pissed himself when he had to manually lower one of the landing pads. You should've seen the look on his face when I told him he had to crank it down by hand."

Max's friends laughed and Nick responded with a tight-lipped smile. Nick was about to ask Zanth his story when the door to the Dry Dock clanged open.

They all looked up as a short, fit, roughly thirty-year-old woman in a tan jumpsuit walked in. She took off her respirator and goggles to reveal blue eyes that complimented her jet black hair. Nick wouldn't have called her drop dead gorgeous, but she was definitely striking. He looked back at his companions and noticed that all their faces had lit up a bit.

"Hey fellas," the woman called out to them, "Wow, look at this. Looks like the gang's all here."

"How are you doing, Lonnie?" Max asked, "It's been a while."

"Sure has, Max," she responded and clapped him on the shoulder, "Doesn't look like much has changed with you."

"Nah," Max responded, "You?"

"Can't complain."

They nodded and laughed and Nick couldn't help but feel like he was intruding on a reunion of old friends. Charlie and Roman moved aside a bit to give her room to pull in a chair while Myra brought over another mug without being asked. Lonnie thanked her with a nod and took a long drink.

"How's business, Lonnie?" Zanth asked.

Lonnie nodded and Nick noted how her short, black ponytail bobbed slightly. He stared into his drink so he wouldn't wind up staring at her.

"Picking up at the moment," she said, "Mr. Winters is back in town. It's safari time again."

"Who's Mr. Winters?" Nick asked.

"Horace Winters, who does not like to be called Horace, is an obscenely rich man who likes to come to Dust to hunt some of the local wildlife," Max answered.

"Yep," she said, focusing her vibrant blue eyes on Nick, "He gets a kick out of fighting the elements and the animals. Thinks the wind and sand makes it real sporty. I drop him in the foothills just beyond Bloom and he spends a few days pretending to be a cold-blooded killer."

"Sounds fun," Nick said with a distinct lack of enthusiasm.

"Who're you?" Lonnie asked Nick, "I don't believe we've met."

"A misguided wanderer," Charlie answered, "Thinks that spending time as Max's co-pilot will let him find some meaning out here in the wilderness."

Lonnie laughed and looked at Nick with wide-eyed sorrow. "Sorry, Nick. I think you may have taken a wrong turn somewhere."

"So I've heard," Nick said, taking a sip of his beer.

"After a few weeks with Max, your hair will turn gray, your knees will hurt, and you'll be lamenting about how things used to be," she said with a smile.

"I am not that old," Max said.

Lonnie arched an eyebrow in his direction.

"I am offended," Max said with mock irritation.

Charlie chuckled, Zanth ordered another round, and suddenly the stories of days gone by filled the conversation.

Charlie told his tale of the failed coolant pump, Zanth told his story of the failed air scrubber, and Roman told the legend of his six days adrift with a failed reactor. Round and round they went, reminiscing about their travails until eventually Max came back to his story about Nick lowering the *Hannah's* landing pad.

"Scared shitless," Max said, "That's how I would've described your expression, kid."

Max's words had started to slur a bit as Myra brought them all another round. Nick looked around the bar, anywhere but at the table. His jaw was clenched shut. Nick was about to call it a night and head back to the hotel when Lonnie's wrist computer emitted a loud chime. She looked at it and frowned.

"Crap," she said. She took a last drink of her beer and stood up from the table.

"Duty calls?" Charlie asked.

"Something wrong?" Nick asked.

"No," Lonnie said with some annoyance, "Winters needs me to go pick him up. The old man probably just forgot something. I need to run out there. I'll see you fellas tomorrow."

"Stay safe, Lonnie," Max said. Charlie and Zanth gave her a wave as she headed away from the table. Nick seized the opportunity to make an exit.

"Are you just headed out and back, Lonnie?" Nick asked, "Think I could tag along?"

Nick blushed slightly as the conversation around the table grew quiet. He was well aware that all ears around him were listening as he asked the only attractive woman he'd seen in this town if he could follow along with her.

"Whatsa matter kid?" Roman asked, "We're not good enough company for you?"

The other men snickered and Nick cast his eyes to the floor. Lonnie smacked Roman lightly on the back of the head.

"You guys are nothing but a bunch of overgrown kids," she said, "Sure, Nick. Come on."

Nick jumped up from his chair enthusiastically and then stopped momentarily as the room swayed around him. Charlie and Max laughed giddily at the eagerness Nick showed in following her.

"Mister adventure," Charlie said quietly.

"Adventure, my ass," Max responded.

Nick ignored them and donned his respirator and goggles as Lonnie threw open the door. She stepped out into the bright evening sun and fairly tepid gusts of wind.

"I don't think adventure is what's on his mind," Roman said just at the edge of Nick's hearing range. Nick shook his head and slammed the door shut. He let out a long sigh as he trudged through the sand toward the subway station.

Nick sat in the passenger seat of Lonnie's sleek, luxurious Vestara-class personal transport. Nick was more than a little surprised to see a Vestara out here. Next to the other scrap heaps on the Windy City Spaceport landing pads, it was a relative jewel in a junkyard. The brushed-silver exterior was smooth, with sweeping contours that arched across the vehicle from front to back.

The interior was as plush and comfortable as the exterior was stylish. Nick practically melted into the seat as the red seat cushions welcomed him into the car with a soft, warm embrace. The Vestara's interior was immaculately clean, a testament to how well Lonnie maintained the small spacecraft.

The vehicle came to life with a soft whir, almost too faint to hear. Nick could tell that the pitch of the engine was an octave higher than was normal for a Vestara, likely because of the membranes that covered the air intakes and exhausts. Other than that, he might as well have been riding in one of the two Vestaras his father owned. He was surprised at how much heartache those memories caused.

He closed his eyes for a moment and lost himself in the comforts of the vehicle.

"You okay, kid?" Lonnie asked.

Nick blushed. "Yeah, just brings back memories of home."

"Where're you from?" She asked, "Not too many people would consider the Vestara to be a comfort of home."

"Valhalla," Nick answered, staring out the front window. Just to their right, the sun touched the eastern horizon. "My father's owned a Vestara for the last ten years. Although I have to admit, I don't think he keeps his as clean as yours."

"Thanks," Lonnie said. She commanded the vehicle to rendezvous with Winters' bio chip and away they went, streaking across the arid, sand covered terrain.

"I'm surprised to see one of these out here," Nick said.

"Well, my clients appreciate a certain level of luxury. I wouldn't be doing myself any favors by flying around in an old scrap heap. Appearances matter for some folks."

"Guess so," Nick said, still a bit uncomfortable with what her so-called clients were doing out here. He knew he was going to invite more ridicule for this comment, but he couldn't hold it in. "I thought hunting of indigenous animals was outlawed by the Republic?"

Lonnie laughed, lines forming around her blue eyes.

"Did you just fall out of orbit, kid? Do you really think anyone gives a damn about what happens out here?"

"I guess not," Nick said.

"Nobody cares what happens out here, not the Conglomerate or the Republic. There's no money to be made on Dust, so we might as well not exist," Lonnie said, wiping a loose strand of hair from in front of her face.

"But this is a Republic world," Nick protested, "They wouldn't just ignore what's happening on one of their worlds."

Lonnie gave him a look that told him he was being absurd.

"Have you seen our fat bastard of a governor?" Lonnie asked.

Nick shook his head in the negative.

"And you won't, unless someone breaks his replicator and steals all his food. That man could care less about what happens around here. He's just waiting to retire, assuming he doesn't have a heart attack first," Lonnie said, "I have plenty of wealthy clients, kid, who count on the Republic looking the other way here.

"Hell, I've had high ranking people from the Conglomerate and the Republic out here for a little safari. Nothing gets an old man's blood pumping like the chance to hunt down a few lesser creatures in the name of sport."

Nick looked away from her towards the almost fully set sun. The talk of corruption should not have been a surprise to him. Wherever there were men with money, there were other men willing to look the other way to get a bit of that money. So his father had taught him; so he was now finally learning for himself.

"Why do this? Surely, there are other ways to make a living?"

"Not on Dust," she replied, "I'm not much of a miner or farmer. I don't have the mind to be a doctor or researcher. I thought about teaching, but I don't have the patience for other people's kids. This has been working out pretty well for me. Pays well and lets me stay around my kids."

Lonnie stopped and was silent. Nick eyes widened slightly at the admission. Kids, more than anything, explained why she was really on Dust. The Vestara sped above the desert floor as the two sat in uncomfortable silence.

"How many do you have?" Nick asked, unable to let the word pass.

Lonnie sighed and then touched a spot on her control panel. A picture of her and two boys appeared on the console. They were young, roughly a year or two apart, but clearly their mother's sons.

"The one on the left is John, the one on the right Joseph," she said softly, "We came out here when I was pregnant with Joseph, shortly after John was born."

Nick was shocked. His cheeks grew red and his brow furrowed in disbelief. He momentarily felt the urge to direct her to stop and let him out.

"How can you do something like that when people across the Republic are dying because they have no food? That's why the law exists. So that we get back to a point where there's enough for everybody? How can you do something like this?" Nick asked.

Nick knew, as all kids were taught, that population control laws and measures had been in place for almost 200 years. Food shortages and resource problems had turned the human race against itself. Colonies died out from starvation and disease, others wiped out local animal populations, while others turned on each other fighting for what food supplies were available. The fledgling Republic was threatened with civil war. Drastic measures were enacted to limit the ever burgeoning human population.

Bio chips were modified to include receptors that altered the normal human reproductive cycle. Desperation had driven a mandate, there was to be no unauthorized reproduction. Adults, married or single, could apply for a parent license. Once granted, the person would be given hormone therapy that allowed for the birth of a single child. Multiple births were a rare exception to the law, though Nick had been taught something in school about how the chips released something that prevented that.

Of course, he knew that with the establishment of the laws came the rise of the black market. He had been taught about so-called Breeder towns, the back alley establishments that used homemade hormone therapies to restore the right to have children. Breeder towns popped up on worlds across the Republic under deplorable conditions. Starvation and disease were rampant, and crime rates sky high as people preyed on each other to obtain the drugs they needed.

The Republic established the Population Protection Division of Republic Security. The PPD hunted down these illegal towns; raids were conducted across the Republic. There were some violent confrontations, with the leaders of those sects painted as crazy, unstable criminals bent on destroying civilization. Nick could vividly remember the days when a PPD officer came to his class to warn them of the consequences of unauthorized population expansion and the threat they would be to the very fabric of society.

Nick remembered the strident discussion of this in his history classes at all levels of his schooling. His teachers had repeatedly made it clear that this egregious violation of human rights was necessary to the survival of the species.

This was sacrosanct. This was law. This was not to be violated.

"Don't lecture me, kid," Lonnie said, "Not until you've had a chance to walk in my shoes."

Nick's face was bright red. His hands trembled slightly. He looked at her with contempt; she looked at him with pity.

"How many?" Nick asked with pointed anger, "How many other families are living out here like this? Is this what Max keeps telling me about when he says that everyone here on Dust is running or hiding?"

"Nick," Lonnie said, sliding her hand surreptitiously to her pocket, "Take a deep breath. Calm down."

"Don't tell me to calm down," Nick said. He shifted in his seat to face her directly and her left hand calmly slid into her pants pocket. "How can you do something like this? Not only do you put other people at risk, but you put your own sons at risk. How can you stand to do this?"

"Put them at risk for what, Nick?" She asked calmly but firmly.

"Starvation, disease, death," Nick said, "Not just for them, but for all of us."

"Look around, kid," she said, "Do you see anyone starving out here?"

"That's not the point," he argued.

"Isn't it? If we were so bad off that the slightest population increase could send humanity spiraling into oblivion, wouldn't you expect us to be dying out here? Wouldn't you expect everyone to be just scraping by? Last time I was at *Nexus*, I don't recall seeing too many emaciated people crawling about begging for scraps. We all seem pretty fat and happy."

"That's because the system is working as intended," Nick said, "Unless people like you doom us all because of your wanton carelessness."

"Don't be so naïve-"

"Don't call me naïve," Nick retorted. His temper was barely controlled.

She spoke softly, almost conciliatory in an effort to calm him. "What do you intend to do, Nick? Where do you go from here?"

"I should turn you in," Nick said heatedly, though the edge of his words had softened.

"To whom? The Governor's office? Do you think they'll lift a finger?"

"Then I'll notify sector security at *Nexus*," he said.

"Do you really think they'll spend the resources to come get me? Do you really think they'll care about one person on one remote world?"

"Why not?" Nick asked, "Why wouldn't they? This isn't just some petty little crime. You could be put away for a long time, have your children stripped away from you. Besides, how do I know it's just you? Windy City could be full of people like you for all I know."

She stared at him coolly, letting a few moments of silence pass between them.

"I don't know that one way or another," she said earnestly, "As far as I know, I have the only unauthorized child in Windy City."

"Why should I believe you?"

"I can't help you with that one," she replied. At that moment, the Vestara's main computer issued a chime. They had arrived at Winters' location. "We'll continue this later."

He nodded curtly. Lonnie was just another person who did whatever she felt like, without regard to those around her. Selfish. Greedy. Like his father.

He sat there unmoving, staring into the darkness that had quickly engulfed them.

"Nick," she said, "I'm not evil. I'm just a mom, a mom who loves her sons very much. I would never do anything to put them in harm's way. If I didn't think I could take care of them, I would have never had them."

"Right," Nick said. He waved his hand dismissively. "Let's go find your client."

He stressed the last word, twisting it with contempt.

Lonnie settled the Vestara at the crest of a small rolling hill. According to the indicator on the wrist computer, Winters was just beyond the crest of the next hill. Lonnie grabbed a couple of flashlights out of the door of the Vestara and handed one to Nick.

"Mr. Winters?" Lonnie called out.

There was no response. She started off down the hill, Nick reluctantly in tow. This was a mistake, he thought, this whole thing. Shouldn't have signed on with Max; shouldn't have run off from home. Shouldn't have come to this godforsaken place.

He trudged ahead, not paying attention to where he was going.

Lonnie gasped.

Nick walked up beside her and followed the focus of her flashlight. Mr. Winters was lying on his back in a pool of blood. His torso had been sliced open from shoulder to waist. Nick had never seen anything like this before. He stood there, mouth agape, unsure of what to do.

Lonnie hurried over to the unmoving body and knelt beside him, her knee dropping into the pool of his blood.

She felt for a pulse on his neck and found nothing. She put her ear to his mouth, but caught no sign of him breathing.

"Damn," she said softly.

"What was he hunting?" Nick asked, looking around for any signs of the predator that did this. He struggled to take his eyes away from the body with its seeping wound or from the blood that was being soaked into the desert floor.

"Dust Devils," she said. Nick looked at her quizzically. "They're like large, feral dogs, except they have a helluva temper."

"Could they have done this?" He asked.

"I don't know," she said, "I don't think so."

An unearthly screech pierced the night air. Lonnie looked up and Nick swung around with his flashlight. The hair on the back of his neck stood on edge. At the end of his sweep, he thought he saw the outline of a figure, but it jumped back beyond the beam of his flashlight.

Nick froze as he heard rustling in the distance. Something was moving fast below them across the dune. He swept his flashlight down, but the thing disappeared again. Out of the corner of his eye, Nick saw Lonnie pull a gun from her pocket. She crouched protectively over Winters' fallen body.

Another shriek erupted from behind him.

"Jesus," Nick gasped, ducking involuntarily. Nick braced himself for an attack but none came. The air was now quiet. Nick breathed again; his hands trembled.

"What the hell was that?" Nick asked.

"No idea," she said, "And I'm not sticking around to find out. Let's get him in the craft and get out of here. Let's get him back to Windy City, then you can turn me in for my crimes against humanity," she said, letting her annoyance show. As Nick knelt by the old man's shoulders preparing to pick him up, he saw a tear streak down her face.

Late that night, Max stepped onto the brightly lit spaceport landing pad. He had too much to drink that evening, but the news of Winters' death had sobered him up. Word had reached the Dry Dock fairly quickly after Lonnie and Nick returned to the landing pad. Tragedies like this were rare, but not unheard of around here.

There had been a murder here a couple of months ago, a crime of passion, but that was the last time Max could remember something like this happening. He knew Lonnie would be shaken a bit and also wondered how the kid had handled everything. He walked out on the pad, wearing his respirator and goggles. The wind that night was mild, but there was still a fair amount of sand being blown around.

Lonnie was going over the Vestara with an ultraviolet light, looking for any unseen stains around the rear passenger door. She found a spot and dabbed at it with a silver cloth in her right hand. She pulled the cloth away and Max watched as the small spot quickly faded.

"What the hell were you thinking, Max?"

He was surprised by her aggravated tone.

"What are you talking about?"

Lonnie stood up and her fierce blue eyes tore into him from behind her goggles.

"That kid is a threat," she said vehemently, "He's a threat to this whole colony."

Max sighed and said, "He knows then."

"Yes, he damn well knows," Lonnie said, wiping the silver cloth across her hands, "He knows about my boys. Did you really think you could bring him here without him finding stuff like this out?"

"Hasn't been a problem before," Max said, looking down at the pad away from her angry stare.

She stepped into his face. "You didn't hire anyone from Valhalla before Max. Christ, you're an idiot."

Max took an involuntary step back and shrugged. "He's just a kid, Lonnie. An idiot kid who doesn't know what he's doing. What do you really think he's going to do? Besides, he may be from Valhalla, but he's trying to get away from his old man. Maybe all this will open his mind a bit."

"Do you know why he's out here, Max? How do you know he's not some Republic mole?"

"You're being paranoid, Lonnie. He's just a confused kid, a little naïve and idealistic, but he'll get beyond that."

"He's a threat, Max. He's a threat to this entire colony," Lonnie said, turning away from him, "If you're lucky, he'll only get himself killed."

CHAPTER 4

Nick awoke still wearing the coveralls that he had donned prior to the delivery to Fracture. His hands were still stained by Winters' blood. He stripped and staggered into the shower. Today, the sonic vibrations did not seem to be enough to shake loose the dried flecks of blood that stuck to his hands. He went to the sink, but minutes after minutes of scrubbing didn't seem to wash the dark red color away.

The image of Winters' body was burned into his mind. Before ever seeing him, he had reviled the man for what he was doing. Alien life, life native to worlds other than Earth, was so far very rare in the galaxy. That life was to be protected, not hunted down for the amusement of the rich. Nick could never have approved of what Winters was doing. However, he didn't wish the man dead.

Lonnie didn't speak to him the entire trip back. She had sat there in the pilot's seat, staring into the night, tears running down her cheeks. They were met at the landing pad by a team of doctors with an incredibly archaic, wheeled gurney. Nick had never seen one before, didn't even know they existed.

The team of doctors loaded Winters onto the gurney and whisked him away. One of them stayed behind, a Doctor Booth, and he took short statements from Lonnie and Nick.

Minutes later, the Doctor was gone, Lonnie turned her attention to cleaning out the Vestara, and Nick was riding the subway back to the hotel by himself. His mind was overwhelmed from the shocks of the evening. He found he could do nothing but stare at the ceiling.

The night's sleep had not helped him much. He struggled even to pick out clothes to put on. Finally, he decided he was too hungry to care, put the dirty, stained coverall back on, and marched down to the cafeteria.

He sat down at the first open table and ordered the same thing he had the day before, this time getting a double order. He turned up the volume of the news broadcast, slumped in his seat and watched vacantly. The same female news anchor stared at the camera while images of another riot played over her shoulder.

"Riots continued on Canis 1 today," she reported, "As Republic security forces tried in vain to keep the peace, Marshall Conglomerate representatives continued negotiations with colony leaders to provide the colony with emergency supplies of military rations. The supplies would provide a stopgap food supply while colony researchers continue to search for viable crops that will thrive in the soil on Canis 1."

"In the meantime," she continued, "The Governor of Katia pledged to send supplies from their reserves to help with the situation on Canis 1."

The image shifted to a middle-aged man with graying temples and dark circles under his eyes. The man looked as if he hadn't slept in a week.

"We're sending what we can," he said in a dry, hoarse voice, "But there's only so much we can spare without putting ourselves at risk."

Nick's food arrived and his stomach audibly growled at the sight of it. The succulent aroma filled his nostrils and he dug into his double order eagerly. About halfway through, he felt a pang of guilt, gorging as he was. The news broadcast continued on in the foreground, with the story having shifted to a new vaccine the Conglomerate was developing for the residents of Midas.

Nick tuned out the broadcast. He wasn't sure if he was bothered more by the image of the dead man that was burned in his memory or the conversation he'd had with Lonnie before that. Both were a shock to him. This was a far cry from the life he knew.

Suddenly no longer able to eat, he pushed his plate away and walked out of the room.

Max stood in front of Sylvia Pritchard's desk in the otherwise empty customs office. His shoulders slumped slightly; his eyes were puffy from a lack of sleep.

"What's the latest?" Max asked.

Sylvia looked up at him with a disappointed smirk and a shake of her head.

"I'm sorry, Max," Sylvia said, "It doesn't look like our link will be restored any time soon. It's not a hardware fault; some sort of software corruption. Damn strange. It could be another couple of weeks."

"Sylvia, you know I can't wait that long," Max said, pleading, "Doc Sinclair doesn't like it when his shipments are delayed."

Sylvia nodded her head in understanding. "I know, Max, I know, but regulations are regulations. I can't release your cargo without clearance from *Nexus*. You know the drill."

Max shook his head in aggravation.

"Can't make any money with my ship on the ground," Max said. Also, the more time Nick had to poke his nose into things, the more likely he was to get into trouble. Need to get him out of here, Max thought, let things cool off a bit.

"I know, Max," Sylvia said, "You've got bills to pay."

Max let out a sigh.

"I know you're doing everything you can," Max said, "Shoot me over a waiver form though. I'll take it by the Governor's office."

"Whatever you need to do," Sylvia said. She tapped her desktop in a few places and a moment later the form popped up on Max's wrist computer. He smiled, thanked her, and headed out of the office.

He took a moment to fill out the form and submit it. He then checked his account balances on his wrist computer just as he had every day for the last ten years. He grimaced as he reviewed his debts owed. He wasn't going to make any money by standing around here.

Max headed out of the customs office and his mind wandered back to the conversation with Lonnie. He wasn't sure what to do with Nick out here. The kid would have to adjust or be adjusted. Spout off again like he did to Lonnie and Nick's stay on Dust might be extremely short. Got to keep an eye on him, Max thought.

Nick had hopped on the subway, which he was surprised to see relatively full. The subway car stopped at Governor's Hall and he briefly debated taking another trip to the neglected chapel. However, he stayed aboard and decided to follow a number of people as they got off and entered Windy City's residential district.

Two or three of the other people gave him an odd look as he stepped off behind them. He looked down at his clothes and for the first time noticed a few spots where blood had been smeared on the hips of his tan coverall. He moved his hand to his sides and tried to obscure the still noticeable splotches. He then lowered his eyes toward the floor and pressed ahead into the main thoroughfare.

He expected squalor and destitution. He expected barely livable hovels with emaciated residents living amongst their trash and waste. He expected the rancid smells of death and decay. After all, these people were poor and isolated. Living outside the regular trade routes of the Conglomerate and beyond the interest of the Republic guaranteed that little money would pass through here, which meant those who lived here were doomed to a harsh and meager life.

Nick was surprised at how wrong he was.

Now, he would never have considered the residential district of Windy City opulent, but it was hardly the dilapidated bastion of desperation that he expected. Immediately after exiting the subway station, he passed by a couple of small shops on his right and left. The store shops were fully stocked with bins of what Nick guessed were local fruits and vegetables. There were a dozen or so people in each shop picking out groceries for their evening meals.

Beyond the two stores, Nick came upon a large square with dozens more people milling about, living lives that Nick would have never expected here. Nick had expected the buildings here to be more repurposed, prefabricated living units, like the Drifter Hotel, or even a repurposed freighter cargo hold, like the Dry Dock. Instead, all of the structures of this district were carved right out of the earth of Dust.

From this central square, Nick could see three main avenues, each ninety degrees from the other, and they each travelled farther into the distance than Nick could see. On the other side of the park, directly opposite where he was standing was a large building with an inscription that read 'Windy City Courthouse.' Opposite that, Nick could make out a school. Around the square were various businesses, a couple of repair shops for replicators or wrist computers, a hardware store that seemed to offer smaller versions of the augers they had delivered to Fracture, a couple more small grocery stores, and police and fire stations.

It took Nick a moment to realize that something was missing from what he normally would have expected. There were no personal transports. Everyone was walking. Nick guessed he could see about two to three hundred people from his current vantage point and they were all on foot, going to and fro.

It also took him a moment to realize that he could see perfectly. While he had expected a dimly lit cave, this was a fully illuminated city carved under the surface of Dust. Some sort of glowing vine stretched across the ceiling of the cavern, covering the majority of it. Each vine emitted a soft, yellowish-white light. It was remarkable. He was so busy gawking at his surroundings that he missed the suspicious glances of a few of the passersby.

He finally picked a direction and started walking down the street to his left. He started passing by what he guessed were individual residences. They would never be mistaken for mansions, but they looked perfectly livable. The street was lined with row after row of homes. Every block or so, he passed what could best be described as wide alleyways that went off to the left or right. Quick glances down them showed more homes carved into the rock.

Nick never noticed that two members of the Windy City police force had been following him for the last couple of blocks. When Nick stopped at the window of a pharmacy, looking at the wares available, the two men stopped behind him.

"Excuse me, sir," one of the men called out sharply.

Nick's mind didn't register that someone was talking to him. A moment later, Nick felt the poke of a stun baton into his back shoulder. The weapon wasn't armed or else Nick would have been left in a heap on the street floor. He turned and saw the two gray-uniformed officers looking at him sternly.

"I'm sorry," Nick said, "Have I done something wrong?"

The smaller man with yellowish skin rolled his eyes and looked to his brown-skinned partner. The taller man looked at Nick like he was the village idiot. Nick fidgeted, trying to wipe dirt off of his coveralls. He looked around at the twenty or thirty people who were passing by in the street and noticed that everyone was giving him a wide berth. Some of the people gave him a brief glance, but quickly looked away to avoid making eye contact.

"You're not supposed to be here," the taller, dark-skinned officer said.

When Max couldn't find Nick at the hotel or the Dry Dock, he checked his wrist computer. In a heartbeat Nick's position popped up on the screen. Max groaned when he saw where Nick had wandered.

He took off at a jog, hurrying to get to the subway. With any luck, he could get there before Nick talked himself into too much of a hole or said the wrong thing to the wrong person. His stomach knotted as the subway seemed to slowly crawl away from the Drifter stop.

A young couple got on the car at the medical center and university stop. The look in their eyes was hollow; Max could tell they were a thousand miles away at the moment, lost in their own thoughts. They seemed to move painstakingly slow. Max gave them a wide berth, checked the wrist computer again, and gritted his teeth in frustration.

As the subway car rolled along, a message arrived that was addressed to both Max and Nick. Someone wanted to talk to Nick about the incident last night. Nick was getting a little too popular for Max's tastes. He switched his display from the message back to the location of Nick. His position had not changed. Stay where you are, kid, Max thought.

"I think you need to come with us, sir," the dark-skinned officer, Officer Freeman said. He reached out to grab Nick by the elbow, but Nick withdrew quickly. The shorter officer drew his stun baton and held it surreptitiously by his left leg. Nick held both of his hands up in front of him in protest and stepped back toward the front window of the shop behind him.

"You're kidding right," Nick said, "I haven't done anything. You've no right to do this."

Freeman sneered at him. He was about to say something when Max called out.

"Nick!"

Nick looked at Max with wide eyes, unsure of what he had stumbled into, while the two officers looked to him with aggravated expressions.

"Max Cabot," Freeman said, "Is this man with you?"

"Yes," Max said, "He's signed on with me for the next six months."

The officer sighed. He locked eyes with Max.

"Do you have proof of employment?"

"Yes," Max responded. He tapped on his wrist computer and held it up. A second later a copy of the profile was visible on Freeman's wrist computer. He reviewed the data briefly.

"Have you informed your employee that this area is off-limits to non-residents?"

"Ah, no, sir," Max said.

"Have you informed your employee that his access is restricted to the Governor's Hall, Dry Dock, the Drifter, and the Spaceport?"

"Look, I didn't mean any harm."

Freeman ignored Nick and continued to stare down Max.

"No," Max responded.

"What's the big deal?" Nick asked.

"Mr. Papagous, I suggest you keep your mouth shut," Freeman ordered, "This residential zone contains a number of bioengineered organisms that are unique to the Dust ecosystem. Those organisms are susceptible to contamination through the introduction of non-native bacteria and other microscopic organisms."

Nick shot the officer a puzzled look.

"I could have you arrested for endangering this colony," Freeman said.

Max said, "I apologize for not clearly explaining the regulations, but we are actually here to meet with Professor Rasmussen, at his request. Nick here was just trying to meet me there and got a little lost."

Max forwarded the message to Officer Freeman. Professor Rasmussen wanted to speak with Nick about the incident with Mr. Winters. Freeman frowned at Nick.

"Why didn't you mention this?" He asked pointedly.

"I didn't know any of this was an issue, Officer," Nick responded, "I just thought I could wander around a bit before we met with the professor."

"Look, do your business with Rasmussen and then get out of here," Freeman said, "Next time, show security the request first and don't wander around."

Nick nodded at the warning and Max exhaled. The two men then turned and hurriedly walked back toward the central square while the two officers watched them leave.

When they were out of earshot, Nick whispered, "Where did you come up with that?"

"I didn't," Max said, "We got lucky. Rasmussen really does want to talk to you."

Nick was thankful for the bit of divine intervention. He followed closely behind Max, still aware of the glances they were getting from the other passersby.

"So was any of that b-s about contamination true?" Nick asked.

"What do you think?"

Nick frowned. He looked around at the surrounding homes and shops and the people passing by. There was nothing notable about any of them. It all looked perfectly normal. Why all the secrecy, Nick wondered.

"Nick," Max said, "I don't want you going off by yourself for a little while. Stick with me during the day."

"Yeah, sure," Nick said.

Professor Peter Rasmussen met Nick and Max in the front lobby of the Biology Department Building of Sinclair University. The building, for that matter the entire campus, was indistinguishable from the other buildings in the residential district. The walls were lined with tile made from the dirt and rock it was carved from. The ceilings were covered in the same luminescent vines that covered the ceiling of the entire district.

The building was fairly small, only two stories high with maybe a half dozen rooms. There was one classroom with only a half dozen desks for students. The rest of the rooms were laboratories and offices. Despite it being the middle of the day, there were no students about.

"Where is everyone?" Nick asked.

Rasmussen smiled and said, "My research assistants are out doing data collection in the field."

"No students?"

"You're new here, aren't you?" Rasmussen said, "This isn't a bustling college campus, Mr. Papagous. Most of my students are adults looking for a new career path. Not your traditional college students. That'll change in time."

"What did you want, professor?" Max asked.

Rasmussen's eyes lit up. "I actually wanted to talk to Nick about this incident with Mr. Winters. Doctor Booth let me examine the wounds this morning and, I must say, they were quite remarkable."

The professor paused and his gaze focused on the far wall of his meticulously neat office. Max shrugged at Nick's quizzical glance after the professor didn't say anything for another couple of seconds.

"Wouldn't you be better off talking to Lonnie?" Nick asked.

"Funny thing," Rasmussen finally said, "She seems to have left the planet."

"Really?" Nick asked in surprise. Max simply frowned.

"I checked with spaceport control after I couldn't find her at her home," Rasmussen said, "It seems she left early this morning. This whole thing must have rattled her."

"I bet," Nick said. Max shot him a look that said to keep his mouth shut and Nick complied.

"You're the only direct witness I can find. Tell me, what did you see out there?" Rasmussen asked, "Any hint of what did this?"

"Just a glimpse. Nothing more than a shadow," Nick said, "It was dark. I thought I caught something in my flashlight, but I never got a good look."

The gleam faded from Rasmussen's eyes.

"That's a shame."

"Why?" Max asked.

"We can't figure out what attacked him," Rasmussen said, a hint of excitement in his voice, "The gash across his chest is too deep to have been made by a Dust Devil. There were also puncture wounds in his torso that are also too deep to have been made by those creatures."

"What else is out there?" Nick asked, "What else could have done this?"

"Nothing that we know of," the professor blurted out, "There are no other large predators on Dust that we know of; this is something completely new."

Nick was surprised at his lack of empathy for the man who had lost his life.

"This thing killed a man, you know."

Rasmussen frowned at Nick and dismissed him with a wave of his hand. "Son, this could be the most important biological find of the last twenty years. Don't get sanctimonious with me. Serves him right for hunting Dust Devils."

"Anything else for us, professor?" Max asked.

Rasmussen's gaze again got lost in the distance. Max was about to get up from his chair when he finally spoke again.

"Yes, actually," he said, "Would you care to go out there again?"

"What for?" Nick asked.

"Show us where you found the body, how it was lying when you found it, see if we can jog any memories loose about what you saw," Rasmussen said, "We'd greatly appreciate it. Any information you can give us could prove invaluable."

Nick looked over to Max who just shrugged.

"Up to you," Max said, "We've got nothing else to do today."

"Guess so, then," Nick said.

Rasmussen beamed. "Excellent, I'll meet you at the spaceport in an hour."

While Rasmussen recalled his assistants from the field, Nick and Max returned to the hotel so that Nick could finally change out of his coveralls. After a quick shower and putting on clothes that were more him, Nick felt refreshed. Max shook his head and gave the kid a wry smile at the sight of the loose-fitting maroon shirt and SecondSkin white pants, complete with his ridiculous metal boots.

"You're going to go out to the dunes in that?" Max asked.

"And I will be impeccably dressed," Nick said. Nick held his head high and walked with a purpose as they made their way to the subway station. Max shook his head and laughed.

"Hope nothing out there decides you'll make a good meal," Max said, "I don't think you're going to be outrunning much."

Nick shrugged. "Let's go, boss."

They hopped on the subway car and Nick's thoughts returned to the previous evening. He stared blankly ahead, hands clasped together as he leaned forward in the seat.

"What're you thinking?" Max asked.

"Just about Lonnie," Nick said as the subway car glided effortlessly on its magnetic rail.

Max grimaced and nodded.

"I'm sure she'll be back at some point. Not too many places for her to go."

"I didn't think I was that big of a threat," Nick said.

"She has no reason to trust you," Max said, "How does she know you're not going to try to turn her in? For the next little while, she'll live in fear that the Republic will come after her."

Nick nodded.

"She shouldn't have had more than one child then," Nick said, "She shouldn't have broken the law."

"It's not always that easy."

"That's why we have these little chips in our necks. They make it easier," Nick said.

"Not everyone believes those chips are right," Max said.

"But they're the law."

"Try not to be so judgmental, Nick, or you're going to find yourself alone pretty quickly," Max said, looking him in the eye, "Try to see things from the other person's point-of-view before you get all spun up."

"What she has done is wrong though, Max," Nick said, "I have trouble getting past that."

"No, what she did is illegal," Max responded, "But not all laws are just."

"Then it wouldn't be law," Nick retorted.

"It's not that black and white, kid," Max said more pointedly, "The Republic has made plenty of mistakes; laws are changed and repealed. There's a reason for that. You need to decide if you think what she did was wrong because your teachers told you it was wrong or if you think it's wrong because you really believe that deep down. Don't let someone else tell you what to think."

Nick laughed and said, "Little bit of irony in that statement."

"There's a difference between learning how to think and being told what to think."

"If you say so," Nick said and stepped off the subway car. Moments later they were on the spaceport pad. Professor Rasmussen and his team were already there, loading equipment onto a rusted hulk of a transport. The craft was older than Nick and painted an awful shade of green.

"Looks like something I threw up once," Nick said.

"College will do that to you," Max said, "Let's get this done."

The craft was as musty on the inside as it was rusted on the outside. With the way it shook when Rasmussen started the drive, Nick had serious doubts about its ability to make the trip in one piece.

"Nick," Rasmussen called out, "Our destination please?"

Nick went into his location history on the wrist computer and sent the coordinates where they landed last night to the craft's main computer. Once again, he was off on a trip across Dust's desert plains as the wind and sand howled around them.

Nick pointed to a spot atop the dune as the late afternoon sun beat down upon them. Rasmussen and his two assistants, a middle-aged man and woman, stood just behind Nick, having followed him up the dune. Nick was not about to admit it, but his legs were tired from the climb. Max was right about the boots.

"That's where we found him," Nick said, pointing, "His head was closest to me and he was lying flat on his back."

The wind had blown away any traces of the body's outline in the sand. There was no longer any trace of their visit last night. Rasmussen had to shout through his respirator to be heard.

"Analyze the area," Rasmussen said to his assistants, "Maybe we'll find some blood or saliva or something below the surface."

The man and woman nodded and went to work. They pulled a case out of the transport and pulled out an instrument with an elongated proboscis connected to a small rectangular box. The male assistant then trudged over to where Nick indicated the body was found and started dipping the proboscis into the sand. The woman monitored the data collection on her wrist computer and gave the man a nod whenever sample data was registered.

Rasmussen meanwhile was looking around the dune and then off into the horizon. His goggles were tinted, so Nick and Max couldn't see where he was looking.

Rasmussen called out to Nick, "Where did you see your shadow, Nick? The thing that eluded your flashlight beam."

Nick took a moment to orient himself in the same position as he was standing last night. He swung around, trying to remember exactly where he had caught a glimpse of the thing. He finally pointed back to the east, where the sun was already inching closer to the horizon.

"Marsha," Rasmussen called to the woman, "Do a survey for tracks and then take samples down the dune for twenty meters in that direction. Let's see if we can find any trace of this thing."

She nodded and set off to work, leaving the male assistant to take samples where the body had been.

"Was there anything else, Nick?" Rasmussen asked, "Was there anything else you heard or saw or felt that could help us identify this thing?"

Nick shook his head, but then he remembered one other detail.

"It shrieked. Can't believe I didn't remember that. It was a high-pitched screech that scared the crap out of me."

Rasmussen listened as he continued to survey the area.

"Did it remind you of anything, any other type of animal?"

Nick shrugged and said, "I don't know. A bird, maybe. It sounded big though, that's for sure."

A chill ran up Nick's spine as he recalled the sound. Involuntarily, he stared at the spot where the body had been. This thing took down an armed man without much trouble, Nick thought, and it took him down from the front. There was no doubt this thing was big.

"Hey professor," Max said, "If this thing comes out at night, I'd rather not be here then. I'd appreciate if you could wrap this up before sundown."

"Probably a good idea."

Nick wholeheartedly agreed.

Two hours later and they were back in their chairs at the Dry Dock surrounded by the usual suspects. Charlie was telling the saga of the leaking water hose, though Nick wasn't paying attention enough to know if this was different than the one told last night or merely a rehashing of the same story with different highlights. Nick had had a couple of drinks in quick succession and was starting to feel their influence.

He sat there quietly while the older men told their stories. He noticed his cup was empty and poured himself another glass from the pitcher on the table. The alcohol in his system had long since killed off any residual nervousness after their trip out to the dunes.

All that time out there and Rasmussen and his team found nothing, no tracks, no traces of DNA, and no other physical evidence of the creature. Nick was glad for that. He had no desire to face whatever struck down Winters. The sun had crept perilously close to the eastern horizon by the time they left and Nick could tell that only he and Max were anxious to get the hell out of there. Rasmussen was filled with overabundant scientific curiosity and clearly felt no danger. His assistants were immersed in their work, willing to do whatever Rasmussen directed them to do.

In that, they were like any other grad student, eager to please their professor and willing to do whatever it takes to gain some esteem in his eyes. Nick had been on that path not too long ago. A life of prosperity lay ahead of him, whatever he desired could be bought with the means at his disposal, or rather his parents' disposal. His parents, his mother specifically, left him to want for nothing.

She was always there when he needed it. She was at every event, every game he played in, every graduation ceremony, every award, and every triumph, but he had left her behind in all this. Nick took a long pull off of the mug of beer he was holding and finished it. He slammed the recycled, transparent aluminum cup on the table a touch harder than he intended.

"Whoa there, champ," Max said, "Don't hurt yourself."

Nick smiled while Zanth poured him another round. Nick gladly took it. He took another long drink, feeling the cool, frothy, golden liquid run down his throat. While Zanth picked up with a story of some other drunken revelry, Nick noticed that the world had gotten a little fuzzy and he thought his fingertips were numb.

He was tapping the tip of each finger on his left hand to his left thumb when the front door of the bar crashed open with a loud clank. An imposing figure stepped through the doorway and lumbered down the steps. The man was well over six and a half feet tall with a solid, thick frame. Nick's eyes were immediately drawn to the misshapen lumps on his forehead and the solid gray plate that covered the left side of his bald head. He wore a menacing, unhappy sneer, but it was his eyes that Nick found most unsettling.

His eyes, an unnatural shade of red, were asymmetrically shaped — one squinting and focused with just a tiny bit of pupil showing, the other open incredibly wide and constantly moving. The movements were purposeful and precise. The eye's field of view swept from one corner of the bar to the other, hesitating briefly at each patron, before passing on to the next.

"Another friend of yours?" Nick slurred.

"Watch yourself, kid," Max said quietly. The conversation at the table had quieted and all heads turned toward the door. Once the big man finished his scan of the room, he began walking purposefully towards Nick, Max, and their compatriots. With each step there was a muffled thud as the lumbering giant put his foot down forcefully with every stride.

Nick remembered his first day here, how Charlie had approached him with a fierce snarl before everyone erupted in laughter. They all had a good laugh at his expense. Nick wasn't about to be played the fool again. He sprang from his stool, stood with his chest puffed out, and blocked the giant's path.

Max immediately reached out and grabbed Nick's arm, but Nick quickly and forcefully pulled free.

"Kid," Charlie said sharply, "Sit down."

"You're not my father. Your ugly friend's not going to get the best of me."

"Kid, trust me," Max said.

"Hey ugly," Nick yelled, too drunk to recognize the collective groan issued by his companions, "Don't you know this bar's only for old, salty space jockeys? Why don't you take your lumpy head and skedaddle on out of here?"

Nick made a little shooing gesture with his hand and turned to flash a drunk smile at Max and his friends. It was then he noticed that they were sitting on their chairs with their heads lowered, staring at the bar. No one made eye contact with him. Just as Nick's brain began to register that maybe he had made a mistake, he felt the giant's hand make contact with his sternum, knock the air out of his lungs, and send him flying across the room.

Nick crashed into a table and chairs, toppling everything, and lay on the floor with a blossoming ball of fire in his chest. Tears formed at the corners of his eyes as he struggled to breathe. Before he could do anything, Nick felt a hand grab the front of his shirt and haul him off the floor. Both of the giant's eyes were fixed on him.

"Tell me why I shouldn't kill you right now," the man growled. Nick struggled to breath, let alone talk. Fear gripped him and all he could do was stammer. The giant clenched his fist and cocked his arm, ready to deliver a thundering blow to Nick's head. Max cleared his throat and stood up, staying out of range of the giant's long arms.

"Francis, he's with me." Max said calmly, "I'm sorry. He's just a kid who's had too much to drink. He doesn't know what he's saying."

Francis' eyes didn't break their lock on Nick, who dangled helplessly a couple of inches off the ground. For a moment, nothing happened and Nick was sure that he was going to get punched again. Francis, however, let him go unceremoniously and Nick once again found himself lying on the floor.

Francis let out a disgusted grunt. "Max, you need to do a better job of picking your help."

Max nodded, but said nothing. Nick thought he heard everyone in the bar collectively exhale; though that may have just been his own huge sigh of relief as he realized Francis wasn't going to beat him to a bloody pulp.

"I'm sorry again, Francis," Max said, "Let's just tend to business, shall we?"

"Right," Francis said with a low grumble. He gave Nick one last disgusted sneer before turning to face Max. "Father expects delivery by noon tomorrow."

"I'd love to," Max said, "I would've delivered two days ago if we'd gotten the forms cleared. I took a waiver to the Governor's-."

"The waiver will be approved by the morning," Francis said. His voice was deep, but it had a slightly metallic twang that was a nanosecond behind his normal speaking voice. "Once you make the delivery, we've got a job for all four of you – a delivery to *Nexus*. We should be able to get you guys loaded up and on your way by tomorrow night."

Francis then extended his arm to the four old pilots and pulled back his sleeve. Each pilot stepped forward and pressed their thumb against the screen of his wrist computer, consenting to the work request.

"Very good," Francis said, "I'll see you at noon tomorrow."

They nodded and Francis headed for the exit. Nick was still lying on the floor, afraid to move and draw anymore unwanted attention. When Francis reached a safe distance away, Max reached over and offered Nick a hand. Nick took it as he continued to watch Francis lumber towards the exit. Just as the giant reached the stairs, a young couple emerged from the shadows of a booth and approached Francis.

Nick couldn't quite hear what the man said as he approached Francis, something about a request for father. Francis stopped and his terrifying sneer transformed into a look of resigned sadness. He seemed to measure the young couple, looking from the man to the woman and back again. Nick realized he recognized the woman; she had been the one crying on the subway this morning. Or was it yesterday morning? Nick couldn't quite remember.

Francis extended his wrist computer toward the couple. The man and woman both touched their thumbs to the screen. An uncomfortable ten seconds passed and then the wrist computer emitted a beep. Francis gestured for them to come with him. The man immediately said thank you; the woman immediately started crying. Moments later, the three of them, Francis and the young couple, exited the Dry Dock and the door swung shut with a bang.

Nick was brushing himself off, finally back on his feet.

"Who the hell was that?" Nick asked.

Max patted him on the shoulder and said, "Another lesson for you, never insult the boss's son."

The others laughed, releasing a bit of the built up tension. Nick did too, but he found himself staring at the door wondering what he had just witnessed. That question never reached his lips. He took a step forward and his knee buckled beneath him. He quickly reached out and grabbed Max's arm for support, but as he hunched over, the room around him started spinning violently. Seconds later, he pitched forward, hit face first into the floor, and the world around him went black.

CHAPTER 5

Pain wracked Nick's chest and he clutched at his shirt. What had happened? The last thing he remembered was the confrontation with that big, ugly guy. He tried in vain to remember the hulk's name, but he couldn't pull it out of the throbbing ache that clouded his memory. Nick remembered being surprised by a thundering fist to his chest and then not much else.

"Lights," he called out. The overhead lighting in the room sprang on with the brightness of a thousand suns or so it seemed.

"Dim," Nick said and mercifully, the brightness of the lights reduced enough that he could open his eyes again. He was relieved to be back in his room at the Drifter, which was a surprising thought in and of itself. He swung his still booted feet off the thin, ragged mattress and onto the metal floor grating. The clang produced when his boots hit the grating made him wince. He stood somewhat unsteadily and slid his feet across the floor in an effort to avoid any more loud noises.

The cramped bathroom held the universe's smallest shower stall and a rusted, stained toilet that hadn't been cleaned in roughly fifty years and reeked of god knows what. Nick gagged slightly at the combination of the odor from the toilet and the scent of stale beer coming from his clothes. His reflection in the mirror showed the effects of the previous night's drinking. Most noticeably, he had a dull red splotch on his right check where he assumed his face had hit the floor.

He gingerly pulled off his shirt to reveal another bruise that had quickly formed. There was a large, reddish, purplish circle right in the middle of his chest. Just lightly touching it caused him to wince in pain. Nick looked dazedly around for his travel pack. It took him a few minutes of searching, but he breathed a sigh of relief when he found some trusty Conglomerate-brand pain medication. He pressed the tube gently to his bruises and within seconds felt relief.

He grabbed a cup of water and sipped tentatively, unsure how his stomach would respond. The water rushing down his throat felt like a flood overrunning desert sands. He immediately started to feel better.

Nick checked the time on his wrist computer. He had a few hours before the hotel restaurant opened up. He was starving and was happy to find a nutrient bar sitting in the bottom of his bag. He tore it open and bit into it eagerly, unbothered by the horribly bland taste and gritty texture.

He sat down on the edge of his bed and said, "Monitor. News. No sound."

A screen embedded in the wall opposite the bunk came to life; Nick squinted as his eyes adjusted to the brightness of the picture. The same blonde-haired woman sat at her news desk, speaking to the audience with a look that was a mixture of solemnity and concern.

Nick couldn't read lips well enough to know what she was saying, but he knew this report very well. This was the news broadcast that had started this chain of events and had sent him off the beaten path. The image had shifted from the reporter to an external view of space from the bow of a cargo ship. Nick remembered what happened next. Pirate ships attacked the freighter, stealing the cargo of food supplies bound for Canis One. Explosions erupted along the hull of the freighter and the pirate attack was underway.

This was not the story Nick cared about though and he ordered the recording to jump to the next segment. Here it comes, he thought. A pit formed in his stomach and the muscles in the back of his neck tightened, sending a fresh spike of pain through his head.

On cue, his father's face appeared on the screen. His father stood there in his perfectly pressed suit, with his perfectly combed and unmoving silver-streaked hair. His father spoke, but Nick didn't bother to turn up the volume; he already knew the script.

"We sincerely regret this tragic turn of events," his father said with a perfectly crafted sympathetic gaze. His father's brow was furrowed just enough to display a bit of consternation though not enough for viewers to doubt his control of the situation. He placed his left hand in his pants pocket; his body language suggesting he was sincerely sorry, though strong enough to show he would not be bowed by this crisis. This was a man whose every action was crafted, every gesture scripted, every word designed to elicit a certain response from the viewer.

He was a fraud. Nick's cheeks flushed and he clenched his jaw.

"Our thoughts and prayers are with those people affected by this tragedy," his father said. Nick choked back the bile that rose in his throat. The only prayer Nick's father had ever said was to the almighty god of corporate profit. Nick had seen his father's files, read the notes to and from his most trusted advisors, and seen the ledgers that showed the potential financial impacts for this disaster.

Nick knew that his father's only concern was keeping the true details of this from the public eye and making sure that the bottom-line of the Conglomerate went unaffected. He would feign remorse, empathy, express a dedicated pursuit of the reasons behind the tragedy, do whatever was needed to keep consumer confidence high, and forge a path to a higher profit margin.

"We will dedicate all our resources towards finding out why this happened and prevent it from ever happening again," his father spoke to the cameras. His father's expression was strong and unwavering. Nick granted that his father had charisma, strength, determination, and drive; what he lacked was any shred of moral decency.

The reporter came back on and filled in more details of the story. Reportedly, a group of unknown terrorists attacked a research facility on Nanuk. Hundreds had been killed before the terrorists accidentally triggered base quarantine protocols. Neurotoxins were released on the compound, killing everyone there.

That was the official story.

Nick shook his head at the memory. Tears welled in the corner of his eyes at the hatred and loathing he felt toward his father. Over the years, he had seen plenty of evidence of his father's greed. This, though, had taken things to a whole new level.

The night he saw this report for the first time he snuck into his father's office, just as he had the night he left, and started reading through his father's files. He found the authorization letter giving the go ahead to conduct human trials on a serum. He found the emails from concerned research scientists warning of the risks of conducting these trials. He found the field reports from those same scientists warning of the abhorrent behavior exhibited by some of the animal test subjects. Just what the serum did, though, was a mystery to Nick. Those details were not in his father's correspondence.

Plenty of other information was.

He had read through all of it, taking in every word. He only stopped to go to the bathroom. He returned to the computer and continued to read, continued to dig. He had no fear of his father catching him; his father was off-world as he often was. The little boy who looked up to his big, strong father during little league games or on career day at school was gone. His mother, his teachers, his priests had raised him differently than this. The father he thought he knew had never really been there.

Two thousand people had died as a result of the Conglomerate experiment authorized and directly supervised by his father. His father didn't care. The last thing he read was a note from Conglomerate Headquarters explaining the potential windfall they would receive from Republic defense contracts as a result of this new serum. This was something worth a potential fortune both as a military asset and as a service to sell to local militia spread across the galaxy. The Conglomerate would make quadrillions if it was a success. His father needed it to get to market right away; everyday that the serum spent in research and development was another day it wasn't earning a profit.

Profit.

It was all his father cared about. Nick sat on the bunk in his rundown Drifter hotel room and stared at the image of his father on the screen. Henry Papagous looked into the camera with a sympathetic smile.

"I hate you."

Max awoke that morning with a bit of a spring in his step. It was launch day and he'd be on the move again. On launch day, the food tasted better, the air was cleaner, and the *Hannah* sang to him. Max always found he got a little grumpy when he was grounded for too long; just the thought of being at the controls of his ship made him smile.

He briefly used the sonic shower to scrape off a layer of grime, made a quick decision that there was no need to trim his beard any further, and had a quick cup of grit-filled, but pleasingly strong coffee. Max threw on his flight coveralls and utility boots and headed downstairs.

He was pleased to see Nick already down there, looking none the worse for wear. The kid seemed to be getting a wakeup call everyday he was here, but as of yet, he seemed to be taking it all okay. Nick was sitting in his seat, facing the news broadcast, and working through two orders of omelets when Max sat across from him.

"Nick, I thought for sure your ass would be dragging this morning. How's the chest?"

Nick gave him a half-hearted smile. "I don't think I've ever felt this much pain in my entire life."

Max laughed again. "Well, you've got more bravado than brains. Picked a helluva person to fight. I think even Charlie would rather ram his head into a bulkhead than have to go toe-to-toe with that guy."

This time Nick's smile was a bit more genuine. "Lesson learned on that one, Max. Who was that guy?"

"Francis Sinclair," Max answered, "Esteemed son of the renowned Doctor Aldous Sinclair, who is of course our primary employer."

Max started laughing as Nick's shoulders sagged. Max could see genuine concern cross Nick's face.

"Don't worry about it too much, kid. Just apologize and move on. We all do stupid things from time to time," Max said.

Nick nodded, wiping at the corner of his mouth with a napkin. Max briefly checked out the news broadcast behind him where a rebroadcast of the pirate attack on the Canis One supply ships was airing.

"Wish you would've stopped me last night," Nick said quietly.

"I tried," Max responded, "You had a gallon of liquid courage in you though. Don't think I've ever seen you so eager to get into it."

"I thought he was another one of your buddies come to give me a hard time," Nick said, "Thought I could throw it back at him."

"So much for that," Max said as his food was delivered. He greedily dug in. He shook his head with a slight smile while he chewed his food; the kid sure had some brass ones to mouth off to Francis like that.

"I'm just glad Francis didn't decide to make you a smear on the floor. Big guy must be getting soft in his old age," Max said, "I was on the wrong end of a fight with him once. Getting hit by him was like being hit with a brick, though a brick had a little more give. My jaw hurt for a full week after that."

"What was the fight about?"

"Something stupid," Max said.

Nick stared at him, but Max looked down at his plate, shoveling food into his mouth.

"What's going on with Francis' head?" Nick asked.

Max shrugged. "Don't know the whole story. Happened before I ever met him. Rumor is that Francis was injured in some kind of experiment back when his father worked for the Conglomerate. Something happened though and they weren't able to regenerate the parts of his brain that were damaged, so Doc Sinclair took it upon himself to fix him up with some cybernetic enhancements."

"I noticed the eye," Nick said, taking the final bite from his plate.

"Yeah," Max said, "Just be sure not to comment on his looks again. He gets a little sensitive about that."

"I gathered," Nick said dryly.

"Anyway, you'll get a chance to see him again here in just a couple of hours."

"What do you mean?" Nick asked with a mouthful of food.

"I guess you don't remember," Max said, "We've got clearance from the governor to deliver our load and get going. We're shipping out today."

Nick put his fork down and paled slightly. Then he abruptly stood up.

"I'll meet you at the ship. Going to stop by the chapel again."

"All right, don't be late. You might want to say an extra Hail Mary or two after last night."

"Very funny," Nick said and briskly walked away. As he left the room, the kid's eyes kept darting back to the monitors. When he was gone, Max turned to see the soft smile of a Conglomerate head honcho, speaking earnestly to some gathered reporters. Max shrugged and turned back around.

An hour later, after finishing his breakfast and packing up the few things he had with him at the Drifter, Max stepped back aboard the *Hannah* and breathed deep. The ship was more of a home to him than anyplace on Dust. Through ten years of work out here, Max had spent more time in the ship than on the planet's surface. While he appreciated the amenities of the Drifter and the company of his friends, it was always a pleasure to return to what he considered home.

He was more than ready to be on his way again, to take another small chunk out of the debts he owed. Max eagerly dropped his bag in his quarters and found Reggie in the cockpit, working through some control system diagnostics.

"How's everything going, Reggie?"

"All systems are nominal," Reggie reported.

"Good," Max said as the robot disconnected itself from his command console, "What's left?"

"Hatch seal inspections and a power core check."

"I'll take care of the inspection; you do the core check. Nick should be here within the hour and I want us ready to lift off. Can't keep the good Doctor waiting," Max said. Reggie nodded his cylindrical, gray head and plodded off down the corridor with a whir and a clank. Max headed for the boarding ramp and got to work.

Ten minutes later, Max was standing next to the closed boarding ramp, waiting for the pressure check to finish, when Nick arrived on the landing platform. An indicator light next to the ramp flashed green and Max received confirmation on his wrist computer that the leak check was successful. The ramp slowly descended. Max gestured for Nick to go on in.

Nick stood there.

"Go on aboard, kid. We need to get moving," Max said.

"I'm not going."

"What? What the hell are you talking about?"

Max slowly turned to face Nick; Nick was not carrying his bag.

"I'm not going, Max. I can't go back to *Nexus*."

"You've got to be kidding."

Nick stood stock still as he spoke. His hands were balled into fists at his side.

"I quit, Max. You can go on without me."

"Bullshit," Max said. His face became flush and as he spoke spittle flew from his lip. "You still owe me for the goddamn augers you broke. You also owe me for the trip out here. You haven't done a goddamn thing to earn what I've given you."

"I'll find a job here," Nick said, "I'll pay you back. But, I'm not going."

"You spoiled son of a bitch. You think you can just do whatever you damn well please out here?" Max yelled, "You signed a contract with me. You can't just walk out on that. You've been nothing but a pain in the ass the entire time you've been here. Have you been trying to get yourself fired?"

Nick looked away, refusing to meet Max's glare.

"You have, haven't you?"

"I…"

"Son of a bitch."

"I just can't go back, Max. I'm sorry."

"Why? Why the hell not?"

Nick hesitated. Max folded his arms across his chest and waited.

"I stole something from my father; he'll be looking for me. I just can't go back."

Max shook his head and smiled menacingly.

"You're a piece of work, you know that. You're a goddamn, hypocritical jackass. You drive off my friend because you judged what she did as wrong, yet here you are stealing things from your father and then you're afraid to face him! Then trying to intentionally screw up so you can get fired! You know what? Screw you. You need to face up to what you've done. Get on this ship and I'm taking you back to *Nexus*. Hell, I'll drag you right to your father and you can learn what it's like to be a man and be responsible for your actions."

Nick jutted out his chin.

"I'm not going."

"Now you listen to me, you little punk," Max said as he jabbed a finger in Nick's direction, "You either get on this ship or I will have you deported. If you didn't get the message through your thick skull, you're not wanted around here. After your little jaunt the other day and your run in with Lonnie, Windy City security would happily kick you off this planet for good. And guess what? They'll put you on the first ship out of town, which just happens to be mine."

"You can't do that," Nick said.

"Oh, I can, Nick," Max said, "I can make it really miserable for you. You don't have a choice here. Get on the damn ship."

"Please, Max."

"Get on-board willingly or I drag you along kicking and screaming. What's it going to be?"

Nick just stood there for a moment, mouth open, looking down at the landing pad deck.

"Max, this isn't just some little fight with my father-"

"I don't give a shit about your family squabbles, Nick. You signed a contract with me. Remember? Then you tried to sabotage my operation. Took money from my pocket. What's it going to be?"

Nick didn't move. Max shook his head in disgust.

"Deportation it is then," Max said, calling up the security comm. channel on his wrist computer.

"No," Nick said, "I'll go. I'll go."

"Well, I guess you're not as stupid as I thought," Max said, "Let's take a walk and go get your bag, Nick. Wouldn't want you to leave anything behind."

An hour later, Max settled into the pilot's seat while Nick took the seat to his right. They hadn't spoken more than a couple of words to each other over the last hour. Max had remained within two feet of Nick all that time. Nick couldn't bring himself to make eye contact with Max. He played around on his console, calling up anything that looked the least bit interesting, while Max went through his pre-flight checklist in silence.

"Good, let's get going," Max said. Max started the launch sequence and within moments, the large freighter rumbled off the landing pad and headed north. Mile after mile of desert sand passed beneath them. Within moments, a rust red mountain range rose from the desert floor. The mountains were jagged, steeply ascending and descending in a rapid succession of peaks. Nick stared at them for a moment, lost in their rugged beauty.

"So, uh, where are we headed?" Nick asked.

Max let out a long, slow breath through pursed lips before responding.

"Nick, you are about to meet the only local celebrity we have out here," Max said as he reviewed the telemetry on his console, "Doctor Aldous Sinclair is almost solely responsible for the success of this colony. He came here just after the Republic and the Conglomerate packed their bags and jumped out of the star system."

Nick nodded as he gazed at the horizon. It was a relief just to have Max talking to him again.

"The story is that Sinclair came here with his power core at full charge, if you know what I mean. He had a real chip on his shoulder, wanted to show the Republic how foolish they were. Much of what you saw back there in Windy City was his design. He engineered the light vines, developed the crops that would thrive at Bloom, designed the machines that dug out the residential district. He's looked at as a bit of a god among men."

Max looked at Nick, whose eyes were focused on a spot in the distance. Nick was trying to piece together what he would do from here. He wasn't ready to face his father and somehow he needed to convince Max of that. He doesn't understand what he's asking me to do, Nick thought.

Max broke up the lingering silence.

"Doc Sinclair has become a bit eccentric over the years. Just wanted to give you fair warning."

Nick looked at him expectantly.

"My advice is to stay quiet, stick with me, and keep your head down. I'll deal with Francis and his old man. You just listen, stay close, and don't do anything stupid. His place is something else…well you'll see for yourself in just a minute."

Nick nodded.

"There it is," Max said, pointing out the cockpit window towards a large mountain that loomed on the horizon.

Nick leaned forward in his seat. There wasn't much to see at first, other than a large black dot that seemed to be embedded in the side of the enormous mountain peak.

Details quickly came into focus. An expansive plateau at the base of the mountain had been converted into a spaceport landing pad. Nick counted a half dozen ships parked there, several of which he recognized from the Windy City platform. Lightning towers dotted the perimeter of the landing pad making the whole site seem like the gaping maw of some beast emerging from the mountain.

Enormous hangar doors were built into the side of the mountain. Large towers flanked both sides of the doors. Two additional towers were placed on adjacent peaks on the opposite side of the landing field.

"You must be able to see for miles from those towers," Nick said.

"Wouldn't know," Max said, "Sinclair doesn't exactly invite people in for tours."

"Place is enormous," Nick said, "Looks like a fortress."

"You've got that right," Max said, "My guess is the structure extends several thousand square meters into the base of that peak. That's Mount Aldous, by the way, it's the tallest mountain on Dust."

"Mount Aldous?"

"Named after Doctor Aldous Sinclair."

"Just a little eccentric then," Nick said.

"Yep," Max responded.

"He built all this himself?"

"He's got a lot of resources at his disposal," Max said.

A robotic voice broke over the communications system. "*Hannah*, this is Sinclair Sanctuary control, we have you on final approach. Please proceed to the landing beacon."

"Copy control," Max replied.

"No folksy charm out here," Nick remarked.

Max shook his head and said, "Doc prefers the company of robotic workers. He's got a virtual army of them. As far as I know, he and Francis are the only two people out here."

"I thought robots were too difficult to maintain on Dust," Nick said.

"Doc Sinclair's a smart man," Max said with a shrug.

Nick shook his head in disbelief as they started to descend.

The moment the *Hannah* settled on its assigned spot on the spaceport pad a swarm of cargo hauling drones approached it. Before Nick and Max could make their way to the entry ramp, the cargo hold was open and the robots were quickly offloading the large, black rectangular crates that filled the hold. Nick caught a brief glimpse of the synchronized ballet as a container was latched onto, lifted onto a conveyor and hauled off towards the large hangar at the far end of the field. The robots worked quickly; Nick guessed they would be done in twenty minutes or less.

A cart pulled up just in front of the ramp. Nick tried and failed to keep his expression neutral as he saw Francis step out. Francis saw Nick immediately and the left side of his mouth curled up in a sneer. In daylight, Francis' deformities looked even more grotesque. The uneven lumps on his head looked to be pulsating slightly and Francis' skin seemed stretched, taught, and unnaturally pale. His mechanical eye fixed its calculating stare on Nick. Nick found it unnerving, but more than anything he felt pity for the large man.

An older man walked a step behind Francis. Despite Francis' misshapen features, there was a hint of a resemblance between the two men. The color of the eyes, the focused stare, the cut of the nose, and the exactness of the mouth gave away their kinship.

Before anyone could say anything, Nick stepped forward within arm's reach of Francis. Francis' hand closed rapidly in a fist.

"L-Look, Francis, I just wanted to apologize about last night. I had too much to drink and I…"

Francis snarled, "Don't talk to me. I have no business with you."

Max put a hand on Nick's elbow and stepped up next to him. "Doc, Francis, no need to rehash bygone events. What've you got for us?"

Aldous Sinclair didn't say anything at first. He calmly but sternly looked from Francis to Nick. Aldous was a tall man, as tall as Francis though not nearly as thick with muscle. Where Francis was a fearsome behemoth, Aldous was stately and refined. His movements were precise; his words clipped slightly.

Nick felt the weight of the old man's stare, suddenly he felt like he was waiting to see if he would make the cut for the varsity team again. Finally, Aldous offered a half smile.

"The indiscretions of youth."

Max nodded and extended his hand in greeting.

"Good to see you again, Doc."

"Likewise, Maxime," Aldous said as the old man quickly consulted his wrist computer, "It looks like this shipment is in order."

"No problems with this one," Max responded. Max then produced a small vial from his pocket and held it out to the Doctor.

Aldous smiled at the sight of the vial, though instead of looking happy, the expression struck Nick as vaguely menacing. "Excellent, Max. Thank you."

Aldous quickly pocketed the vial and then pressed an unseen button on his computer.

"Payment has been transferred, as usual," Aldous said, "The next job is a big one. Most of the cargo is in-orbit at Platform Alpha. We should have everything launched within the next two hours. You'll load up at the platform."

Max nodded.

"Very good then," Max said, "We'll be on our way in just a few minutes. What are we carrying anyway?"

"Something I've been working on for the Conglomerate for some time. The results of some weapons research I've been conducting."

Max raised his eyebrows in mild surprise.

"Doc, I didn't think you were still doing work for the Conglomerate."

Aldous' smile faded, his eyes momentarily gained a sharp focus, and he calmly replied, "This is something I owe them, Maxime. I'm just glad to finally have it ready."

Max said, "All right, then. We're going to do a quick inspection of a few things and then be on our way."

Aldous nodded and turned back toward the cart. Francis stared at Nick for an extra moment before slowly turning and leaving. Nick exhaled and felt his hand tremble slightly in relief. He opened and closed his fist repeatedly in an effort to regain composure. He finally took his eyes off of the cart as it departed the landing field. Max had opened a panel on the underside of the ship just beneath the cockpit and was inspecting some wire harness connections. Nick walked over behind him, somewhat detached from the moment.

Without looking away from what he was doing, Max said, "You okay, Nick?"

"Yeah," Nick responded, though his voice was unfocused.

"Don't let Francis rattle you like that," Max said. He was satisfied that the connections were tight and he closed the access panel. "Francis isn't going to beat you to a pulp on sight, though it might be best if you just keep your distance from him. Your apology would've gone over well with most reasonable people, but Francis, well, I don't think his mind's all there."

Nick nodded. He looked over to his left and saw Charlie waving to them from across the pad as he boarded his ship. Nick gave a wave back. While Max checked inside another access panel, Nick stood and watched Charlie's worn, battered freighter lift off the spaceport pad and then start rapidly climbing towards the upper reaches of Dust's atmosphere.

Moments after Charlie's ship disappeared from view, Nick heard a resounding boom reverberate around him. He quickly scanned the skies for the source and found a large pill-shaped container rocketing towards the sky.

"Rail launcher?" Nick asked.

"Yep," Max responded, "Doc Sinclair had a giant one installed on the other side of the mountain peak."

Nick continued to stare at the object until it too disappeared from view. He then turned back to see Max closing up another panel.

"Why not just load up here?"

Max frowned as he found a couple of frayed wires.

"Sinclair's probably got a heavy payload for us. This'll save some wear and tear on the engines," Max said. He pulled a small canister from his belt and sprayed the exposed wiring.

"What are you checking anyway?" Nick asked.

"Noticed on the way up that one of the landing pad position indicators was stuck on retracted. Figure it's either a bad connection or a bad sensor. If this doesn't fix it, I'll have to ask Reggie to swap out the sensor."

Nick wasn't listening. He was still looking around, taking it all in. The cargo haulers had long since emptied the *Hannah's* hold and disappeared from the landing pad. Three other ships also were being prepped to leave, but other than that, the pad was empty. The spaceport was so large; it would not have been out of place in several other more developed worlds. Yet, according to Max, only the old man and his son lived here.

"I don't get it," Nick said as he continued to stare, "What the heck goes on here?"

Max walked up to him, wiping grime from his hand on his pants, "I told you, Nick. Doc Sinclair is a bit eccentric. He really goes all in for everything he does. I don't think moderation is in his vocabulary."

"But how the heck can he afford to do all this?"

Max looked around and shrugged. "The man's services have been in high demand for years. Supposedly, he did a lot of genetics research for the Conglomerate. Came here a wealthy man."

"No doubt," said Nick.

"Come on," Max said, "Let's get going. We've got a long day ahead."

"What's on your mind, Nick?" Max asked as he took a bite of what the food processor called beef stew.

It tasted fine, Nick thought, but the oatmeal-like texture seemed off. After a couple bites, Nick struggled with eating any more. He put his spoon down after he realized he was just pushing the brown paste around his bowl.

"Sorry, premium food is not in the budget," Max said after Nick remained silent for a minute.

Nick cracked a smile, "It's not that, although I have to say I don't think I've ever eaten anything like this."

Nick's voice was a bit weary, exhausted from the long day spent loading the cargo and getting underway.

"I'm sorry, Max."

Max didn't say anything at first; he took a long drink of water from his cup.

"I'm sorry for what I've done and how I've acted," Nick said, staring at the table in front of him, "I've had a tough go of it lately. Haven't been myself."

Max nodded as he listened.

"You did pretty well today once we got going," Max said, "I appreciate the apology, but that's not going to make up for what you've done."

"I understand," Nick said, reluctantly taking a bite of the brown goo. "How long have you worked for Sinclair anyway?"

Max thought for a moment. "Just over ten years now."

"Man, not sure I could handle his creepiness for so long," Nick said. Aldous had been polite enough and business-like when they met, but there was still something about him that Nick didn't like.

Max chuckled a bit at the remark.

"I told you Aldous is eccentric, but I don't think you have anything to worry about. The man's done a lot for Dust; he's done a lot for a lot of people in this corner of the galaxy."

"Why has he exiled himself on Dust, then? If he's so magnanimous, why not operate a bit closer to civilization?"

"Different strokes for different folks, Nick. Not everyone feels comfortable with the hustle and bustle of Earth or the other more established colonies. Besides, operating out here gives him a bit more freedom than he would have under the bright lights of the Conglomerate or the government's watchful eye."

Nick looked at Max skeptically. His experiences with his father taught him that given enough money, ethics were merely a minor inconvenience when it came to the Conglomerate's scientific progress.

"Something just feels off about him."

Max looked annoyed. He swallowed the bite in his mouth and then slammed his fist on the table.

"Kid, stop looking for things that aren't there. Sinclair's a bit of an oddball. So what? Don't be so quick to judge."

Nick recoiled a bit.

"Sorry, Max," Nick said softly, "I'm probably just tired. Mind's looking for conspiracy theories."

"Nick," Max said, looking into his almost empty bowl, "I owe a lot to that man, more than I can ever really explain. Guess we're both a bit tired tonight. Why don't you do a quick walkthrough of the hold? I'll clean up here."

Nick nodded, pushing his bowl toward Max. He stood up and walked towards the galley exit, boots clanging off the floor grate with every step. He put a hand on the hatchway and hesitated. He framed his question carefully, not wanting to strike another nerve with Max.

"Hey, what was in the vial you gave him, anyway?" Nick wondered, "He seemed awfully excited about it."

Max didn't bother to turn around, keeping his back to Nick.

"He did light up, didn't he? Think it was some genetic data on some animals, birds or something. Can't say I really understood what it was. Doc's been trying to adapt some of the local wildlife, thinks it can help with the terraforming."

Nick nodded and walked away. The ship had been configured for night mode, so the hallway lighting was a dim red. Nick had been told that the lighting effect was designed to help his body keep normal rhythms in this artificial environment. It was supposed to be soothing, readying him for sleep. Nick just found it annoying because he could barely see where he was going.

Thankfully, the living quarters section of the *Hannah* were fairly small so it only took Nick a minute to reach the cargo hold hatchway. Nick was sure that Reggie could have done this or maybe Max could have done it from the cockpit based on sensor data, but he sensed Max was looking for a nice way to end the conversation. Knowing that you were spending the next three days locked up in a glorified tin can with only one other person and one old maintenance robot meant you needed to be able to give the other person space when they needed it.

Nick walked between row after row of giant rectangular shipping containers. The crates came up to his waist and were longer than he was tall. Nick's curiosity was peaked, but he saw no quick way to take a look at what was inside. He guessed that Max would probably not appreciate him poking his nose into the containers, creepy doctor or no creepy doctor.

All told, there were roughly one hundred containers locked up in the hold. Faint red track lighting allowed Nick to see as he wandered up and down the rows. Green lock indicators at the ends of each container told him they were being held tightly in place. The only thing that caught Nick's eye in the inspection was an open access panel. Max or Reggie probably forgot to close it while looking into something or other.

Nick closed it with a louder than expected clang. He stood there and listened as the sound echoed throughout the chamber. Then finally, the hold was again silent.

Then, Nick heard a thud from the nearest stack of containers. The hair on his neck stood on end as he quickly activated his flashlight. There was nothing to see in the compartment; nothing moved under the gaze of his flashlight beam.

Great, Nick thought, now I'm hearing things. The hair stood up on the back of his neck as the fact that he was all alone in the dark cargo hold took hold of him. Surrounded by mysterious black containers, stacked so high that they created a bit of a maze, he realized he could no longer see the exit. His heart started beating a bit faster.

Nick took a deep breath and tried to calm himself. Nothing like getting a good case of the willies, Nick thought.

"If this is how I am on the first night," Nick said to himself, "By the end of this trip, I'll be huddled in the corner of my quarters, hiding under a blanket."

Nick chided himself for being a little scared and started to walk back. Despite his efforts, his pace heading out was noticeably quicker.

CHAPTER 6

Nick lazily pushed the leftover maple syrup and brown sugar flavored oatmeal around his bowl. At least for this meal, the food's consistency and texture were right, but he was pretty sure that the maple syrup and brown sugar were never derived from a tree or plant. It didn't help that the remnants in his bowl had long since grown cold. The thick, sugary food paste stared back at him, testing his fortitude. The food was winning.

He dropped his spoon in the bowl with a noisy clank and looked up at the movie playing on the monitor. He couldn't remember the name nor did he know what was going on. It was merely noise in the background. Nick's eyes became heavy as he listened to the rhythmic thud-thud-thud of Max's feet on the treadmill.

A moment later his head jerked up and his eyes snapped open. Nick cleared his throat and sat up on the bench. The lounge of the *Hannah* was fairly well equipped, with a solid library of programs, movies, music, and games as well as the treadmill and some resistive exercise equipment. Still, there were only so many shows he could watch before he felt the urge to get up and do something. Anything.

If this was how bored he was on their first full day in transit, then he was going to be pulling his hair out by day four. Max's footsteps suddenly stopped and Nick looked up to see him wipe the sweat off his face with a towel before taking a seat on the other end of the couch.

"So, do you get used to the boredom?" Nick asked.

Max shook his head with a bit of disdain.

"How can you sit here and claim to be bored when you're watching one of the greatest movies of all time?"

"This?" Nick said with a nod of his head towards the monitor.

"Yes, this!" Max said, "That's Farely Lane. She's one of the best actresses of all time, not to mention one of the most beautiful. Plus this is *Valhalla Reborn*! It won best picture in '48. This movie is about your damn home planet! How can you not like this movie?"

"That was five years before I was born," Nick commented, "Can't say I've ever seen it."

Max's face took on a pained expression and he said, "How can you have been raised on Valhalla and never seen this movie? I would've expected someone raised there to have a better cultural background."

Nick laughed. "This isn't really the kind of culture that's valued there."

Max rolled his eyes. "I should've guessed that the high and mighty of Valhalla would think a movie was beneath them. I'm sure you've enjoyed a night at the symphony while sipping on tea in a real china cup made from naturally-grown tea leaves."

Max was more right than Nick cared to admit. Valhalla was a wealthy world; its citizens expected to be among the cultural elite. Most performances there were live action plays, symphonies, or other similar events; a movie would be considered too mundane.

"How can you not have watched a movie about the settling of your own homeworld, anyway?" Max asked.

Nick shrugged.

"I guess they didn't think this was accurate enough to teach in our history class," Nick said with a hint of sarcasm.

Max shook his head and said, "You don't know what you're missing, Nick. I guess you have some catching up to do on the movie library then."

Nick tried to change the subject.

"Where are you from, Max?"

Max's eyes were glued to Farely as she glided across the screen, "Churchill. Lived there until I got my first job as a maintenance tech for Conglomerate Fleet Services at the ripe old age of 18."

Churchill was not a world that Nick was familiar with. He had heard of it, believed it was mostly an industrial world, but that was all that stuck out in Nick's head.

"Can't say I know it very well."

"Not surprised," Max replied, "It's probably not significant enough to be covered in your geography lessons."

Nick had a hard time figuring out if Max's disdain was real or not.

"Didn't mean to offend. When I get control of the curriculum, I promise we'll add it to the first week of Colonial Astronomy."

"Be sure to mention my name," Max said with a smile.

"Why'd you leave?" Nick asked.

"I've always wanted to be a pilot. To be at the controls, flying through the stars, that was my dream. I even signed on with Central Exploration for a while; wanted to be a planetary scout."

"I take it that dream didn't go far."

"Their budget was cut and I was laid off; some bean counters decided we'd done enough galactic exploration. I got lucky and found a job with a shipping company; worked for them for about ten years. That was where I met my ex."

The words hung in the air for a moment, before Nick realized what Max had said. Max continued to impassively stare at the screen. He didn't look away as Farely tended to some ill colonists. Nick wrestled a moment with whether to turn the conversation elsewhere. In the end though, he realized they would be spending a lot of time together over the next few months. If they couldn't talk about each other, what would they talk about?

"What happened with her?" Nick asked.

Max hesitated; this time he did look away from the screen. For an instant, pain flashed across his face, but was quickly replaced with a neutral expression.

"Our daughter died," Max finally said, looking at Nick, "Things weren't the same between us after that. Shortly after our little girl's death, I bought the *Hannah* and started doing runs out here. I told you kid, everybody out here is running from something."

"I'm sorry," Nick said. He knew he had nothing to be sorry for, but he couldn't think of anything else to say.

"Don't be," Max said earnestly. Max tried to act as though the memory hadn't gotten to him, but clearly it had. He stood up from the couch.

"Losing her was the hardest thing I've ever been through."

Max returned his gaze to the screen, but Nick could see his eyes had glossed over a bit.

"I think I'll go get cleaned up," Max said and left the room.

Nick awoke from a nap with a start as he heard a bang come from the corridor. He was up in an instant and quickly poked his head out of the hatchway. There, he saw Max, toolbox in hand, crouched down in front of an access panel that he was unfastening.

"What's going on?" Nick asked somewhat groggily.

"CO_2 levels are higher than normal," Max said matter-of-factly, "I'm going to take apart one of the air scrubbers and see if I can figure out what's wrong."

"Shouldn't the, uh, ship be able to tell you where the problem is?" Nick asked as he stepped into the hallway.

Max shot him a look that said don't be an idiot.

"Of course, genius, but I'm not getting anything useful out of the computer. Means we've either got a scrubber problem, a sensor problem, or any of a dozen other possible problems."

Nick nodded and sidled slowly over to Max. He watched as Max wormed his way into the exposed maintenance crawlspace. Once he was in there, Max was wedged in the cramped space in what looked to be a fairly uncomfortable position.

Nick gave him a wry smile, "So, what's the point of having a maintenance robot if you never let it do maintenance?"

"You're doing a great job channeling my ex-wife. Try making your tone of voice a little more acidic," Max said. He turned on a utility light and the beam illuminated a maze of pipes and hoses, shiny canisters, dirt-stained wiring, and a few odd bits of duct tape. "Reggie is running some diagnostics on the gas analyzer. I figure while he's doing that I can do this. Besides, time for me to change out some filters in this anyway. And it gives me something to do so I don't have to sit around watching movies with you."

"Mind if I help?" Nick asked, crouching down next to him.

"Not really room for two sets of hands in here," Max said, "But you're free to watch. Call up the schematic and follow along."

Nick tapped a button on the wall, "Schematic. Air scrubber. Uh, Port Air Scrubber."

A holographic image appeared in the corridor just in front of Nick. The three dimensional projection was the same maze of hoses, canisters, and wires that Max was now elbow deep in.

"Highlight filters," Nick commanded. Four points were highlighted yellow on the projection. "Show access."

The projection started moving and a listing of steps appeared immediately to the right.

"Audio?" The computer asked.

"Please don't," Max said, grunting as he tried to pull apart a connection.

"No," Nick responded. The animation of the maintenance procedure proceeded at an almost dizzying speed, theoretically giving Nick an overview of what Max was doing. Nick could have slowed it down, sped it up, or stopped at any given step, but he wasn't really interested in what he was watching. He sat next to Max and watched him methodically pull apart various connection points, inspect the ends of each, check for any other signs of damage, and ultimately move on to the next part.

Max disconnected a hose and the connector on the end of it was corroded and worn. Flakes of metal came off as Max ran his fingers over the end of the connector. The black rubber seal around the edge was tattered and torn. Max wormed his way back out and handed the part to Nick.

"Go make another one for me, will you?" Max asked. "You can get the part number from the computer."

Nick nodded and headed to the small engineering room that separated his quarters from Max's. He stood before the replicator and called up the holographic schematic of the air scrubber. He found the part number and commanded the replicator to make another. Within five minutes, the new part had been printed and he dropped the old one in the recycle bin.

Max continued checking connections for another twenty minutes before Nick spoke again, "So how did you lose your daughter?"

Max looked at Nick blankly for a moment before the question sank in. He frowned, the creases on his forehead deepening slightly. "Nick, this is not Zen and the art of spaceship maintenance. You are not my psychotherapist. You've already gotten more out of me than your last two predecessors did in over two months on the job. Let's talk about something else."

Nick nodded. Max took a moment to look at where he was in disassembling the scrubber. After taking a moment to scrutinize what connectors were currently disconnected, Max dived in again, pulling things apart.

"All right," Max said, breaking the silence, "Tell me why you're afraid to face your father. What'd you take from him that made you set off halfway across explored space and take up on a rig shuttling back and forth for the benefit of the armpit of humanity?"

Nick hesitated a moment as he eyed Max uncertainly.

"It's nothing, just stupid stuff."

"Bullshit, kid," Max said, "Stupid disagreements don't get you out here trying to sabotage my operation just so you can get fired. What are you running from?"

Nick watched as Max disconnected a small cylindrical piece, threw it in his toolbox, pulled a clean one out of the box, and installed it. Nick took a deep breath and let it out slowly.

"My father is, well, he's the Vice President of Research and Development for the Conglomerate."

Max disconnected another small cylinder and threw it in his toolbox. He stopped for a moment and looked Nick in the eye.

"Christ, kid," Max said, wiping at his hands with a rag, "Vice President of Research and Development? Wish you would've told me that in the interview."

"You never would have hired me," Nick said, meeting Max's piercing stare.

"Damn right," Max said, "Do you have any idea what people back on Dust would have done to you if they'd known you were the son of a high ranking official in the Conglomerate? You think you had it rough when you were being questioned by those cops in Windy City? If I had turned you in and they had discovered that little nugget, I don't think you would've ever seen the light of day again."

"I don't see it, Max. Dust is no threat to the Conglomerate."

"Do you remember the park, Nick? Do you remember what you saw there?" Max said.

Nick thought for a moment and shrugged.

"Nothing remarkable. Just people going about their lives."

"All right, true enough. What didn't you see? What do you see every day on the news broadcasts that you didn't see there?"

"Poverty, hunger, unhappiness."

Max again locked eyes with the young man, "Who do you think provided all the food we ate there? Who do you think built the homes? Hell, who made that park?"

"I don't know. The Republic? The Conglomerate?" Nick responded, "Who normally provides that stuff?"

"Do you think they would spend the resources to make sure folks on Dust lived comfortably when people on other worlds are fighting, protesting, rising up like they are?" Max asked, "How many times do you have to be told that the Republic and the Conglomerate gave up on Dust a long time ago?"

"Then where did it all come from? How has that place managed to thrive when so many other places are falling apart?" Nick asked.

"They did it all on their own, Nick. They grow their own food. They take care of their own there," Max said, "They did it all with the help of Sinclair. He's responsible for almost all of that. He engineered the crops, he created equipment that could survive the environment, he's created that way of life. He is almost single-handedly responsible for turning Dust from a dying husk to a thriving community. And no one there wants anyone in the Republic or the Conglomerate to know anything about it."

"That doesn't make any sense," Nick protested, "If they knew what was going on there, I can't imagine them not celebrating it. If Sinclair can create thriving crops and food in this place, he could do it anywhere."

"And if the Conglomerate found out about this place, they would shut it down immediately, lock Aldous up for illegally modifying local wildlife, and tear apart this colony faster than you or I could blink. They'd claim patent violations left and right, shutting down any production or farming. They'd claim patent rights over the seeds in the soil and the gaskets on the augers. Every dime that Sinclair earns is a dime stolen from their pockets or so they would have you believe," Max said.

"I don't believe that, Max."

"It's all about profit, Nick," Max said, "The Conglomerate is twice the size of any other corporation in the Republic. They make more money in a year then almost every planet in the Republic save for Earth. They use that money to control the Republic. They control the trade. They control the prices. They control the people. The breakthroughs on Dust would be a very clear threat to that control.

"And don't think Dust is the only colony that's like this. There're other places, other worlds, where people have gotten wise to the Conglomerate's ways. You've seen it yourself on the news. Those food riots on Canis One weren't just about people being hungry. Who do you think convinced the Republic to stop colonizing new worlds? The Conglomerate did. And they did it because their influence is already being subverted in places like Dust. Keep expanding and they lose more of their grip on society."

Nick nodded, but he couldn't believe it. He had seen the greed of his father firsthand, but that didn't condemn the entire company. He stood in the corridor silently, staring blankly at the opposite wall as thoughts swam through his head.

Max eyed him for a minute before continuing his work.

"You didn't answer my question," Max said, "Why did you run away from your father? If he really is a Vice

President for the Conglomerate, you should be spending your nights sleeping on a bed made of money."

Nick took a seat on the floor and leaned his back against the wall. He pulled the data crystal out of his pocket and held it up. The lights in the corridor refracted through it casting a rainbow of light on the floor in front of him.

"See this crystal, Max?"

Max looked up with a grunt.

"It holds every record I could find on his computer, records of the experiments he authorized, of the human testing he authorized. Records that show he is responsible for the deaths of thousands all in the name of profit. The only thing he's ever cared about is making a goddamn dollar. To think, I used to look up to him."

"Pretty serious claims."

"Aren't you the one who just said the Conglomerate would shutdown everything on Dust for profit?" Nick asked.

"And aren't you the one who had trouble believing a corporation would do something like that? Tell me, Nick, where's the truth here? Is your father the outlier? The one bad apple in an otherwise good company. Or is your father just a reflection of the values of that company?"

"My father authorized human trials of some kind of serum. He's responsible for the incident on Nanuk," Nick said, "And he did it all against the advice of those under him. I've seen the memos. He did it."

"And I would bet that any other manager in that company would have made the same decision," Max said.

"But it was my father that did it and I hate him for it."

"Did you ever talk to him about it? Stand up to him? Find out what he really did?" Max said as he started to reconnect some of the hoses he had taken off.

Nick shook his head. "No…I couldn't stand to even look at him."

"Well, you're going to have to soon. You can't run from this, from him, forever."

"And I bet I don't live beyond that day," Nick said, "He'll see to it."

Max laughed. "Being a little melodramatic aren't you? I don't think I've ever met a man your age who didn't hold some kind of grudge against his father. Isn't it possible that maybe you're overstating things a bit?"

"We'll see soon, won't we?"

Max looked away from the scrubber and looked Nick in the eye. He chewed on the inside of his lower lip for a moment as he looked over the kid. After another minute, Nick carefully put the crystal back in his pocket.

Max asked, "Does he know you have the data?"

"I think so," Nick said, nodding his head, "He sent me a message the day we left *Nexus*. Made it sound like he knew."

"So give it back and walk away, Nick. Close that chapter in your life. Don't worry about him; get on with your own life. Do the things that you think are important. Be the good person you wanted him to be."

Nick nodded but didn't respond. He stared at the wall opposite him. It wouldn't be that simple, he thought. His father wouldn't let it be that simple. His father would want him to know the consequences of his actions. That was one of his favorite phrases. It was something Nick heard more and more of as he grew up.

Max crawled out of the small maintenance area and reinstalled the panel that covered the air scrubber.

"Activate Port Air Scrubber."

A few soft clicks were audible as the device restarted.

"Reggie, status?" Max asked.

"The gas analyzer appears to be working nominally," Reggie's voice came back to them over the intercom.

"CO_2 levels?"

"Still above normal," Reggie responded, "And rising slightly."

Max cursed and scratched the back of his head.

"What are you thinking?" Nick asked.

"I'm thinking that with three full days left in this trip we can't just let the carbon dioxide levels continue to rise. At this rate, we have about a day before it'll become a problem."

"So you've got backups, right? Something else that can get the air cleaned up?"

"Sure," Max said, "But I don't like mysteries on my ship. Everything that occurs on a ship is explainable; there is no such thing as an unexplained event. Something has to be driving the levels up."

"So what could it be?" Nick asked.

"Computer," Max said, "Scan for vital signs on-board. How many people are you picking up?"

After a slight pause, the computer responded, "Only two life forms detected, both currently in the crew quarters section."

Max frowned. "Well, that rules out a stowaway."

"You know," Nick said, "I heard a strange thump in the cargo bay last night during inspection. I thought it was just my imagination."

"Only way to fool the scan would be with some pretty thick shielding," Max said.

"What about those containers? Are they thick enough to do it?"

Max thought for a moment.

"It's possible. Those cases are sealed, though, and Sinclair would've told me if we were transporting something biological," Max answered, "Let's take apart the starboard scrubber and then we'll do a sweep of the bay. All three of us. We'll have a look at those containers, but I don't think they're it. Like I said, Sinclair would've told me."

Nick reclined in the co-pilot's seat, half asleep, entirely exhausted and listened to Max and Reggie go back and forth on the carbon dioxide issue. The three of them had been attacking the problem all day. Max and Nick had completed the same overhaul of the starboard scrubber.

When that yielded no results, the three of them did a slow meticulous search of the cargo bay. They started with the containers but could find no openings in the cases that could emit any gases. The seals on the containers appeared to be airtight.

Then they searched the rest of the hold, inch by inch, looking for any traces of a stowaway. Max had admitted that this was an unlikely cause for the spike. One extra body on-board was unlikely to cause elevated carbon dioxide levels.

After they completed the sweep, they did a check of some of the plumbing for the environmental systems. Carbon dioxide collected by the scrubbers was routed to a water generator that took the oxygen from the carbon dioxide and combined it with hydrogen to make water. They found no leak though, no unexpected source.

Max had grown more frustrated as the day went on.

"Reggie," Max said scratching his forehead as he leaned forward on the pilot's console, "What possibilities are left over?"

Reggie stood in the back of the cockpit, almost invisible due to the low light levels. Only one green power indicator on his chest revealed his presence.

"We have eliminated the most likely candidates," Reggie intoned, "A concentrated source would be needed to cause the rise of CO_2 levels that we are seeing, a tank of the gas perhaps."

Max frowned and rubbed a lump on his forehead that he suffered when he bumped his head on the edge of a container.

"Nobody's used tanks of CO_2 on-board spaceships in over 500 years, Reggie," Max said, "I don't think that's what Sinclair has in those crates. What else you got?"

Reggie spoke through some unlikely causes – off-gassing from the containers, sublimation of a dry ice deposit – but could come up with nothing that seemed plausible.

"Increase the air scrubbers to full capacity, Reggie, and activate the backup system," Max ordered. Reggie nodded and left. Max let out a frustrated sigh.

"You need to relax," Nick admitted.

Max immediately gave him a stern look. "I told you earlier that nothing happens on this ship without me understanding how or why. Mysteries are for books and movies, not for interstellar spaceships."

Nick nodded and turned his attention to the stars outside the cockpit window. They both sat there in silence for the next ten minutes. Max finally leaned back in his pilot's seat and propped his feet on the console.

"Giving up?" Nick asked.

"If I sleep on it, something'll come to me."

Max gave Nick a sympathetic look.

"What?" Nick asked.

"This situation with your father is pretty tough. You should've talked to someone about it," Max said, "No need to go it alone."

Nick nodded. "I know, but it's not something I can trust just anyone with."

"It took guts to tell me all that this afternoon. I don't know what to tell you though. The good guys don't always win."

Nick grimaced, "I know that. I just wish I could do something about it."

Nick sat there a moment more, but then got up and stretched. There was no more to be done and Nick decided he might as well hit his bunk. He gave Max a nod and headed to the hatch. He placed his right hand on the frame to steady himself as he stretched when Max spoke again.

"My daughter was ten, Nick," Max said as he continued to stare at the stars, "She was spending a day around a hangar with me, just enjoying some time at work with Dad. A cargo hauler's proximity sensors failed. It ran over her with a full load. She died in minutes."

Nick stood there, speechless. Before he could think of anything to say, Max started again.

"I held her broken body in my arms and cried over her until the medics arrived. There was nothing that could have been done. Accidents happen, I was told. Not my fault, I was told."

Max shook his head and swallowed hard.

"It should've never happened," he finally continued, "So I make sure nothing like that will ever happen again. I know every part of this ship, every nuance, every eccentricity. I can never let anything like that happen again."

Max tapped a couple of buttons on the console and a picture of a smiling, happy ten-year-old appeared above the console. She looked like any other happy kid. She had long, curly brown hair, a slightly gap-toothed smile, and a mass of freckles on her cheeks. Max squeezed the tears out of his eyes.

"You're not supposed to outlive your kids," Max said softly, "I'd give anything to have her back. A day doesn't go by when I don't wish I had done something differently that day."

"I'm sorry, Max," Nick offered weakly. He couldn't really understand Max's pain, but he could easily see how strongly the rugged and strong-willed man was affected. He could think of nothing else to do or say, so he stood there in the hatchway in what felt like a silent vigil for the long departed little girl.

"So am I, Nick. So am I."

CHAPTER 7

Nick slept exceptionally sound that night. Opening up to Max had lifted a burden from his chest; he could breathe again. With a bit of a spring in his step, he grabbed a quick cup of coffee from the galley and made his way to the cockpit, where he could hear Max and Reggie chatting.

"What's the data telling you, Reggie?" Max asked.

"There's a 99% probability that the containers are the source. All other sources have been eliminated."

"Good morning," Nick said as he entered. Max once again had his boots up on the console with his fingers laced behind his head.

"Good morning, sir," Reggie replied. Max simply gave him a nod as he chewed on the inside of his lip.

"How are the CO2 levels this morning?" Nick asked.

"Present readings show the carbon dioxide levels are at three millimeters of mercury and holding," Reggie said.

"We've got nothing to worry about, Nick. At full capacity, the ship's systems can handle over a hundred people being on-board. I just don't like to run things at full capacity; causes too much wear and tear."

Max suddenly swung his feet down to the deck with a loud clang and stood up.

"Come on," he said, "Let's see if we can find out what we're carrying."

Nick quickly chugged down half his cup and scampered after Max and Reggie. Max stopped briefly in the corridor to grab a tool bag from his quarters. Moments later, the three of them stood staring at a stack of five of the jet black crates.

"Any ideas on how we break into it?" Max asked. They had found no seam, no exterior control panel, no air vents, and no access ports. The crate looked like one solid block of metal.

"It's possible Doctor Sinclair used a shape memory alloy to construct the box," Reggie said, "The actuator to get the material to change its shape could be a communications signal of some sort. I could try a range of frequencies, sir, and see if there's any response."

"Are we sure that's a good idea?" Nick asked. "These are supposed to be weapons, right? I'd hate to accidentally set something off."

Max frowned. "I feel like I'm violating the Doctor's trust just poking around this thing. I hate not knowing what the hell's causing this though. Reggie, if the box is sealed, are we just seeing off-gassing?"

"Possibly," Reggie said, "I could attach some sensors to the crate in order to confirm that."

"Do it," Max said. Reggie trundled back to the forward section of the ship and returned a few minutes later with two palm-sized, flat cylinders. Reggie tapped a couple of spots on the face of the cylinder and a couple of indicator lights came on. Reggie then placed the sensor in the middle of one side of the crate.

"It should take-"

There was a slight crackling sound and small tendrils of electricity washed over the sensor. It detached from the crate and fell to the ground.

"That was odd," Reggie said.

Max had a tight-lipped grimace on his face. Reggie configured the second sensor and moved to attach it to the crate.

"Not sure that's a good idea," Nick said. As the sensor made contact with the crate, bolts of electricity immediately washed over the sensor and then arced across Reggie with a loud crackle. Max and Nick winced at the bright flash and loud squelch that Reggie emitted.

A moment later, the flow of current stopped and Reggie dropped to his knees.

Max ran up to him. "Are you okay?"

Reggie didn't respond. A red indicator light appeared on his chest. Another light appeared next to it, blinking rapidly.

"What now?" Nick asked.

"He's rebooting," Max said, "Should be back on-line in a minute."

"Well, I don't think we should try that again," Nick said.

"I wholeheartedly agree, sir," Reggie responded.

Max cracked a smile and slapped Reggie on the shoulder. "That was a close one. Don't have time to replace all of your processors today. Log all that, Reggie. Let's note the issue and we'll take it up with Aldous when we return. Let's leave these things alone for now."

"Any reason not to trust Sinclair on this one?" Nick asked. "Whole thing seems strange."

"Aldous Sinclair is a good man, Nick. He's done more-."

"I know," Nick interrupted, "You've told me. But, do you really trust him?"

"He's done a lot for my own family, Nick. So, yes, I trust him. I'm sure there's a good reason for all of this."

Nick was taking a nap on the couch in the lounge when Max woke him with a nudge.

"Wake up, kid," Max said, "We're almost at the jump point."

Nick blinked, trying to clear the sleep from his eyes and the fog from his mind. He got up slowly. A minute later, they took their seats in the cockpit, taking the time to strap themselves into the seats. Nick looked up just in time to see a bright flash of light out the right side of the window. Max checked the display. Two ship transponders continued to broadcast.

"Looks like Charlie just jumped," Max reported, "We're last in the cue."

Nick nodded. He reached forward and tapped on his console initiating diagnostics on several of the *Hannah's* critical systems. The main computer ran a health status check, followed by the jump controller, and the reactor controller. Within a minute, they all came back in the green. Nick gave Max a thumbs-up.

Max initiated the reactor spin-up. A countdown timer appeared on his display. In thirty minutes, they would be ready to jump. Nick felt a little tightness in his gut in anticipation of the jump. He found out on the trip from Valhalla to *Nexus* that he was one of the ten percent of people who didn't handle them well. He knew he would feel a few minutes of disorientation afterwards and more than a little bit of nausea. Nick had skipped lunch, just to be sure.

"You okay, Nick?" Max asked. "You look a little pale."

Nick tapped his foot nervously on the floor as he poured over the telemetry data on his console. "Just not a fan of the jump."

"Do I need Reggie to fetch you a bucket?"

"Very funny," Nick said.

At that moment, Reggie's voice broke through the intercom, "Propulsion systems nominal. Report ready for jump."

Nick's attention turned to the jump beacon that floated roughly fifty meters ahead of them. Blinking red and green lights on either end of the beacon held Nick's gaze. It was just about that time. The countdown clock flashed red as it fell under one minute remaining. Nick double-checked his restraints then waited for the jump to initiate. His right hand was holding on to the edge of the console so tightly that his knuckles were white. Max smiled at him.

"What?" Nick asked.

"Nothing, kid," Max responded, shaking his head.

As the timer hit zero, Nick felt himself being pulled forward, stretched through space-time. The cockpit filled with an almost blinding white light. Then, seconds later, it was over. Nick's stomach heaved. He blinked his eyes and breathed deep, willing himself calm. Sweat broke out along his forehead and he began to doubt that he would be able to hold it together.

Within a minute, the feeling passed and Nick began to breathe normally.

"You know, Nick," Max said, "Not really good for a spaceship pilot to suffer from jump sickness. This might not be the career for you."

"I'm fine," Nick said, slightly agitated.

"You sure you can handle it?"

"I'm good," Nick said.

It took only a few minutes for Nick to feel like they were back in civilization. He could make out dozens of blue and white thrusters firing against the backdrop of space and stars. Whereas Max and his three friends were piloting the only ships departing Dust, new ships were arriving every five minutes at this *Nexus Station* jump beacon.

The ship's computer established a connection with the local network and emitted a chime. At that moment, Nick's wrist computer started beeping and vibrating. Nick looked at the display; dozens of messages were filtering in. Two messages were from his mother, imploring him to come home. A couple of messages were from friends, wondering where he had gone. The rest were from his father.

You can't hide from me.

I'm getting close, Nick. Hope you're ready to see me.

You're an ungrateful, little brat.

Stealing is wrong, Nick. I thought we taught you better than that.

Message after message scrolled across his display. His father became increasingly irritated with the passage of time. With each message he read through, his mouth dried out a little more until his tongue felt like a dried up, but swollen piece of meat. Nick read the last message.

You must realize, Nick, that your actions will have dire consequences.

Nick tried to swallow.

"You okay? You look a little pale again."

Nick nodded weakly. "I'm okay."

"Bullshit," Max said, "What is it?"

Nick gritted his teeth and stared at the face of his wrist computer for a moment. His fist was tightly clenched. He slowly released it and stretched out his fingers.

"Messages from my father," Nick said, "He's still looking for me."

Nick touched a spot on the face of the screen and the messages were projected above the cockpit console. Max read them for a moment before letting out a long, slow whistle.

"Your old man is a piece of work, Nick."

"Yeah," Nick said, nodding.

"You'll be better off facing him; getting this over with. Then, you can put it behind you and start figuring out what to do with the rest of your life. You'll be glad when it's done."

"I'm sure," Nick said with little conviction. His right hand started trembling and he hid it from Max's view. "If you don't mind, I need a few minutes."

"Sure thing, kid. Nothing to it from here anyway," Max said. Max laid in a course for the shining silver dot on the horizon that was *Nexus Station* as Nick got up from his chair. Nick dazedly walked down the hallway to his room and closed the door behind him.

Max stared out the cockpit window as dozens of ships from dozens of colonies converged on *Nexus Station*. His eyes were focused on the spot where Nick's messages from his father had just been displayed. The content of the messages stunned him; he couldn't fathom sending anything like that to his own flesh and blood.

If his daughter was still alive, she would've been about a year older than Nick. She would've been the one trying to find her place in the universe; she would've been trying to assert her independence. Nick didn't need to be threatened; he needed guidance. He needed someone to show him a good example.

Max sighed and shook his head. He was about to get up and head to the lounge when Nick popped back into the cockpit.

"What needs to be done around here?" Nick asked. "I could use something to help pass the time."

Max looked the young man over for a minute. Nick's jaw was clenched; his expression resigned. Whereas so many other times Nick's gaze was cast at the floor, now he locked eyes with Max ready to get on with things.

"You can change out some of the urine processor filters in the head," Max said, "It's a bit of hazardous work, but I always like to change them out before I hit *Nexus* so I can stock up on a fresh supply."

Nick frowned slightly but smiled back at Max. "I shouldn't have asked."

"It's not too bad, Nick. Less gross than it sounds."

"I'll do it," Nick said.

"Want me to walk you through it?"

Nick shook his head. "I'll follow the procedure. If I run into problems, I'll let you know."

"Sounds good," Max said. Nick turned and left and Max was once again in the cockpit alone. *He's still just a kid*, Max thought.

"Maisha," Nick said, "If I could go anywhere in the galaxy, I'd go to Maisha."

Max gave him a slow whistle and said, "Nothing like reaching for the stars on that one, Nick."

Max looked down at the virtual cards he had been dealt. He had a pair of jacks with the dealer program showing another jack. Max looked around the table at the three-dimensional, photorealistic projections of Charlie, Roman, and Zanth. They each had lost most of their money and were down to their last few dollars. Nick was in a little bit better position, but his eyes looked tired and heavy. They had been playing for the last hour, trying to make the final stretch to *Nexus* bearable.

"Think about it though," Nick said, "A world untouched by human hands. The only world we've discovered with a developing intelligent civilization. But they're primitive, in their relative stone age. You could get away from all this crap, roll back time, and live like our ancestors did thousands of years ago."

"In the heat," Charlie said.

"Or cold," Zanth added, "With no connectivity."

"You can pry my ability to watch robo-ball from my cold, dead hands," said Roman.

"Not me," Nick said, "I'd love to sail across those open seas, hike up those mountains and just take it all in."

"Max, it sounds like he's got your first date all planned out," Charlie said.

"Very funny," Max retorted, "Way to pick a place you can never go. Maisha is off limits to anything and everything. It's the one thing the Republic's done right."

"Have you ever been there?" Nick asked.

Max nodded in the affirmative, "I delivered a shipment of spare parts for an observation team that was doing some sort of migration study. They had set up shop on Maisha's moon. They were shut down though after their grant ran out. No idea if anyone's ever been back there."

"What was it like?"

"From space? Just another floating marble," Max said, "Just like all these other worlds. From that high up, every planet is beautiful. You have to get close to the surface to see any scars that humanity has left behind."

"That's the great thing about Maisha," Nick said, "No scars."

"Don't you guys give him a hard time for being a romantic," Charlie chided, "Kid, keep on dreaming and maybe you'll find a better lot for yourself than we have."

Nick called but Max took the hand.

"I think that's it for me," Roman said, "I want to get a little shuteye before we reach the station."

The others agreed and the game came to an end. They each said their goodbyes and then Max deactivated the game link.

"That was fun," Nick said, "Thanks for setting that up."

Max shrugged. "Something we like to do whenever we get the good fortune of making a run together."

Nick stretched and yawned, extending his arms as far behind his back as he could.

"Think I'll try to get some rest," he said as he got up from the table.

"Nick," Max said and then he hesitated as Nick looked back at him with tired eyes. "If you're not ready to do this, to face your father, I understand."

"I…I don't know."

"I think your father needs to calm down a bit, judging by those messages," Max said, nodding towards Nick's wrist computer, "You can stay on-board the ship. It'll probably be a day or so, but I think you can survive cooped up in this can that long."

"Won't they pick my chip up with a scan?"

"I have ways around that, Nick. You wouldn't be the first person I've had to, uh, be discrete about."

Nick let out a long, slow breath and shook his head. He stood there for a moment without saying anything. Max watched him; he could see that Nick was trying to figure out the right thing to do. Finally, Nick stood up straight and looked Max in the eye.

"Thank you, Max. Thank you. Whatever I can do to repay you, let me know."

Max gave him a smile. "You've earned your keep, kid. We'll get through this."

CHAPTER 8

"Contact Echo-Sierra-Victor-Two-One-Five-Alpha this is Nexus Control, we have you on final approach," the controller's voice boomed over the cockpit speaker, "You are clear for docking port one-niner."

"Copy, one-niner," Max replied. *Nexus Station* loomed in front of them; its cylindrical shape completely filled their view. The curved surface of the station facing them was littered with brightly lit docking ports cut into the smooth gray exterior of the station. Just at the edge of their view, Nick could see the jagged forms of control towers that dotted the edge of the cylinder's rim. The station dwarfed the *Hannah* and the hundreds of other ships that buzzed around it like a swarm of very organized bees.

Nick spared a quick glance at the traffic around them. A dozen or more ships were on parallel trajectories, each headed for a different docking port. Floating just above and below their plane of approach, Nick made out the silhouettes of a couple of security patrol ships with the Conglomerate logo prominently emblazoned on the sides of the ships.

"Time to slip on that necklace, Nick."

Nick plucked a silver rope off the top of the console and placed it over his head. The necklace was heavy; he felt a tug around his neck as it dropped into place.

"That should shield you from any long range scans. This whole run should be by the book; we'll be in, offloaded, and on our way within a day," Max said, "Nobody'll even know you're here."

"My father will be looking for me, either himself or with some hired help."

"That's why you're wearing the necklace. Also, turn off your wrist computer," Max said with surety.

"Uh, right," Nick said. He fumbled with the controls for a moment before remembering how to deactivate it.

Docking port 19 now entirely filled their field of view. The *Hannah* silently passed through the port's thin atmospheric field and adroitly settled onto its landing pads. With the slightest thump, they were down. Nick and Max unstrapped themselves and headed into the corridor.

"Reggie," Max called out, "I want you to do another calibration of the gas analyzer once the cargo's unloaded. Also, check the cargo bay seals for any signs of wear and tear."

"Yes, sir," Reggie responded.

"Max, he's not going to give up easily," Nick said.

"These kinds of arguments happen all the time, Nick. You're not the first person to have a falling out with their father."

"This isn't just a falling out, Max."

"Look, do you want my help or not? I'm happy to go back to the old plan and just drop you in his lap."

Nick shook his head. "Sorry, Max. Just nervous."

"It'll be all right, Nick," Max said, "If things get hairy, there's a maintenance crawlway under the floor grating that Reggie can let you in and close off behind you. The crawlway goes to the reactor; get close enough to that and no one'll be able to detect you even at close range. Reggie can show you where it is once I'm out of here."

Nick nodded. Max picked up a small backpack.

"I gotta check in with the dock foreman. Stay out of sight for the next little bit while they're unloading the ship. I'll be back tonight," Max said.

"Thanks, Max."

"No problem. Don't sweat this; it'll be a piece of cake."

Max bounded down the ramp into the brightly lit, cavernous docking bay. An overweight, balding woman approached. Her hair was cropped short and she had a lump of something rotten-smelling stuffed into the side of her cheek. She chewed as she reviewed data on her wrist computer.

"Good to see you again, Phyllis," Max said.

She nodded in his direction and flashed a frightening smile, teeth stained and crooked. "Max, we've got a problem with your shipment."

"Come on now. Don't give me this crap," Max said, "I sent you the purchase record."

Phyllis consulted her data. "Yes, and it has a purchase order number that's ten years old. Conglomerate is refusing payment; say they don't know what the hell this is."

"So what the hell am I supposed to do with this stuff?"

Phyllis gave him a humorless smile, "This is where you made my day real special, Max. Because your purchase record says that you're carrying weapons, I have to take it off your hands and put it in secure storage until we get this sorted out."

Max rolled his eyes, "Come on, Phyllis. Time is money here."

"Sorry, Max, nothing I can do."

"Did you check on Charlie's purchase record? Or Roman's or Zanth's?"

She nodded as she tapped on her tablet, "Yep, all of them. We've got the same problem for all four of you. So you're all stuck here until we get this cleared."

"Great," Max said.

"I'm sure we'll get it taken care of quickly. We've already put in the call to Sinclair. Suspect he just got the purchase record confused. I'll buzz you once we get this cleared. Go grab a beer with your friends; we'll get this sorted out."

"You know the link's down with Dust," Max said, "How long are you going to hold me on this, Phyllis?"

"Rules are rules, Max," Phyllis said with a shrug, "Nothing I can do. Maybe the Conglomerate'll figure this out on their end then. Otherwise, you're going to have to wait until we can get in touch with Dust."

Max nodded; his lips pursed in frustration.

Phyllis pushed a spot on her wrist computer and a dozen cargo haulers emerged from a door on the far side of the port. A moment later, he heard a thunk as Reggie opened the cargo bay doors of the *Hannah*. Max watched as the robot haulers got to work, disconnecting containers from their attach points in the *Hannah's* hold. Nick was nowhere to be seen.

"Hey Phyllis," Max called out as she walked away, "I don't want a delay like we had with those vats of nanomachines. Keep me in the loop if you think it's going to be more than a couple days."

"I'll do what I can, Max. No promises."

Max looked around and scratched the back of his head. He'd have to come back and break the bad news to Nick later. Might as well go grab a drink, he thought.

He boarded the lift and a selection of levels appeared on his wrist computer. A dozen images appeared on the display with small icons for the things that could be found on each level. Engineering levels made up the lower levels, just below the hangars. Above them were the main concourses, commercial districts, a couple of residential districts, and finally the administration levels.

Max selected the main concourse and the lift started moving. A moment later, the doors opened and Max scowled at the throng of people. He tentatively tried to step forward into the flow and was bumped into by a man in a shimmery suit talking away to a picture of a woman on his wrist computer.

Max cursed at the man under his breath before joining the flow. At least he knew where he was going, he thought as he narrowly avoided running into a group of tourists who were milling around an interactive map.

Moments later, he stepped through the faux wood doors of The Mechanical Horse. Max let out an audible sigh of relief at the quiet of the bar; a noise dampening field muted the cacophony of the concourse crowd. Max looked around. The bar was well lit and about half full. The walls were adorned with faux antiques and reprints of news images from the last two hundred years.

Charlie and Roman were sitting at a table directly beneath a news story celebrating the anniversary of the moment when humankind had finally defeated the common cold. The two men saw Max enter and waved him over.

"Where's Zanth?" Max asked as they settled in at the table.

Charlie shrugged and said, "Who the hell knows? Probably still arguing about having his cargo impounded. Where's Nick?"

"Avoiding the crowds," Max said.

Charlie nodded knowingly and put down his drink. "I guess there's hope for him, yet."

"He's coming around," Max said as he took a long sip of the ice cold drink. He reviewed the menu and selected something absent-mindedly. He glanced over at the monitors which were showing a rundown of stock market ups and downs.

His food was being brought out by a robotic server when a squad of security officers burst into the bar. Two of them immediately flanked the door; two rushed into position to guard the exit into the kitchen. The lead officer quickly walked up to the robotic bartender and whispered something to it.

"Now, what's going on here?" Roman asked. A moment later, the bartender pointed at their table.

"Don't like that," Charlie whispered, "You do anything I need to be aware of?"

"Nothing besides bringing in a cargo hold full of weapons. You?" Max said.

Charlie frowned. "Don't remind me. Hope this bullshit gets sorted out quickly."

The lead officer walked up to them quickly with three other officers taking up position around the table.

"What's the problem officer?" Max asked.

The lead officer ignored the question and looked sharply at Max.

"Are you Maxime Cabot?" he asked. His eyes narrowed and no hint of a smile graced his face.

"Yes," Max responded, "What's this about?"

The officer extended his arm and held out his wrist computer. Max pushed his thumb on the pad. Within moments, his picture appeared on the pad and confirmed his identity.

The lead officer nodded his head toward his compatriots. They stepped forward and grabbed Max by the arms.

"Hey, what the hell's going on?" Max asked indignantly.

"Maxime Cabot, you're under arrest," the officer said, "For the possible kidnapping of Nicholas Papagous."

A pit formed in Max's stomach.

"This is some kind of mistake," Max said, his facing turning red with anger. The guards started immediately leading him from the table.

"Save it for the Captain," the lead officer said sternly, "Nicholas' father reported him as missing, possibly kidnapped, two weeks ago."

Max sat on a small, silver metal chair in a cold, sterile, white-walled room. Bright lights in the ceiling reflected off the high gloss paint that coated the walls making it very difficult to see. The harshness of the light made him squint, while the heat the lights generated made him sweat. Max focused on keeping a level head. He took several deep breaths, slowly stretched out his neck, and then rolled his shoulders. He had been sitting in this chair for close to an hour.

Finally, the door opened with a whoosh and, to his dismay, a familiar face stepped into the room. The man standing in front of Max was of average height and build with pale complexion and a reed-thin mustache decorating his upper lip. At the sight of Max, his beady eyes narrowed and the right side of his mouth curled up in a sardonic smile.

"Ah, Christ," Max blurted out as the man stared down at him with disdain.

"Well, Max," Captain Yeon started, "What kind of trouble have you gotten yourself into now?"

"Jin, you've got no damn reason to hold me in here!"

"You'll address me as Captain Yeon, Mr. Cabot. And I have plenty of reason to hold you here. You've gone too far this time. This time I don't need your wife to press charges. This time we'll be able to cite you for more than just public intoxication."

Yeon flashed him a malicious smile.

"What the hell are you talking about?"

Sweat poured from Max's forehead; the room felt like the temperature had rapidly climbed ten degrees. They're probably doing that on purpose, Max thought. Yeon's forehead was perfectly dry.

"Mr. Cabot, you are the last person known to have been in the company of Nicholas Papagous. He left this station with you a little over a week ago. His father, Henry Papagous, has declared him missing and he is deeply concerned that his son has been kidnapped. So, where is young Mr. Papagous?"

"I don't know," Max said.

"How can you not know?"

"Because I left him behind on Dust. It was what he wanted," Max said as he met Yeon's glare.

Yeon stared at him icily. "How did you come to travel with the young Mr. Papagous?"

"I recruited him here two weeks ago!" Max yelled, "He signed a damn contract! You want it? I'll call it up right now!"

"Mr. Cabot," Yeon said, shaking his head and speaking slowly, "Any fool with some level of familiarity with work contracts can forge the necessary documents without much effort. I'll ask again. Where is Nicholas Papagous?"

Max didn't answer; he just stared straight ahead.

"You don't have to tell me anything, Max," Yeon said icily, "We already know that he left with you. That's enough to get me a warrant to search your ship, which we will be doing right about now. If we find him there, we're going to spend a lot of quality time together."

Nick felt like he was being cooked in a microwave. There was barely enough room in the crawlspace for him to lift his head up and be sure that he was not, in fact, on fire. The orange glow that illuminated the compartment wasn't helping his perception of being cooked. Sweat poured down his face. The hum of the reactor was loud enough that he couldn't hear anything going on outside the crawlway. He leaned his head back on his bag and closed his eyes.

Somewhere out in the corridor, sector security agents were combing the ship for him. Nick had been sitting in his room reading through some of the ship's manuals when Reggie popped his head in. Security was trying to break into the *Hannah*.

"We have 4.3 minutes to get you in the reactor maintenance crawlway," Reggie had said.

Nick shot up, wide-eyed, and grabbed his travel bag with all his things stuffed inside it. Reggie adeptly removed the four fasteners that held the panel in place. Nick grimaced at the sight of the size of the opening, but he crawled in as fast as he could. Once he got far enough into the crawlway, the light from the corridor disappeared as Reggie fastened the cover in place.

Now, he just needed to wait. He instinctively looked at his wrist computer to see the time, forgetting that it was off.

Nick sighed. If security was searching the *Hannah*, they must have also picked up Max.

"Just sit tight," he whispered.

But time was crawling. Questions flooded his mind. How long would they hold Max? How long would he have to wait in here? What if they posted a guard in the ship? When could he get out? How long has it been? How can Max be sure they can't detect me? Who else has Max smuggled in this ship? How much time has gone by?

He sipped on the straw of a drink bag.

Suddenly, Nick felt like he was ten years old again and hiding in his closet. It was where Nick went whenever he was in trouble. His father would come home and sit on the edge of his bed, hands clasped in front of him as he leaned forward. He would yell for Nick to come out, to come and accept the consequences of his actions. Nick hated that phrase.

"Why am I doing this?" He asked. "Why should I be afraid of him?"

Max was right. He should just face his father, hand the data back to him, and be on his way. He could live his life and turn his back on his father. He could go live the life that he wanted, not the one his father wanted for him and not the one his mother was shamed into living.

"I am not afraid of him," Nick said. He wormed his way back out of the crawlspace; his clothes soaked with sweat. His foot hit the crawlway cover. He lifted his boot just a few inches and started pounding on the cover.

Max looked up as Yeon opened the door again. Max's expression was one of practiced weariness. He was just waiting for this annoying ordeal to be completed. Yeon's expression, though, was unsettling. There was a hint of glee in his sneer and an upturn of his eyes that told Max they had found something.

Yeon looked at his wrist computer and seemed to want to start laughing.

"You really screwed up this time, Max. Did you really think we wouldn't find him?"

Max grimaced and leaned forward in his chair.

"He was literally pounding on the little crawlway access panel with his foot. When we pulled him out, he was covered in sweat and babbling away about something. We're having him looked at by the docs right now."

Max closed his eyes and rested his head in his hands.

"That's right, you degenerate son of a bitch, we're going to nail you for this."

"I don't suppose he told you he wanted to be in there?"

Yeon laughed. "I must have missed that part."

Max had to steel himself from yelling out in frustration.

"Good thing his father is already en route. We'll be able to close this up pretty quickly. I'd say you're looking at thirty maybe forty years."

"You're making a mistake," Max said, "This is all a misunderstanding."

"Oh, I'm sure," Yeon said with a grin.

Nick sat in a small, uncomfortable chair in the unnecessarily cool office of the overly formal man who was taking his statement. Officer Raji was a stout, rigid man with no discernible personality or sense of humanity. His face seemed to be set in a perpetual blank stare; his eyes betrayed no emotion. He was as robotic a human as Nick had ever met. Raji sat at the desk, entering information on Nick into the computer. The desk was tilted just enough that Nick could not see the words he typed on the touchscreen built into the desktop.

"How did you get the contusion on your chest?" Raji asked, looking up only briefly from the display.

Nick hesitated for a moment, surprised at the question.

"What contusion?"

"The body scan showed some unhealed tissue damage in your chest. Did Mr. Cabot assault you will you were in his custody?"

"No, I was in a bar fight on Dust," Nick said, "I had a little too much to drink and shot my mouth off to someone I shouldn't have."

Raji entered the response on his terminal, "Did Mr. Cabot threaten you?"

Nick sighed in frustration, "No, for the tenth time, Max has done nothing to me. I was not kidnapped. I was not held against my will."

Raji eyed him with his blank expression. Nick couldn't tell if he was making any headway or not.

"Your blood test results show elevated levels of carbon dioxide in your bloodstream. This can be caused by being in an environment, say an enclosed space, with poor ventilation and elevated carbon dioxide levels. How long were you in that crawlway, Nick?"

Nick's frustration got the better of him and he yelled, "Damn it, I was not held against my will! I asked him to hide me away!"

"And why would you do that?"

"Because I was afraid to face my father. I ran away from him and I didn't have the courage to stand up to him."

Raji entered the response on his terminal and looked at Nick impassively.

"Look," Nick continued, "I signed a contract to work for Max for six months. I'm sure he's got a copy of it in his files."

Raji blinked but otherwise stared silently. "Cabot is being interviewed by Captain Drake. I'm sure they will go over that."

"Ok," Nick said, frustration continuing to mount, "You have me now, right? Can't I just tell you that I'm fine and don't want to press charges?"

"I'm afraid that's not possible," Raji said, "How do I know you're not suffering from the psychological effects of your incarceration. A doctor will be available in the morning. You're going to have to do a full psychological screening before you're deemed healthy enough to be trusted. Beyond that, we'll need to clear up the kidnapping charges with your father. He was apparently en route when we contacted him with your whereabouts."

"I bet he was," Nick said snidely.

Raji nodded and said, "Yes, he's on his way. He said he'll be here by tomorrow evening. We have explicit instructions to hold you until he arrives and has a chance to speak with you."

Nick leaned his head back abruptly in the chair, whacking the back of it on the cold metal. As he continued to answer procedural questions from Officer Raji, he remembered that his wrist computer was still shut down. Nick activated it and within moments a message popped up.

Found you! Looking forward to catching up! - Love, Father.

Nick clenched his fist and shook his head.

"Something wrong?" Raji asked.

"Nothing at all," Nick said. He punched in a reply and sneered as he hit send.

Looking forward to it, too. About time I did this. - Nick

CHAPTER 9

While Max spent the night huddled in the corner of his holding cell, trying to shield his eyes from the bright overhead lights, Nick was shuffled from one room to the next. Oh, the officers said they were trying to find him a quiet place for him to rest, but it seemed every time he was on the verge of sleep someone found a reason to move him.

By the time he was dragged in to the psychiatrist's office, his eyes were heavy and red-rimmed and his skin felt clammy, coated with a dried layer of sweat. Nick always tended to sweat a bit more when he was over-tired. He also had a bit of a splotchy five o'clock shadow as patches of uneven fuzz blotted his face. He felt gross.

The attending doctor, a very fit and attractive young woman, Doctor Paige Barckowitz, looked up from her comfortable, brown, synthetic leather chair and appraised Nick with an unyielding stare. Nick sat opposite her, focusing very hard on keeping his eyes focused on her eyes or other parts of the room and nowhere else below her neckline. With her long, silky brown hair and deep blue eyes, Nick found her absolutely stunning.

She didn't waste any time with small talk and jumped right into the questions.

"Tell me about your relationship with your father?"

"Strained," Nick responded, his voice distant and shaky, "We haven't gotten along well these last few years."

Nick had spent half the night thinking about what he would say when he finally confronted his father. He had struggled to find anything that wouldn't result in some punches being thrown.

"Have you tried to run away before?" Paige asked.

Nick smiled and absentmindedly picked at the seam on his pants.

"You could say that."

Paige was just about to ask another question when the lights turned from white to red. Within seconds he heard booted footsteps running down the corridor past the office.

"What's going on?" Nick asked, trying to turn around and face the doorway.

"I'm not sure," she answered, her tone as curious as Nick's. She got up and walked over to her desk. There, she looked at the display built into the desktop and tapped the intercom. While she was at the desk, the door to the office slid shut. A click was heard as the door locked.

"Captain, what's going on?"

"Doctor Barckowitz, we've got a security situation. We're on lockdown," the Captain's voice came through. He was breathing heavily and Nick could hear the rapid clangs of many pairs of boots ringing off the metal floor. "Don't have much info at the moment. We'll give the all-clear as soon as we can."

Nick watched her type a few more things into the desktop. She stood there for several minutes, trying to access something. The frustration on her face grew.

"What is it?" Nick asked. She looked up with a bit of a blank stare.

"Oh," she responded, "I was just trying to access some of the security camera feeds to find out what was going on. I can't access anything though."

Nick stood up from his chair slowly and made his way toward the desk. She locked eyes with him for a moment and he gave her a sheepish smile. Her stern, stone-faced expression stopped his approach.

"Well," Nick asked, "Now what?"

"We'll take a break for now and continue once the all-clear is given," she said, "Might as well have a seat and get comfortable."

Nick sat back down, but he was restless. They sat in silence for several moments while Nick fidgeted in the chair. Paige continued to fiddle around with the desk, looking for more information. He watched her for a few moments while her eyes were glued to the desktop. She was gorgeous, someone Nick would have been too nervous to talk to back home. He felt compelled to talk to her, to strike up some conversation where he could learn more about her, but he felt this was a ridiculous time to do that. Eventually, Nick gave up on the idea, leaned his head back, and closed his eyes.

Once again, he heard booted footsteps running down the corridor on the other side of the door. Both Nick and Paige looked up and stared in the direction of the sound. Suddenly, a loud bang reverberated through the room as something slammed into the wall adjacent to the door. They both jumped slightly at the sudden sound.

Then, they heard the screech. An inhuman cry came from the corridor; a high-pitched, hair-raising sound that caused Nick to clench the arms of the chair. He had heard that sound before. His mind flashed back to the scene in the desert, looking over the mangled body of Mr. Winters. He remembered the blood that had seeped from the old man's wounds. He remembered the glimpse, the passing shadow, which passed through the light of his flashlight that night. He remembered that inhuman screech; it was an unforgettable sound.

Nick's sense of dread grew as they heard another scream, this one far too recognizable as that of another man. The scream suddenly stopped and there was another bang, this one slightly softer than the first.

"What the hell was that?" Nick asked.

"Quiet," she said, raising a finger to her lips. "If we can hear them, they can hear us."

They heard nothing else though. They both sat there for another tension-filled couple of minutes, but there were no further sounds. Nick had had enough sitting around. He quietly got up and walked slowly to the door. He pressed his ear up against it and listened. There was nothing to be heard. He turned his head and was startled to find Paige standing right behind him.

"I don't hear anything," he whispered, "Now what?"

"We wait," she said.

"For how long?"

"As long as we need to," she said and returned to her desk.

"Don't you want to know what's going on out there?"

"Don't be an idiot," she said, "What do you think you'll accomplish by blindly charging out there? Let the professionals handle this one."

Nick blushed. She didn't call him 'kid' but she might as well have. He could hear it in her tone of voice. He looked away from her back toward the door. Despite her protests, Nick was very anxious to get the door open. He didn't like being trapped in this room, but he saw no recourse except to sit and wait it out. He plopped down onto the floor next to the door and leaned his back against the wall.

"Has this-"

Nick's question was cut short by a high-pitched, warbling siren. The red lights in the room returned to their normal white, a pair of red flashing lights appeared over the door, and the door slid open.

"Evacuation alarm," she yelled over the din of the siren, "We need to get out of here!"

She quickly yanked open the bottom left drawer of her desk and pulled out a stun gun. It was a slim, gray, egg-shaped projectile weapon that fit into the palm of her hand. Nick had seen them used by the police before, but only on the news. He eyed it nervously as she stuffed it in the inside pocket of her blazer.

Paige looked up from the desk, took a step toward the door, and froze. Her face went pale and her mouth hung open in shock. Nick pulled himself quickly off the floor and turned to look. The wall opposite the door in the corridor was covered by a long splatter of blood.

Cautiously, he poked his head into the corridor. Several bodies were strewn across the floor. To the immediate left of the opening lay the body of a young male security officer. His head had been reduced to a bloody, mutilated stump atop his body. The rest of it seemed to be smeared across the wall on their side of the corridor. That explained the bang on the wall, Nick thought.

There were two other bodies down the corridor to his right. One had a gaping hole burned right through his chest; the other bled out through a series of savage lacerations on the head, neck, and chest. A pool of blood covered the floor.

The siren continued to wail in the background. With the flashing lights in the hallway, the noise of the alarm, the sight of the carnage, the smell of burned flesh, and the general shock of the scene, Nick's mind became overloaded and he suddenly dropped to one knee.

He was about to fall forward into the bloody mess that remained of the officer to the left of the door, when he felt Paige's hand grab him firmly by the shoulder. He felt her other hand pat his other shoulder and he straightened up. He could feel the warmth of her breath on his shoulder as she spoke into his ear.

"Come on. We have to get out of here!"

He nodded and pulled himself to his feet. Nick turned to face the Doctor for just a moment; her face was taught with grim determination.

"Just stick close to me, all right," she yelled, "I'll lead the way."

She started to charge past, but Nick reached out and grabbed her elbow.

"I can't leave yet," Nick yelled. Her brow furrowed as she looked at him without comprehension. "Security picked up someone else, a friend of mine. He's being held here somewhere. I have to find him."

She shook her head. "No way. We need to get out of here. We don't have time for side trips."

Nick wasn't going to give in on this one. He couldn't abandon Max. He was the reason that Max was picked up and he would make sure Max got out of here.

"Then, I will go without you," Nick yelled. He steeled himself mentally and then started down the hallway to the right. He stepped around the bodies and grimaced as he was forced to take a step in the pool of blood. He reached the end of the hall and hesitated as he tried to figure out if he should go left or right. He saw nothing that would help him make the decision.

He decided to go left, stepped forward, and felt a hand on his shoulder. Nick nearly jumped out of his skin. He pulled away from the touch and spun around, putting his hands up to defend himself. He let out a sigh of relief when it turned out to be Paige. She gave him an aggravated glare and pointed to the right.

Moments later, they came across two more bodies in the corridor, one with a giant hole burned through the head and the other with an arm ripped off and a severely broken neck. Nick tried not to look at the bodies as they continued on. Eventually, they arrived at an emergency stairwell and descended one floor.

They stepped around another corpse as they exited the stairwell. They had yet to see any evidence of what had done this. Nick had an idea what it was though, or at least, he knew where it was from. The rising levels of carbon dioxide on the ship, the now ominous words of Doctor Sinclair, something about sending the Conglomerate something he'd been working on for a long time, the crates that they could not break into, and that blood-curdling unforgettable screech all pointed to a conclusion that Nick struggled to accept. There were a hundred of those crates on the *Hannah*, Nick thought, and who knows how many on the other ships Sinclair dispatched.

Nick tried to push the thought from his mind as they walked past a row of offices. They took another right and stopped. Paige stared straight ahead, unmoving. Nick noticed that her hand trembled slightly as it hung by her side. She started to reach inside her blazer pocket when Nick stepped around her.

It took Nick's brain a moment to understand that he was seeing something real. This was no special effect, this was no costume; the creature that lay ahead of him was real. His mind struggled to find the familiar in what he saw.

The creature was incredibly large. Must be at least a foot taller than me, Nick thought. The skin of its body was jet black from its feet to the base of its neck. The thing looked mostly like a man with two arms and two legs, but so much of it was inhuman.

Nick couldn't help focusing his attention on the toes. Instead of normal human toes, there were three black, pointed claws, like those of a large bird. The claws on the feet were short and narrow, but Nick noticed that the ones that replaced its fingers were long, thick, and ended in a razor-sharp point.

All around the thing's body, Nick could see fine, black down settling onto the floor. The thing's entire body was covered in feathers. It had been cut in several places; red blood poured down its torso.

As Nick crept slowly closer to the prone creature, he noticed more unsettling features. Large wings protruded from its back. Finally, Nick saw a wiry neck and the enlarged head of a bird-of-prey where the head and neck of a man should have been. He stopped a moment and just stared; his brain could hardly comprehend what it was seeing.

The head lolled unnaturally to the left, dangling down onto the torso. Its black eyes lay open and unmoving, reflecting a distorted image of Nick back at himself. Nick noticed a slightly bulbous, silver plate that covered the back of the head. This creature was made and not born; it was an abomination. This was the thing that had killed Winters, that they had brought here, and had now been unleashed upon this space station.

Nick didn't dare get too close for fear that the creature was still alive. Paige motioned for him to turn left past the creature. It took Nick several moments to work up the courage to get close enough to the thing to turn the corner. Nick closed his eyes, steeled himself, and took another step closer to it.

It wasn't until then that Nick noticed the large rifle with the custom grip that lay next to the beast's right hand. It was a long, dull gray weapon of a type that Nick had never seen before. The trigger and grip seem to have been molded to the creature's talon-shaped hands. He thought briefly about picking it up, but he didn't dare reach down far enough to grab it. That would have put him within arm's length of the beast.

He rounded the corner, stopped about ten feet away from the creature, and waited for Paige to join him. Nick found that he could not take his eyes from the grotesque thing that lay there unmoving. How many of them were there? He shuddered at the thought of a horde of these things marching through the station's corridors.

Paige finally rounded the corner a minute later. She was visibly trembling. Where Nick couldn't take his eyes from the creature, she couldn't bring herself to look at it at all. It looked like it was taking all her strength not to run away. Her white-knuckled fists were balled tightly at her side. This time, Nick put a hand on her shoulder and she inhaled sharply. She let the breath out slowly and opened her eyes again.

"Your friend should be in one of these rooms," she said, her shaky voice barely audible above the continuing siren. Nick walked up to the nearest door and tried to trigger it by placing his right hand on the access pad. Nothing happened.

"Locked," Nick said. He was surprised they didn't open when the evacuation order was given.

"It wouldn't be good if the detainees ran free. It's assumed the responsible officer would escort them to safety."

"That assumes the responsible officer is still alive," Nick responded, "How do we get in?"

"Any officer should have the appropriate access," Paige replied. The next gruesome step quickly became apparent.

"I don't suppose that includes you," Nick said.

She shook her head negatively. "Sorry. I'm an independent advisor, not an officer."

"Great," Nick said. He looked back down the corridor. The last uniformed body he remembered seeing was about twenty meters back, just around the corner. Of course, that meant crossing paths with that thing again.

"Wait here," Nick said. She didn't argue. Nick set off and again gingerly walked past the creature. He found the mangled body of another guard, a stout woman who had a gaping hole blown in her midsection. The wound was cauterized, apparently the product of the rifle the creature carried. Nick was thankful that she had not suffered wounds from those pointed talons.

He grabbed the corpse's still warm wrist and then hoisted the body over his shoulder. He was lucky; she couldn't have weighed more than 150 pounds. Still, she was at the upper limit of what Nick could handle by himself. His first steps with the dead woman over his shoulder were tentative and clumsy. Maneuvering around the creature proved especially difficult as Nick struggled to do anything other than shuffle his feet along the floor.

As he rounded the corner, his foot glanced off the creature's toe. Nick froze; his breathing stopped. When the creature didn't stir, Nick exhaled slowly and trudged on. The body hit the floor with a loud bang as he dropped it from his shoulders, a bang that betrayed the respect he was trying to show the dead officer.

"Sorry," Nick said.

"Let's just get this done."

Nick nodded and placed the dead woman's hand on the access pad. The door slid open, but Nick was disappointed to find the room empty. It took three more tries, lugging the body from door to door and using her stiffening hand to deactivate the door lock, before they found the room Max was in.

Max sat huddled against the far wall, knees pulled up to his chest, arms folded across his knees, with his head back and his eyes closed. Nick could see that Max was gently rocking back and forth to keep himself calm. With the siren still in alarm, Max didn't hear the door slide open and continued to sit there with his eyes closed.

"Max," Nick yelled above the din, "Time to go!"

Max lifted his head up and blinked his eyes. He stared for a moment, trying to figure out if this was real or some strange torture-induced hallucination. Finally, his mind pieced together where he was, who he was looking at, and what was happening. His first reaction was pure relief.

"Oh, thank God," Max said and began to slowly get of the floor. Nick walked over to him and extended a han' which Max gladly took. Max got up off the floor with groan and a pop as a couple of joints protested his ti sitting on the floor. "I was beginning to think I would n' get out of this room. Nick, you picked a helluva tir grow some balls. What the hell are you doing in anyway?"

"Now's not the best time, Max," Nick yelled, "We to get the hell out of here!"

Max clutched at a sore spot on his back and hunched over slightly.

"What are you talking about? I've been sitting on this floor for the last six hours. Where the hell is Captain-"

Max's jaw dropped in disbelief and his eyes bulged.

"Holy shit."

Nick spun around to see what caught Max's eye and the world seemed to move in slow motion. Paige was still standing in the doorway, watching Nick and Max, when Max's faced turned into a white sheet. Before Paige could turn to look, she heard an inhuman screech behind her. One of the creatures was there, looming over her. Its wings flared; its beak opened in a terrifying call to attack.

Its head tilted quickly to the side and bobbed slightly on its elongated, scrawny neck. Green and red indicator lights blinked on the silver cap that covered the back half of its head. Its arms, which seemed unnaturally long now that 'ick saw it standing upright, were tensed and ready to strike.

econd later, it did with deadly results.

'aige had just turned to face it and was bringing her hand her jacket pocket when the three claws of its right 'wung with frightening speed. The creature's 'ed slash easily ripped through her clothes and the 'th. Wounds quickly opened diagonally from the ' her chest up through the left side of her face. 'ards from the blow and a quickly expanding 'ossomed beneath her.

'reamed. He lunged in her direction. Max 'ifting his gaze and quickly and firmly 'lder, preventing him from moving any 'esome wound, Paige was still trying to 'veapon in her pocket. The creature took a sudden step forward and embedded its claws in her chest. Within seconds, she stopped moving.

Max quickly assessed the situation. When the hideous creature once again roared and flared its wings, Max charged forward and grabbed the metal chair in the center of the room. Max screamed with deadly intent as he swung the chair with all his strength.

He swung low, attempting to knock the creature from its off-balance perch. The blow connected with the thing's legs. It fell backward and its claw was violently removed from Paige's chest, spattering blood across the wall. The thing landed on its back with a jarring thud, but it reacted to the attack with blinding quickness. It launched its right leg out striking Max right on the sternum. He staggered back, the wind knocked from him and searing pain filling his chest.

Max felt blood pooling on the front of his shirt. He had no chance to look down and check the wound as he desperately tried to dodge a swipe from the now recovered creature. Max lost his balance and fell backward next to the small table in the room. The creature suddenly leaped onto the top of the table and screeched again. His claw flared and Max rolled for the underside of the table. The blow caught his calf and ripped open a long gash.

Max screamed in pain.

Nick could do nothing but gape for a moment. When the creature jumped on the table and pressed the attack on Max, he finally found the sense to move. He remembered the gun in Paige's pocket and dove toward her. Nick scrambled while the creature's attention was focused on Max. Nick reached into the blood-soaked pocket with a grimace and found the slim, gray stun gun. His hands trembled mightily as he brought it to bear.

The creature grabbed Max's wounded calf, dug its claws in slightly, and forcibly pulled him out from under the table. It held him up in the air with one hand; its right arm reared back to deliver the killing blow. Nick pulled the trigger, but his hands were shaking so badly the shot missed high and to the right. He quickly fired again and this time the tiny dart hit the creature square in the back. The creature jerked its head towards Nick, then a second later its hold on Max weakened and both the creature and Max tumbled to the floor.

Max curled his head up just enough so that he took the impact on his shoulders and wound up flat on his back. He gasped at the pain and gritted his teeth. Nick watched as the older man fought through the pain and hobbled over to the now-broken chair he had used to club the creature down.

Max didn't sit down; instead he picked it up again and walked over to the creature.

"What are you doing?" Nick yelled.

Without responding, Max swung the chair with all his might so that the back legs of the chair made contact with the creature's neck. He swung again and again until the brute force of each swing started to tear through the skin and muscle of its neck. Finally, its head flew off, leaving a ragged bloody stump behind. Nick paled as he watched Max brutally decapitate the creature. When Max was finished, he threw the chair down and collapsed onto both knees, breathing heavily.

As both men sat on the floor staring at each other, dazed from the encounter, the alarm mercifully ended and the room was silent. Nick sat there with a look of utter revulsion on his face. With the room silent, the dead body of Paige right in front of him, gore from her and the creature spattered around the room, and the bloody stump of the creature's neck pointed straight at him, Nick had to focus on not becoming unhinged. His head bobbed as a wave of nausea passed over him. His stomach wouldn't hold; he turned his head and threw up all over the floor.

"Sorry, kid," Max said, "I didn't know how long that stun dart was going to keep it out. Didn't want to take the chance that it was going to get up in thirty seconds and do to us what it did to her."

Nick wiped his mouth with his sleeve. He wiped away the tears that welled in his eyes from his upheaving stomach.

"No argument from me," he said, "What is that thing?"

"I was hoping you knew."

"No," Nick said, shaking his head and wiping vomit from his lips, "But I know where it came from."

"Where?" Max asked through ragged breaths.

"We brought it here," Nick said, "They were in the delivery from Sinclair."

Max looked at the young man skeptically. "You sure about that?"

"That sound, Max," Nick said, looking the older man in the eyes, "That screech. It was the same sound I heard in the hills on Dust. That's what killed Winters. And now Sinclair has unleashed his pet on all of us."

"You're jumping to a lot of conclusions there, kid," Max said shaking his head, "I can't believe that Sinclair would do this. He's not that kind of man."

"How do you know? How can you say that? Just because the guy did some nice things for the colony doesn't mean he couldn't do this."

"I just can't believe he would do it," Max said.

"Just like I couldn't believe my father would cause the death of thousands."

"Yeah, let's talk about that later," Max said as he tried to scoot closer to Nick. He grimaced and clutched his thigh as he tried to move. Ragged chunks of flesh dangled from the wounds on his calf. Blood stained the entire lower portion of his pant leg. Nick winced at the sight of the wound.

"Looks bad," Nick said.

"It'll be all right soon as I can pop some regen pills," Max said.

"Max, we need to get out of here," Nick said, "Get someplace safe."

Max nodded his head as he looked around the room. "What's it like out there?"

"There are bodies all over the place in the hallway," Nick said, "There's one more of those things right down the hall, dead though. We didn't see anybody else."

Max exhaled slowly. "Depending on how many of them there are, this could get real ugly."

"Max, we brought them," Nick said, "If there was one in each container on our ships, there are hundreds of them here. I don't get it. Why did he do this?"

"Nick, I just can't accept that Sinclair would do this, not without proof."

Nick shook his head in disappointment as he got to his feet. "You need to open your eyes on this one."

Max immediately shook his head. "Sinclair's eccentric, but he's not a monster, nor does he make them."

"What was in those containers, Max? How do we know it wasn't those things?"

"I just can't believe it, kid. That's just not him. Sure he doesn't have a lot of warm feelings for the Conglomerate or for the Republic, but he's not a murderer."

"That's what I thought, too," Nick said.

Max wiped sweat from his brow with his sleeve, leaving a streak of blood across his face.

"Thanks for coming after me," Max said, "Now help me up and let's get the hell out of here. We can sort out all this crap once we're safely back at the ship."

Nick legs were shaking a bit; he took a deep breath to calm himself. He realized he was still holding the small stun gun in his hand and jammed it in his back pocket. He reached a hand toward Max and the older man clasped his forearm. Max groaned as he tried to get to his feet. His leg buckled slightly as he tried to stand on it.

"Can't put much weight on it," Max said. Nick quickly moved in to support him and Max wrapped an arm around his shoulder.

"Well, I don't think we're going to win any races," Nick said.

"Let's just hope we don't come across any more of those things," Max said.

They started down the hallway, both taking a long look at the creature that lay dead at the turn in the corridor.

The hallways of the security station were littered with the bodies of fallen officers, support staff, and other detained civilians who were unlucky enough to be caught in the rampage of the monstrous creatures. Blood was spattered across the walls and pooled on the floor; dismembered body parts were found in random corners. With each grisly discovery, Nick's stomach threatened to upheave again, but each time he found the focus to control that impulse.

Throughout the rest of their journey through the security station, they only saw the body of one more of the creatures. They cautiously walked past it only after finding a few heavy office knick knacks to throw at it and ensure it wasn't about to jump up and grab them. Neither of them dared to breathe while they crept passed it.

Soon after, they found a pressed and folded officer's shirt, never worn, sitting on the corner of a desk. Max took it and tied it around his bloody calf, turning it into a makeshift compress. It was in that office that Nick finally saw a chink in Max's emotional armor. Just behind the desk, lay the body of a small boy in an unnatural, broken position.

"Christ," Max said.

Nick had to look away, focus on something else.

"Kid was probably just lost," Max said, "Looking for his parents."

Max knelt next to the boy, gently crossed the boy's arms across his chest in a more natural position, and closed the boy's eyes. When Max got up, Nick could see him fighting back tears.

Max hobbled over to another fallen officer, the nameplate on her shirt read Garcia, and accessed a floor plan of the police station on her wrist computer. He looked up and gestured over to Nick, who helped him back to his feet.

"There's a surveillance room just down the hall," Max said, "Let's get a look at what's going on out there."

Nick nodded. They found the room within moments. Walls on both sides of the room were filled with a variety of camera feeds from throughout *Nexus Station*. The images on the feeds were terrifying.

The creatures had spread across multiple levels. Fifty or so were sweeping across the concourses that connected to the hangars, another couple dozen were just getting off lifts into the residential districts, while another image showed them sweeping through the engineering sections. In all the images, people, security officers and civilians alike, were fighting back. Most were ill equipped to confront these creatures, who had clearly been bred for slaughter. The results were gruesome.

Nick struggled to watch. He looked away from the scenes of people valiantly defending themselves and an image on the far left of the array caught his eye.

"Look," Nick said, pointing.

The image showed the inside of a large storage vault. There, scattered throughout the facility, were hundreds of open containers of the same size and shape that Max and Nick delivered yesterday. But there was something else going on; something else was crawling out of the containers. Small, gray robots, just over half the size of an adult, were emerging from the containers and assembling in the chamber. They were waiting for something.

"Do you believe me now?" Nick asked with anger in his voice.

Max pursed his lips; he was at a loss to explain what was going on. The kid was right though. They had brought these things here.

"Yes," Max said softly, "I believe you. Now, we need to get the hell out of here."

"Go where? The ship? Let's just wait it out here," Nick said.

Max shook his head and said, "No, we need to get out of here, get off this station."

"That's crazy," Nick said. He gestured at the monitors, "You want to go out in the middle of that fight?"

"Not really, kid," Max said, "But if we're right and we delivered those things here, do you really think anyone will believe us when we say we didn't know what we were carrying? Do you really think they won't hold us responsible for this?"

Nick hesitated. "But we need to tell them the truth. They need to know who's behind this."

"Which they'll do when they forcibly yank the memories out of our minds, turning us into walking vegetables," Max said, "Maybe your family will help buy your way out of this, Nick, but I need to get out. You're welcome to join me."

Max started to hobble toward the exit. Nick watched him struggle to make progress, but he knew better than to question Max's resolve. Nick knew that Max was right. Max would be held responsible for this. Nick might too, depending on how he resolved things with his father. Max had made it out the door of the room and into the hallway when Nick rushed to his side.

"We're not done with this conversation," Nick said, taking some of Max's weight, "But we can continue it on the ship."

"Sounds good to me."

Some part of Nick's brain expected them to enter the main concourse of *Nexus Station* and see life as it should be, with a chaotic throng venturing to and fro on business known only to them. He expected normalcy. Instead, as they passed through the main entrance of the police station, Nick and Max were greeted with a display of carnage and devastation the scale of which neither man had ever experienced nor conceived.

There was no throng; there were no shoppers, no tourists, no bureaucrats, no lost children or wandering pets, no young lovers, no concerned parents, no discrete rendezvous, and no backdoor business dealings. There was only death and destruction. It was clear that when the evacuation alarm sounded, there wasn't enough time for people to flee this section of the station. The marauding creatures had swept through the crowd mercilessly, indiscriminately killing anyone or anything in their path.

For as far as they could see, the corridor was filled with the remains of the dead, walls coated in viscera and blood as if it were a hastily applied paint job. At odd intervals they saw the black forms of one of the creatures sticking out from the sea of torn flesh and blood.

Max's good leg buckled and Nick winced as he tried to stay upright and support the heavier man's body weight. They slammed into the bulkhead next to them and Nick's right foot wound up in a pool of blood. He recoiled and paled, looking like he was going to lose his lunch again.

"Come on, buddy," Max said softly, whispering for no reason other than to respect the dead.

Nick reached out and grabbed hold of the wall with a white knuckled grip. His stomach let go again with a tortured wretch that echoed throughout the mostly silent corridor. When his stomach finally stopped heaving he looked up at Max, who seemed almost on the brink of tears. The corridor was silent as Nick tried to recompose himself. It was then that he heard the faint echoes of weapons fire and the screams of battle. There was still fighting going on up ahead, somewhere beyond the curve of the corridor.

The thought of taking even one step through the remains of these unfortunate victims was almost too much for Nick.

"What now?" Nick asked through clenched teeth.

Max just shook his head as they looked around. After a few moments, he pointed to a door on the other side of the corridor.

"Over there, kid," Max said, "Maybe there's something in there."

Nick sure hoped so. Because with each careful step, desperately trying to avoid stepping on the remains of the dead, Nick was becoming more convinced that there was no way through this. It took a few moments to make their way across the hall, but they were rewarded with an unlocked door. As the door slid open, the light inside came on.

The room was small and gray, lined with plastic shelving and stocked with cleaning supplies, tools, and spare parts. Most importantly, a small sled, designed for carting a maintenance tech, some tools, and spare parts, sat in the middle of the closet. Max grinned. He eagerly limped over and pressed his thumb to the ignition pad. The sled started to hover about a foot above the floor.

"Thank God for small miracles," Nick said.

"You ever drive one of these before?" Max asked.

Nick shook his head, keeping his mouth shut guaranteed that nothing else would come rocketing out of his stomach. Excess saliva pooled in his mouth, he swallowed it down and his stomach cramped.

"Well, no time like the present to learn how," Max said.

"I can't think of a better time for a learning opportunity."

Max laughed. "Next time we're in an unforeseeable emergency situation, I'll make sure we practice everything we need to do beforehand."

Nick gave Max a weak smile. His stomach seemed to settle slightly from that brief release of tension. He grabbed onto the handle bars at the front of the sled and hesitated as he tried to figure out what to do.

"You control it by standing on the pressure plate," Max said, "Just lean in the direction you want it to go. Pretty simple."

"Right," Nick said.

"Have you seen the simpletons they hire as maintenance techs these days? If they can figure it out, so can you. Hop on."

Max gingerly lifted his leg over the toolbox that covered the back half of the sled and then plopped himself down. The sled bobbed slightly with the sudden added weight. Nick stood there for another moment, figuring out where all the controls were.

"Let's get going before one of those things finds us," Max said.

Nick nodded. Color had returned to his cheeks and his breathing had steadied. If he was going to die today, it would not be because he was afraid to drive this little yellow and black maintenance sled. Nick grasped the front handlebar and found his balance point. He leaned forward tentatively and the cart slowly moved forward. The grisly overcoat of blood and body parts on the floor seemed to have no impact on the sled's ability to move about. Immediately after he pulled the cart out of the closet, he brought them to a stop.

"Where am I going anyway?" Nick asked.

Max consulted his wrist computer. "Looks like we're a kilometer and a half away from the lift to our hangar bay."

Nick nodded and started to turn to the right. He overturned and then overcorrected, before finally figuring out how to get the cart moving in a straight line.

"Few more turns like that and I'm going to lose my lunch all over the back of this thing," Max said.

"Until this sector gets cleaned up, I don't think anyone will notice if you do," Nick said.

They were moving along smoothly. It would take about six minutes for them to reach the lift. As they moved along, the number of dead and dismembered seemed to drop and the number of dead creatures seemed to rise. The sound of fighting grew louder with each passing moment. If they came upon one of these things again, they were ill equipped for a fight. Nick brought the sled to a stop.

"Something wrong?" Max asked.

"What's our plan if we have to go through these things to get to the lift?" Nick asked.

Max chewed on the inside of his lip as he thought for a moment.

"You still got that stun gun?"

"Yes." Nick nodded, digging the small gray ellipsoid out of his pocket.

"Give it to me," Max said, "You steer, I'll shoot. If we see one of those things, give it as wide a berth as you can. Hopefully this will knock them out long enough for us to get clear."

"And if there's more than one?" Nick asked.

Max sighed. "How the hell should I know? I'm a damn freighter pilot, not some secret commando in disguise. You got any bright ideas?"

Nick shrugged. "Is there anything in there?" He asked, pointing to the tool chest Max was sitting on.

Max opened it up and rummaged around, finally pulling out a large pipe wrench. "Well, this'll slow someone down," he said handing it to Nick.

Nick was surprised by the weight of the wrench and almost dropped it, clanging it off the sled, "If I can manage to pick it up and swing it."

"We'll have to make sure you hit the weights once we get back to the ship. Look, this sled probably weighs about 500 pounds plus another 400 between the two of us. All that weight moving at about fifteen kilometers an hour ought to be enough to knock one or two of them out of the way. Aim for the smallest one you see and I'll shoot as many of these darts as I can to help clear the path."

Nick nodded, silently mulling over any other options. He had no better ideas; his brain was just filled with an incessant whirring sound. It took Nick a moment to realize the sound wasn't in his head. As they waited, the sound grew louder.

"What is that?" Nick asked.

Max shrugged and was about to tell the kid to keep moving when a silver-gray mass became visible several hundred yards behind them. Within seconds, it became clear that it wasn't one solid mass, but rather the same group of small, gray robots they saw assembling in the surveillance video.

"More well wishes from Sinclair," Max said.

Nick decided not to wait any longer and got the sled moving forward again at its plodding pace. Nick tried to steal some quick glances back; the gray robots continued to gain on them. Every so often, a couple would break off from the pack and head toward the sides of the corridor.

"Nick, if you can move this crate any faster, please do so," Max said.

"What are they?" Nick asked, leaning as far forward as he could.

"Pilot drones," Max said.

"What?"

"Very basic robot pilots," Max said, "They're used to ferry ships on very simple routes."

"So?" Nick asked.

"They're Sinclair's design. He's trying to steal some ships," Max responded.

"Great," said Nick.

The fighting they had heard in front of them finally came into view. Nick's mind filled with dread as it took in the scenes of the skirmish. A crowd of the black-winged vulture-human creatures was pushing steadily forward. Nick watched as they broke through a firing line of security officers and the two sides started tearing each other to shreds. Just beyond the combatants, Nick saw a crowd of people fleeing in terror.

Some in the crowd tried to assist the security officers in any way they could, throwing whatever they could find, firing off weapons scavenged from the dead, and some launching themselves into hand-to-hand combat. Those fools were quickly torn apart by the savage beasts.

Nick watched as the creatures raised their elongated, silver firearms and let loose streams of blue-tinted energy. Their aim was indiscriminate; holes were bored through officers, store fronts, signs, and civilians, leaving nothing but death and destruction in their wake. The security officers were fighting bravely, but with their line broken they stood little chance against the creatures.

Nick was relieved to see that the main throng of combatants was about ten meters beyond the door to the lift that would take them back to the *Hannah*.

"Do you see this?" Nick shouted.

Max said, "Get us in that elevator, kid, and beers are on me for the week."

Nick couldn't help but smile. He leaned forward pushing the sled as fast as it would go. The humming servos of the pilot drones had grown incredibly loud; there must have been at least a hundred of the slender gray robots. To Nick's dismay, he wasn't the only one who heard the din. Several creatures turned and looked back toward them. Nick and Max were spotted. The creatures raised their rifles.

"Hold on," Nick said, though he wasn't sure holding on would do either of them any good. It was all he could think of to say. The creatures opened fire and streaks of blue energy filled the corridor around them. One bolt struck a trailing drone and a shower of sparks erupted from its chassis as a hole was burned through it.

Nick watched as the creatures tried to aim their rifles at the sled. Their manual dexterity was lacking and none of them could accurately lead a target with a shot. They relied on sheer volume of fire to overwhelm their target. Suddenly, a shot burned into the corridor wall just to the left of Nick's head, and he no longer felt so confident about their chances.

All it takes is one lucky shot, Nick thought. He tried to slip the sled from side-to-side, but it was comically slow in doing so.

"I don't think this is helping," Max said.

"How about you start shooting instead of criticizing my driving," Nick said.

"Easier said than done, speedy," Max retorted. He couldn't twist himself around to get a decent shot off. Nick finally quit bobbing back and forth and headed straight for the opening of the freight lift. The lift door yawned open, a tantalizing ten meters ahead of them.

Suddenly, the creature closest to them leapt, covering the roughly four meters between it and the sled in a single bound. It landed on the front edge of the sled with its beak inches from Nick's nose. Nick let out a yelp as the weight of the creature pitched the sled forward and drove it into the floor. The creature grabbed at Nick with both arms in a panicked flail as the sled handlebar pushed the creature into the floor.

Nick screamed in pain as the creature's talons pierced the skin of his torso. He heard a terrible, wet squelching sound as the handlebar of the sled buried itself in the creature's chest and continued to push farther into the nightmarish thing as it skidded to a halt.

Nick tried to immediately climb out from under the cart; afraid the weight of it would snap the handlebar and send it crashing down on top of him. He wiggled free, his midsection now covered in the blood of the creature, but his pant leg snagged on something. He turned to see what he was caught on and heard the clang of another one of the creatures as it landed in front of him. He looked up to see it flare its wings and unleash its devilish screech.

Max, thrown forward over both Nick and the creature when the cart tipped, was ready with the stun gun. He was propped against the wall of the lift, grimacing in pain, as he fired off three of the tiny darts from the stun gun. Before the creature even finished its wail, it slumped to the ground.

Nick yanked on his pant leg with all his strength and it ripped free. He crawled forward as fast as he could, getting into the lift just as two pilot drones rushed in. Max selected the hangar on his wrist computer and the doors began to close at a painstakingly slow pace. Nick still lay on the floor panting, blood welling up on the sides of his torso, as he watched the doors slowly slide shut.

When the doors sealed and the lift began moving, Nick laid his head on the floor and exhaled slowly in relief. He tried to sit up, but it hurt too much to move. Max limped over to him and held out a hand.

"Well done, kid, but we're not out of this yet," Max said as he nodded towards the two drones they shared the lift with. The drones paid them no attention; they hovered in complete silence.

"What are you thinking?" Nick asked.

"They'll make a break for the ship, but Reggie won't let them leave without us. If they do intend to take the ship, we can at least find out where they want to take us before we turn them into spare parts."

"Whatever you say, boss," Nick said with a wince.

The lift came to a stop and the doors opened. Max and Nick tentatively poked their heads out far enough to get a look around the hangar. The pilot drones floated past them and did a quick scan of the hangar looking for available ships. Within seconds, one of the two took off towards the *Hannah* while the other set off towards a ship at the other end of the bay.

Nick turned his attention away from the drones and noticed that Max was pointing towards the far end of the hangar. Nick made out three dark shapes; a few of the creatures had been on the loose in here. Max gestured and took off at a fast hobble, slightly doubled-over in pain. They passed a row of empty, gray shipping containers and Max paused. There on the floor lay the dead body of Phyllis. She had been cut to pieces by the talons of one of those godforsaken creatures.

"Shit," Max said, "I've known her for more than ten years. She was a good, honest, hard working woman."

"I'm sorry, Max," Nick said, "Come on. We've got to get moving."

Nick gestured at him impatiently and stabbed his finger toward the creatures. One of them had turned towards them and was awkwardly lumbering in their direction. Nick once again helped Max support his weight and they moved as fast as they could towards the ship. Nick could hear the creature screech when they finally reached the ramp. Reggie stood at the top of the ramp, ready to close it as soon as everyone boarded.

"I am relieved to see you, sir," Reggie said.

"You have no idea how glad I am to hear your voice, Reggie," Max said as he knelt on the floor, "Do me a favor and go get the med kit. And where's that drone?"

"Right away, sir. The drone is in the cockpit. I have currently locked it out of all the ship's systems; however, it is running a strong decryption algorithm and will probably have access within the next ten to fifteen minutes."

"Computer," Max called out, "Run a bio scan on the ship."

"Scan reports three biological organisms present on the ship," the computer responded.

"Crap," Nick said.

Max frowned.

"What is the location of the third organism?" Max asked.

"Cargo hold."

"Well, at least we found out now before it had a chance to kill us in our sleep," Max said, "Reggie, get me that kit and bring me my atomizer!"

Max's voice echoed off the corridor walls. Reggie's affirmative response returned a moment later.

"Atomizer?" Nick said, "I didn't think anyone still used those."

Max smirked at him. "I used to run a route through pirate-controlled space. It came in handy on one or two occasions. Now it just gathers dust in my storage locker. It'll get the job done, though."

"We should just vent the hold to space," Nick said.

"I'm with you on that, but let's make sure we're bagging one of the bad guys, first."

Reggie returned and handed Max a silver bag and a small pistol. The bag opened at Max's touch and he rummaged through it for a minute. He pulled out a vial of black pills, took two, and handed the vial to Nick. Nick glanced at the label, emblazoned with the Conglomerate logo, before pouring out two more pills and taking them.

"How long do these things usually take to work?" Nick asked.

"They'll get you patched up in about an hour, though they've got a helluva kick."

"Wonders of modern medicine," Nick said, struggling to get back to his feet.

Max had the gun reassembled. "Reggie, you lead the way. Nick, stay behind me. Let's find this son of a bitch and get him off my ship."

The three of them trudged toward the aft of the ship. Reggie's feet and Nick's metal boots clanged heavily off the deck. They sure weren't going to sneak up on anyone, Nick thought. The hatch to the cargo hold slid open and Reggie cautiously stepped inside. It seemed even Reggie was concerned about running into one of those creatures.

Reggie saw nothing and gestured for Nick and Max to follow. Just before they entered, Max remembered to give the stun gun back to Nick. Nick nodded in appreciation. He quickly checked the ammunition counter on the top face of the gun; there were only a couple of shots remaining.

As the three of them entered, Reggie commanded the lights to full brightness. The hold was largely empty with only a couple of places to hide. In the far right of the hold, a few crates of spare parts were stacked about three meters high and in the back left was a relatively small closet used for storing tools and more spare parts. Those were the only two possible hiding spaces.

It occurred to Nick that he would be surprised to find one of these creatures hiding. They didn't seem to have that cunning nor did they seem to have any sense of fear. Still,

Nick didn't dare relax. After what they had just been through, he allowed that anything could happen.

The spare part crates were fastened to the far right wall of the hold. There was a small gap in the between the crates; it took only a quick check to see that there was no one hiding there. Nick breathed a sigh of relief that there was nothing there, but looked in apprehension towards the storage closet.

The closet door was open; the darkness inside it was unsettling.

"No light in there?" Nick asked.

"Remind me to fix that later," Max said.

The trio walked up to the room as quietly as their wounds and wardrobes would allow. Max and Nick flanked the sides of the door and Max gestured for Reggie to go in first.

Reggie was in there for just a few seconds when he called out, "Captain, I have found our third passenger."

Max and Nick stepped in, weapons still drawn, to see Reggie with his flashlight beam focused on the shivering, slight frame of a small girl. Both men let out a sigh of relief and lowered their weapons.

"Thank God. I don't think I could've handled another round with one of those things," Max said.

Nick walked over to the girl and knelt in front of her. "Are you okay? Are you hurt?"

The girl, maybe twelve years old, shook her head. As Nick approached, she hugged her knees tighter to her chest. Her face and hair were covered in a spatter of blood. Nick recognized her designer clothes; the girl's parents had been well off.

"What's your name?" Nick asked.

She didn't answer.

"Reggie, how much time until the drone breaks through the encryption?" Max asked.

"About five minutes."

"What are you thinking?" Nick asked.

"Let's find a safe place for her in the hangar," Max said, "We need to get out of here."

Nick looked at Max in stunned surprise. "You're going to leave her here?"

"You got a better idea, I'll listen," Max said, "But I'm a wanted man now, Nick. With what's about to come down on us, we can't afford to be bringing on stragglers. This is not a refugee ship."

"I can take care of the kidnapping charges," Nick said.

"Nick, look around. Who's going to get blamed for what happened here? If I'm not executed, I'm going to be put away for a long time. We need to get out of here and I don't know where we're going. This is not the safe place for her to be. I'm sure we can put her in the hangar control room and lock her in and she'll be perfectly safe."

"Would you look at her?" Nick said.

The girl pulled her legs in tighter and was visibly shaking. The girl's face had turned a pale white.

"Please don't make me go back out there," she whispered.

"This isn't happening, Nick. She can't stay and I'm not debating it," Max said firmly. He turned to leave and said, "Reggie, do what I asked."

"Yes, sir."

Reggie started toward the little girl. Nick put his hands gently on her shoulders and knelt down in front of her.

"What happened to your parents? Are they here on the station?"

"My mom…she's…she's dead," the girl said softly, "Please don't make me go back out there."

Reggie tried to grab the girl's hand, but she pulled away from him and crawled back.

"Max, damn it! We can't just leave her here!" Nick yelled, getting to his feet.

"I'm not debating this, Nick. End of story. We need to get the hell out of here. If you don't like it, you can get off too."

Max had walked halfway across the hold and didn't stop to face Nick.

"Max, how can you possibly turn your back on her? What the hell's wrong with you?" Nick yelled, "What if this were your daughter? Would you be so willing to throw her life away?"

At this, Max did stop and slowly turned around. The look on his face was one of pure malice.

"Don't you dare say that," Max growled, stepping closer to Nick, "She's better off here. She shouldn't be on this ship!"

Nick gestured toward the hangar. "Do you remember what's out there? We can't just lock her in a room and hope she'll be okay! Who knows when or if they'll have this situation under control! Might as well just put her out the airlock!"

"That's what you wanted to do two minutes ago, remember? What are we supposed to do with her, huh? You want me to hold her hand and walk her to a security officer? Might as well put the cuffs on myself, because they're sure as hell not going to let me walk away! If her mother's dead, then she needs to find her father! Not go tromping around with us."

"Max, we need to go to security. Tell them we know who's behind this; clear this up now. Running just makes it look worse," Nick said.

"Do you really think they're going to stop and ask questions before they lock me away? Do you really think I can say, gee, sorry officer, I didn't know I was launching an attack on the station? Christ, you're an idiot."

Nick and Max now stood less than a foot apart. Reggie now stood at the doorway of the cold storage room with the girl's hand firmly in his grasp. The girl had fresh tears in her eyes. Nick looked back at her and his resolve strengthened.

"The day your daughter died," Nick said, "Don't you wish someone had been there to help? Don't you wish that if someone could have done something to prevent it that they would have? Don't you have to do the same thing here?"

The malice on Max's face quickly shifted to rage and he punched Nick right in the jaw. Nick fell backwards. Max glared at him; his face beet red. Max took a few deep, forceful breaths, his chest noticeably rising and falling, before turning and stomping off.

"Get them both out of here, Reggie," Max yelled as he walked out, "Get that piece of shit off of my ship."

"Max, you can't run forever," Nick said, but Max ignored him and continued walking.

"Let's go, sir," Reggie said.

"Come on, Reggie," Nick said, "You can't let him do this."

"I can only follow orders, sir," Reggie said. Reggie held the girl's hand and with his other arm, grabbed Nick firmly by the elbow.

With the small drone hovering in front of the pilot's seat, Max plopped into the co-pilot's seat in the cockpit with an annoyed grunt. He looked out the window of the cockpit at the mess of crates, robots, and ships and tried to calm himself. Even after all these years, he could still hear his wife nagging him about walking away from an argument. Max let out a slow breath and focused on the creature that was now bobbing away from the ship.

They could make it, Max thought. They can easily get to the hangar control room before the creature gets there. Then, they could ride this whole mess out in there until security gets a handle of things. They won't be in any danger. Then Nick can face his father like he wants to do and move on with his life. It'll all be good for the kid.

But Nick will also talk to security about all this. He will tell them where the creatures came from, who delivered them, and who was responsible for all this. He may try to tell them that it wasn't Max's fault, but there's no way they will believe them.

Max needed time to sort all this out, time without the Republic hunting him down. The only way he could get that time was by keeping the kid from talking to security. He reached over and activated the intercom.

"Reggie," Max said, "Change of plans. We're getting out of here. All of us. Everybody strap in. Reggie, release the encryption and let's see where this pile of scrap is going to take us."

Within seconds, Max could feel that the engines had started the liftoff sequence. Moments later, the *Hannah* took off with a lurch. The drone applied too much thrust on the port side. Max shook his head in annoyance.

Max watched his console display with a sense of dread as the drone plotted the ship's next course. They were headed back to Dust; their course back to the jump beacon was now set. Max fumed. He was angry at the world. He was angry at Nick for so blatantly using his daughter's memory against him. He was angry at Sinclair. After years of dedicated service, paying off a debt he could never truly repay, Max had been deemed expendable.

To hell with them, Max thought.

Max leaned forward in the seat and activated a view of the station from the rear of the ship. Max watched as dozens of random vessels - cargo ships, luxury yachts, construction barges, even a few defense frigates - launched from *Nexus Station*. Max shook his head in disbelief. How long had Sinclair been planning this?

The Republic would not stand idly by while Sinclair attacked the innocent civilians on *Nexus Station*. They would retaliate with full force once they figured out who was responsible for all of this. Bloodshed was coming to Dust.

Max continued to watch the display as he tried to hail another ship.

"*Beau*, this is the *Hannah*, do you copy?"

Max waited a moment but received no response.

"*Beau*, this is the *Hannah*. Charlie, are you there?"

He tapped another spot on the display.

"*Wounded Duck*, this is the *Hannah*. Are you there, Roman?"

He repeated the calls several times over the next half hour but never received a response. His shoulders slumped and he sat back wearily in the chair. He looked over at the smooth finish of the drone, its single blue-glowing eye focused on the cockpit display. Max hated that robot with every fiber of his being, hated that it was in his chair, hated that it was piloting his ship, and hated that Sinclair thought it would replace him. At that moment, it represented every unholy thing in the known universe.

Max got up abruptly, his boot clanging loudly off the deck, and headed for the maintenance closet. He rummaged around for a bit and pulled out a socket wrench, hammer, and a cold welder. He then poured himself a cold beer from the galley and chugged it down. He wiped his mouth with his sleeve, left the empty beer mug, and stormed off toward the cockpit.

CHAPTER 10

Max's head bobbed and he jerked himself awake. He had nodded off only briefly; his Captain's chair wasn't conducive to anything other than short naps. He looked around at the various pieces of scrap that had been the drone. The floor of the cockpit was now littered with bolts, wires, circuit boards, grease, and all sorts of other components. It would take some time to clean all this up. Max stood up and headed to the galley to get a cup of coffee.

The little girl was there. She was looking around for something. She found the bowls and pulled one out. She turned around and froze when she saw Max. Her hands started to tremble; a look of fear passed over her face. She took a step back towards the cabinet.

"Please don't get mad," she said.

Max had to blink to keep tears from forming. He reached toward her and she tried to recoil again.

"I'm not going to hurt you," Max said, "I'm sorry for earlier. I'm not mad at you."

She stood unmoving, dirt streaked across her cheeks, still wearing the shirt with her mother's blood. Max offered her a slight smile.

"Can I help you?"

"I was starving," she said, "Just looking for something to eat."

Max held his hand out and she tentatively handed him the bowl. He stuck the bowl under the food processor and waited as the gray goop was dispensed.

"Sorry I don't have anything better," Max said, "I used to have real oatmeal, back when…"

He stopped. Back when my daughter used to come with me, he was about to say. This girl didn't need to hear that though. Max coughed. He gestured for her to have a seat and set the bowl down in front of her.

"What's your name?" He asked.

"Eleanor."

She greedily tore into the paste, too hungry to care about the taste or texture.

"Where are you from, Eleanor?" Max asked as he grabbed a cup of coffee.

"Roosevelt," she said.

Max had to laugh. "Were your parents historians?"

She nodded. "My dad is. Why?"

"No reason," he said, shaking his head, "What were you…uh…doing out here?"

"Going to a robotics fare," she said, "My mom was…"

Max could easily see the fright on the little girl's face. She stopped eating for a minute and looked up at Max. He could see the tears starting to fall.

"When she fell, when she hit the ground because one of those bird-things got her, I just turned and ran. It felt like they were right there, right behind me. I could hear their claws scraping against the floor as they followed me. I just wanted to find a place to hide."

Looking her in the eye was heartbreaking, so Max wandered over to the sink behind her and fiddled with some of the dirty dishes.

"I wasn't angry at you, Eleanor. I promise," Max said.

"I was so scared," Eleanor said through a veil of tears. Max stood behind her and put a hand on her shoulder. He could feel her shake with every sob. The horror and terror of the day before came pouring out of this scared, little girl as she sobbed, gasped, and shook.

"My mom," she said with a heartbreaking whine. Then she turned toward Max and before he could stop her, she hugged him fiercely.

For the first time in over ten years, Max held a little girl in his arms and he nearly lost himself. The feeling of protectiveness that flooded back to him was overwhelming. He found himself pulling Eleanor in tightly, wrapping his arms around her to protect her from the harsh reality of the world.

Nothing he could do would change what had happened and they both knew it. Eleanor stood there in his embrace and cried for her lost mother until there was nothing left to come out of her. Max would've stood there for as long as she needed, holding her tight to let her know that she was not alone in this world. He would do whatever he had to do to return this little girl to what remained of her family.

"Let's send a message to your father. Let him know you're all right," Max said, and the two of them went to his quarters. Max sat Eleanor at the small desk in his room and activated the video recorder that he seldom used to record his personal logs.

"Go ahead," Max said.

Eleanor nodded, sniffed, and wiped tears from her eyes. She tried to compose herself as best she could. Max could see the strength in her, the resiliency, and a feeling of pride welled up inside him. Eleanor reminded him so much of his own daughter and once again tears threatened to overwhelm him.

"Hi, Daddy," Eleanor began, her voice trembling slightly, "I don't know if you've heard about what happened, but if you have, I just wanted you to know I'm all right. I'm on a ship. But mom, mom didn't…"

She tried to continue, but couldn't. Max slid into view behind Eleanor, crouching down so that his head was roughly level with hers. Suddenly, Max realized that he hadn't trimmed his beard in several days, hadn't showered, hadn't slept, and looked generally unpleasant.

"Uh, sir," Max began and then turned to Eleanor and asked, "What's your Dad's name?"

"John," she said.

"Uh, John, my name is Maxime Cabot. I am a freighter pilot who picked up your daughter during the incident at *Nexus*. Your daughter is safe aboard our ship and we'll get her back to you as soon as we can. I have to take one short trip before we can bring her back to Roosevelt.

"I have to go get my own daughter, first."

Nick awoke screaming, covered in sweat. Images from the day before were burned into his mind - the blood, the bodies, the dismembered body parts, and the awful visage of those creatures. He rubbed his eyes and then his temples trying to clear the thoughts from his mind. His hands trembled slightly.

The sides of his chest itched slightly from where one of the creatures had dug its talons into his side. Though the muscle and tissue had been rebuilt and repaired, the area was still tender and sore to the touch. His jaw also ached from Max's punch; he slowly worked it back and forth to try and clear some of the stiffness and pain.

Max came in and sat on the couch opposite him. Max had heavy bags under his eyes, the left was bloodshot and the right seemed to be twitching slightly. His hands and clothes were covered in bluish grease which he was slowly wiping off on a rag. Nick noted a streak of red on the rag as well. Max had gashed the palm of his right hand on something. A fresh scar was visible where the meds had closed the wound.

For a moment, Max sat there and just stared at him.

"Nightmares?" Max asked as he slowly, hypnotically wiped the rag back and forth across his hands. With each swipe, the fabric picked up globs of goop from his hands and ultimately, left them spotless.

Nick nodded. "Can't get the images of those people out of my head."

"I doubt you ever will, Nick. Seeing something like that can scar a man for a long time."

"I take it you didn't sleep at all," Nick said with a bit of a yawn.

Max nodded again and threw the rag on the table between them. "Did a lot of thinking last night. Trying to figure out what to do."

"Thinking and tinkering, again?" Nick asked with a slight smile.

Max gave a little chuckle as he inspected his hands for any leftover grease. "I took that bastard drone apart bolt by bolt. I gave the central processor to Reggie; see if he can decode its programming, find any other surprises. I think I'll give the rest of the parts to the little girl as a present."

"Eleanor," Nick said, "How's she doing this morning?"

Just after takeoff, Nick and Reggie had set Eleanor up in his quarters for the night. They gave her Nick's bed and the girl passed out by the time her head hit the pillow.

"Okay," Max said, "For a kid who watched her mother get slaughtered right before her eyes yesterday."

Nick shook his head in sorrow and disbelief.

"Where is she now?"

"Playing around with Reggie," Max said, "She seems to have a thing for robots. I warned Reggie to make sure she doesn't come at him with a screwdriver."

Nick smiled halfheartedly and the two men sat in silence for a moment. Nick got up and walked over to a dispenser on the wall behind him. He tapped a command into the control pad and seconds later a cup of coffee was in his hands.

"So, what now?" Nick asked.

"Don't ever use my daughter's memory against me again," Max said, "If you do, you can get off the ship wherever we are and I never want to see you again. Do you understand?"

Nick nodded.

Max sighed and looked at Nick hesitantly. Nick could almost hear the wheels of thought turning in Max's head. Nick took a sip of the coffee. He wasn't fond of the taste but the warmth that trickled down his throat and then filled his stomach calmed him made him feel more at home.

"We're going back to Dust," Max finally said.

Nick's eyes went wide. He slowly lowered the cup and said, "Are you crazy? We can't go back there! What the hell are you thinking?"

Max looked at him sternly.

"Nick, the second we tell sector security who is behind this, they will descend upon Dust in droves. The lives the people on that colony have lived will be over. That whole place is going to be locked down and torn apart as they get to the bottom of what's going on there.

"I need to get some things and get out of there. Disappear for a while. Maybe the Republic will think I died on the station and not coming looking for me. Once I've got what and who I need, I'll drop you and Eleanor off and you can contact whoever."

"Let's just fire off a warning message to your friends and be done with it," Nick said, "No need to go back there in person and risk being food for one of Sinclair's pets."

"Nick, I need to go there. I want to pick up my ex-wife and…and someone else," Max said. He looked down at his clean hands and the fresh scar on his palm.

"This is about more than just your family, Max. What happens if Sinclair launches another attack while we're busy taking care of the one or two people you've deemed worthy of saving?" Nick asked angrily. "How many more people have to die before we go to sector security and explain-"

"Explain what, exactly? That we unwittingly unleashed a terrorist attack on that space station? I'm sure they will be understanding and not hold us accountable for that in any way."

Another spark of anger flashed in Nick. "I guess it would be difficult to explain how someone who worked for Sinclair for ten years didn't see this coming."

"What are you saying, Nick? Think I had something to do with this?"

"I just find it hard to believe that someone you trusted so much could do something like this without you having any idea what was going on," Nick said, "I mean, it's not like he did this on a whim. You don't create those things, create those weapons, and unleash them without a lot of planning. Without help."

The words hung in the air. Max's hand curled into a fist; his muscles tensed.

Nick was ready to get punched again. He didn't agree with Max on this. "The longer we go without reporting what we know the more likely it is that someone else gets hurt."

Instead of throwing a punch, Max let out a long sigh and ran his hand through his graying hair.

"Sinclair's been involved in a lot of things that weren't always within the law," Max said, "You've seen plenty of evidence of that. But he's done more to help people than I've been able to show you, more than I can explain with words. If I ever thought this would happen, I would've never worked for him."

Nick said nothing in response. He looked down at his hands again and then down at the floor.

"Just let me pick up two people and then we'll send a message to sector security," Max said, "That should give them enough time to prevent Sinclair from getting any ships out loaded with those things."

Nick didn't like it, but Max was right, that should give them enough time. Nick forgot about the cup of coffee in his hand and accidentally spilled a drop. The hot liquid burned his thumb slightly. He took a sip and watched Max out of the corner of his eye. The old man was standing there, staring at some undefined point, thoughts running through his head.

"What is it, Max?" Nick asked, "What aren't you telling me?"

"Nothing, kid," Max said. He stood up from the couch, leaving before Nick could press him further.

Nick frowned. "And what about Eleanor? Are we just going to drag her along with us, another member of the crew now?"

"First opportunity, we'll take her to her father," Max said, "But that has to be later. Whatever is going to happen on Dust, it's going to happen fairly quickly and I need to get there first."

The *Hannah* arrived at the jump beacon late that afternoon but faced a three hour wait due to the number of ships in the queue. Max sat in the pilot's chair with his feet propped on the console and a toothpick between his lips. He watched as ship after ship jumped to the Dust system. So many ships were on their way, more than Dust had ever seen at one time, but that was not where Max's mind was.

He could think of almost nothing except Eleanor and the strong hug she gave him that morning. She had felt so small and frail in his arms. He wanted to hug that little girl and protect her from all the evils of the galaxy, to hold on to her until he knew she'd be safe. He wanted to do for her what he failed to do for his own little girl.

Max held his daughter's broken body in his arms that fateful day. He screamed for help, but there was no one there who could do anything. He had held her fiercely, long past the moment when her life slipped away. His little girl, who looked up to him for everything, who would be by his side at all times, was gone.

He drank that night, drank himself into oblivion, until he passed out on the living room floor of their tiny two-bedroom apartment. It was the only way he could get the tears to stop and the only way he could get rest.

Within a week, the arguments with his wife had started. She wouldn't come out and say that she blamed him, but it was the moments of silence after certain questions, the sidelong glances during conversations, the terseness of certain responses that told him how she felt. She was as devastated as he had been. Her only daughter, the only child they were allowed to have, had been ripped away.

A month later they applied for a special exemption to have a second child. Their appeal was denied. After the denied appeal came in, he went out to drink again and returned home to find his wife sitting on the couch, waiting for him. She sat there in a nondescript night gown and stared at him with red-rimmed eyes.

"There are other options," she had said, wiping at the tears with the back of her hand.

He looked at her through a drunken fog, trying to understand what she was saying. He leaned heavily against the doorframe that separated the living room from the kitchen.

"We still have access to her cord blood," she said, "Margaret told me about someone else who went through this. Said they found a doctor out on the fringe…"

"No," Max said as understanding dawned on him, "I can't do it. I couldn't look at her again."

"God damn you!" She screamed, "I want my daughter back, you son of a bitch!"

He recoiled; her fury astounded him. She slapped him that night, the first and only time. He had known at that moment that their lives were about to go on separate paths. She just had one condition for the divorce.

Max stirred from his thoughts as Reggie came tromping into the cockpit with Eleanor in tow. She looked up at him warmly. He could tell that sadness lurked just beneath the surface of her emotions, but she was a strong kid and her grief barely showed. It took Max a moment to realize he was staring at her.

"What's up?" He finally worked up the courage to ask.

"We've finished parsing the code from the drone," Reggie said.

"We?" Max asked.

Eleanor shrugged and said, "Reggie let me help with breaking down some of the lower level algorithms."

"She's quite good, sir," Reggie said.

Max couldn't help but smile. "Whatever fuels your engines, kid. Anything of interest?"

"Quite a bit," Reggie continued, "Detailed instructions for the next phases of the plan, contingency instructions if they are intercepted by Republic or Conglomerate forces, and a database of potential targets for future missions. It was ready to receive its next set of instructions once it reached Dust orbit."

"Christ, you're killing me with all this, Reggie," Max said, "I can't believe this. What the hell is Sinclair thinking?"

"I cannot answer that, sir," Reggie said.

"Well, did you get anything useful?"

"Quite a bit," Reggie responded, "Instructions to run the reactor at maximum output and shorten the trip back to Dust."

Max frowned, running the reactor hot would allow them to travel faster but it would put them at greater risk for a core meltdown.

"I want us to blend in Reggie. Run us as close to maximum as we can handle, but prepare to kick in safeguards at a moment's notice. Anything else?"

"They carried a worm that would wipe the memory banks of the jump beacon."

"Trying to cover his tracks," Max said with a wry smile, "Won't take the Republic too long to reconstruct where they're headed, but it might buy him a few days."

"There are some other things, sir," Reggie continued, "Some commented out code that I don't understand. It has something to do with the astronavigation algorithms, but its exact purpose is unclear."

"Keep working on it," Max said, "Let me know what you figure out."

With a little over an hour to go before the jump, Nick joined Max in the cockpit and started fiddling around with stellar maps on his console. He scrolled and zoomed, panning through star system after star system. His head rested on the palm of his hand as the soft white light from the console gave his face a pale glow.

"I have to admit I underestimated your father," Max said, "But if I hadn't been picked up by security, I would have been on that concourse somewhere during that attack. Funny how those things work out."

"I tried to tell you," Nick said, "My father's a pretty relentless man."

"He could get in a lot of trouble for what he did, lying about you being kidnapped."

Nick shook his head.

"No, he'll walk away from that pretty easily," Nick said, "My father's been using the Republic to get what he wants for years. He'd find some way to explain it away. He always does."

"That data you have must be pretty sensitive to pull a stunt like that."

"I told you I stole his files, everything related to the projects his department was working on. All sorts of internal memos, data sheets, you name it. Do you have a crystal reader? I'll show you."

"No," Max said, "Though I bet…"

Max stopped and Nick looked up from what he was doing.

"What?"

"I was going to say, I bet Sinclair has one. Doesn't matter anyhow."

Max waved his hand for Nick to continue and the young man nodded.

"Well, once we're done with this run, I'll drop you wherever you want. Then, if you want to chase your father down, that's up to you," Max said.

"He wants that data so bad; I guess I'll give it back to him," Nick said with a shrug, "I don't know what else to do with it. That's why I let security know I was in the crawlway; I just wanted to get it over with."

"You'll feel good when it's all done, Nick," Max said, "I-"

Max's console beeped loudly. He reached over and accepted an incoming transmission.

"Emergency message," Max said.

"This is Commander Dorn," a strong female voice erupted from the speaker, "I am commanding officer of the Fifth Fleet of the Republic. I am declaring Martial law in this sector. All ships are ordered to shut down their drives and await inspection by Republic Forces."

Max turned off the message and checked the position of the fleet on his console.

"They're a day out," he said, "But that's not the real problem. They're going to lock down the jump beacons."

"So, now what?"

"This isn't my first flight, kid," Max said, "Sit tight."

Max started furiously accessing command menus on his console. He was drilling down through submenus when his face lit up.

"What is it?"

"Time to declare a medical emergency," Max said, "How do you feel about having a heart attack?"

"I'm disappointed that I didn't keep myself in better condition," Nick quipped.

"Nice. This'll bump us to the head of the queue. Now, cross your fingers and hope we can get out of here in time."

Max opened up the intercom.

"Reggie, get Eleanor strapped in. We're about to jump. Hurry."

There was no time to wait. The countdown clock on Max's console jumped from 55 minutes to 20 seconds. This would strain the engines, but Max didn't have time for a proper spin up. Just before the count expired, Reggie's voice came over the comm.

"She's secure."

The countdown clock on the pilot's console hit zero, they felt the pull of the jump, and with a flash, they were back in the Dust system. Nick's face paled after the jump and Max couldn't help but shake his head and laugh.

"Do you get seasick, Nick?" Max asked, "Maybe you should consider a career on a boat. Might be less nausea inducing for you."

"You're not helping. And, no I don't," Nick said through gritted teeth.

"Not trying to help," Max said.

Max's smile disappeared as his console display suddenly filled with patches of red and an alert tone sounded in the cockpit. Max silenced the alarm and quickly started reviewing the data.

"Crap," Max said, "Put a little too much strain on the power system with that emergency jump. We just blew out a power distribution unit."

"How bad is it?"

"Not too bad," Max said as he scanned the data, "Backup units are on-line. Looks like everything came up fine. Just gives us something to do on the trip to Dust."

Max reached for the intercom.

"Reggie, I need you to start checking out the primary power string. Find out what box in the line we need to replace."

"Will do, sir," Reggie responded.

Max turned his attention to the area of space around them. Intermixed among the sea of stars were the red flashing lights of dozens of other ships, all on the same return trajectory as the *Hannah*.

"That little trick to get out of the system was interesting," Nick said, "You're quite the smuggler."

"Thanks," Max said. It took him a minute to realize that may not be a compliment. "I've smuggled some people in before."

Nick nodded but didn't respond.

"Like Lonnie and her two kids," Max said, "But I swear that's it."

"Doesn't matter, Max. Let's just do what we need to do."

"Sounds good to me," Max said. He stood up and stretched; his muscles and mind were weary from the physical and emotional drain of the day. The energy pill he had taken a few hours ago was rapidly wearing off and the fact that he hadn't slept much over the last two days hit him like a brick wall.

"Holy crap, I'm tired."

Nick shot him a knowing smile.

"Get some rest," Nick said.

"You look like you could use some, too," Max said. Nick's eyes were puffed with dark circles underneath them.

"Yeah," Nick said, "I'm having trouble sleeping without having nightmares."

"Well, feel free to have a few beers. Always helps me sleep when I've got too much on my mind."

Max didn't stick around to hear Nick's reply. He went to his quarters, closed the door, and fell asleep in his coveralls.

CHAPTER 11

Nick awoke again in a puddle of sweat as the images from *Nexus Station* continued to haunt his dreams. He sat upright and rested his head in his hands. He glanced at his wrist computer; it was still early. The ship was hauntingly quiet as everyone else still slept.

Should've taken Max's advice, he thought. But Nick had never taken a drink alone in his life and wasn't about to start now. Besides, Max's advice may not be all it was cracked up to be. Max was holding something back; that much was clear. And his admission to smuggling and the subsequent defensiveness made Nick question how much Max really knew about what was going on here.

Nick needed to clear his head. He walked, barefoot, down the corridor, trying to make as little noise as possible. Even Reggie was offline, plugged into his recharging station that was nestled into the side of the corridor just before the entrance to the cargo hold.

Nick kept quiet as he entered the vast, empty hold. The room was dark, save for emergency lighting placed at regular intervals around the hold. Nick kept the lights off and paced around the hold. He wasn't sure what he was searching for, just a spot that felt right. He finally squatted down in a spot in the middle of the hold.

After the events of the past few days, Nick's nerves were raw. He couldn't relax; he kept expecting something to jump out at him from the shadows. He knew that was ridiculous, but it didn't stop him from feeling like something was about to get him.

Nick kneeled on the unforgiving metal floor, the grating digging into his knee. He prayed for the first time in days. He whispered the words he knew by heart as he recited the Lord's Prayer. He then recited the Apostle's Creed, then a Hail Mary, and he methodically went through every prayer he could remember.

When his memory was exhausted, he found silence in his mind. He found calm. He prayed for guidance, for evidence that Max wasn't leading them down the wrong path. He needed to see something from his captain, something that could reassure him that Max knew what he was doing. Max hadn't been the same since they had found Eleanor in this very room.

Nick could see the sorrow and pain in the old man's face every time he looked at the girl. Old wounds had opened up for him. He couldn't help but wonder if Max was leading them the wrong way.

"Please, Lord," Nick said, "Help me find strength and courage."

Nick eventually made his way back to the lounge and tried to watch John Doe, a movie about a man trying to rediscover his lost memories. It was billed as a hilarious comedy about a man rediscovering his sense of self. It was awful. Nick gave up on the movie and turned on the latest news recording. This was just more of the same - riots, starvation, colonies struggling to survive, but hey

Conglomerate stock was up. Nick got sick of it all and turned off the screen.

After spending some time in the cockpit taking in the view, he found Eleanor in the cargo hold with Reggie. She was tinkering with a little robotic creation built from the scrap of the pilot drone. Reggie did not have the capacity to become emotionally attached to someone, but he was volunteering to spend plenty of time with the little girl. Nick wondered if deep inside Reggie's circuits, the robot engineer found some measure of satisfaction in comforting her.

It was heartwarming to watch the little girl play, but Eleanor's constant refinement of her toy's decision making algorithms was a little too tedious for Nick's taste. Eleanor was clearly a bright little girl and Nick envisioned she would have quite the future in robotics, computer science, or something similar if she stuck with her current passion.

Nick eventually left the two of them in the hold and decided to return to the cockpit. As Nick made his way forward, he caught a glimpse of Max working intently at the console in his room. From the corridor, Nick couldn't see the images on the shiny glass surface; he could merely see Max tapping things here and there, dragging something across the surface, and finally zooming in to check some details.

"What's going on?" Nick asked.

Max was massaging the temple of his forehead with his left hand while he worked with the right. The puffy, dark circles underneath the older man's eyes had faded somewhat after his long rest last night. Nick was relieved to see Max looking a little better. Max stared blankly at Nick for a moment.

"Just trying to iron out the plan is all," Max said. He turned his attention back to the console.

Nick could now see a picture of Dust on the screen. The planet slowly rotated on the display while yellow lines representing the *Hannah's* trajectory were superimposed around the planet. Nick watched as Max jabbed at a triangle that represented the ship's insertion point into Dust orbit and dragged the triangle to a point on Dust's night side.

"Mind filling me in a bit on what that plan is?" Nick asked.

As Max moved things around, numbers on the left side of the display updated in real time. Nick recognized a few of them, velocity, thrust, thruster firing times, but the details behind them were far beyond what Nick had learned in school.

"Well," Max said slowly as he moved another point on the display around, "The sheer number of ships coming in ought to help us slip through relatively unnoticed. Still, I'd like to give us whatever cover we can, so I'm trying to figure out how to give us a night time approach."

Nick nodded and asked, "But where are we going?"

"According to the data Reggie was able to pull out of the drone's brain, all these ships will be rendezvousing with Sinclair's orbital platforms. There's enough ships that we ought to be able to slip into the atmosphere without drawing too much attention."

"Then what?" Nick asked.

"Good question," Max responded, "Look at this."

Max expanded the image of Dust and then rotated it so that the main continent of Dust was centered on the screen. He tapped another spot on the console and icons appeared showing each of the planet's settlements. Max tapped another button and a layer of cloud cover appeared over the continent. The clouds were enormous and covered the central plains of the land mass, including all of Windy City,

Fracture, and Bloom. Bright flashes of light danced across the clouds.

"Lightning?" Nick asked.

Max nodded. "Never seen a storm like that. Wind speeds are incredibly high. I don't know a pilot alive who could land in those conditions."

"Surely it'll clear up in a day or two," Nick said.

"I'm not so sure," Max said, "If you wanted to prevent the Republic from landing troop transports, this would be a good way to do it."

"They're controlling the weather?" Nick asked.

"I told you those lightning storms were a byproduct of the terraforming process. Well, they can adjust the air flow rate through the terraforming stations and generate a hellacious storm like this. Safe bet that Windy City knows trouble is coming."

Nick just stared at the display for a moment. The giant, swirling storm was mesmerizing.

"Max, what, exactly, are we going to accomplish here?"

Max let out a long slow breath through pursed lips and scratched at the back of his head.

"We're going in and getting two people out," Max said, "I've told you that."

"Your ex-wife and who else?" Nick asked. He waited for Max to respond. Ten seconds passed, an eternity of silence.

"I don't have time for this, Nick. We've got to get crackin' on replacing those power units."

"No, Max," Nick persisted, "I want to know who we're risking our lives for."

Nick stood in the open doorway, arms folded across his chest.

"You think you can intimidate me, Nick?"

"You're not answering the question."

Max shook his head in annoyance.

"Another little girl, all right. My wife's daughter."

"Seriously? I guess I shouldn't be surprised at this point. Is that what Sinclair did for you?"

Max simply nodded, but didn't respond.

"You don't understand, Nick."

"I understand that you're risking our lives by going back there and you're also risking the lives of who knows how many more by not turning in Sinclair."

"Look, we settled that. We make the call as soon as we have them. I'll drop you off right after that. You're free to turn me in then, too."

Nick shook his head.

"That's not what I care about," Nick said, "I just want to make sure Sinclair doesn't get a chance to launch another attack. I just want to do what's right."

"So do I, Nick," Max said.

Nick let the hostile edge in his voice fade away.

"So, if we can't get into Windy City, where do we go?"

Max tapped the rotating image of Dust and it enlarged and unfolded into a two dimensional map of the surface. A flashing icon in the southern portion of the largest continent indicated the location of Windy City, while another far to the north of that was Mount Aldous. Max touched a point to the northeast of Mount Aldous, a spot right along the coast of the main continent. A little warning indicator popped up on the display with the words 'quarantine zone' flashing in red. Max dismissed the alarm.

"Resurrection?" Nick asked.

"Yep," Max said with an uncertain frown, "That's where my ex lives. And a few other people who like to go undisturbed."

"So the whole quarantine thing?"

"A good story for the rare tourist. Keeps people from sticking their nose where it doesn't belong," Max said.

"I guess I'm not a tourist anymore," Nick said.

"Let's just say I don't think you're high up on the threat list anymore."

Nick lay in a crawlspace, back against the floor, installing a replacement power converter unit in the alcove above his head. He looked to his left at the three-dimensional projection of the power converter unit he was working on. He double-checked the placement of each connector going into and out of the box. Everything looked good. He swung the access panel closed and wiggled his way out of the crawlspace.

"This one's done, Reggie," Nick said as he wiped a river of sweat from his forehead, "What do we have left?"

"Two power control modules and one more converter unit," Reggie reported.

"Well, that's progress right? I'll let Max know."

Nick pulled off a pair of thin work gloves and stuffed them into a pocket on his coveralls. He hated the tan utility clothes, but he had to admit there were times when function was more important than style. He grabbed a quick cup of water from the galley and headed for the cockpit. He could hear voices; Max and Eleanor were talking about something.

Nick crept up to the cockpit hatch silently, listening to what was being discussed. Max seemed to be telling a story in the dimly lit area. From the corridor, Nick could see that Max was sitting in his favorite position with his feet propped up on the console. He could also see Eleanor's tiny feet sticking out from beyond the edge of the co-pilot's seat. In between them, the picture of Max's long-dead daughter hovered over the console.

Nick stared at the poor little girl's picture, at the innocence of her smile and the happiness on her face. Max was telling her story again.

"Her name is Hannah," Max said, "She's daddy's little girl. Always loved to be around me, to be around the hangar. At one point, she wanted to be a pilot herself someday. Her mom hated that. I don't think that's where she's at now. She's also incredibly strong; loved gymnastics. She's always hopping and jumping and twirling around. Are you into that at all?"

"I'm not really into sports," Eleanor responded, "I've tried lots of things, but didn't like any of it. I like robotics a lot better. My dad always comes home with lots of part kits for me. Last month, he even brought me home Neural Networks Programmer 3.0, that was super fun."

Max laughed. "I bet. You're pretty good at that."

"What does she like to do?" Eleanor asked.

"Well, she loves to get her hands dirty. She's gotten in trouble so many times for getting grease all over her clothes. If she doesn't wind up being a pilot, maybe she'll be an engineer, designing her own ships."

Max hesitated a moment. His next words were almost a whisper.

"Always loved to help me out."

Nick stood still just outside the cockpit and kept quiet. The conversation was off; something wasn't right about it. Eleanor's presence had awoken something in Max that Nick wasn't sure the older man could handle. As Nick listened, he couldn't tell if Max was talking about his daughter that died or the girl they were going to pick up.

Have to wonder if he's losing his grip, Nick thought. It was just another reason that this whole trip didn't sit right with Nick.

But what could he do? Max was bigger and stronger than he was, so if Max has lost it, overpowering him was out of the question. Then, he remembered the stun gun. Nick was fairly certain he left it in one of the drawers in his quarters. He slowly, silently walked away from the cockpit, leaving them to their conversation. Eleanor had been sleeping in his room ever since she came aboard, but she didn't spend much time in there.

Nick was relieved to see that the gun was exactly where he had left it. He checked the display on its top face, two shots remained. That would be good enough, he thought. If it came to it, he would be able to take Max down with this. His aim better be good though; he wasn't likely to get a second shot.

Nick put the stun gun back in the drawer and slid it closed. He stepped out in the corridor and stared for a moment in the direction of the cockpit. He wiped the sweat from his palms on his coveralls and pursed his lips as he tried to figure out what was going on in Max's head. Nick decided it was best not to think about it right now.

"Okay, Reggie," he called out, "What do you want me to do next?"

Nick's fingers ached as he tightened the last fastener on the final power control module that needed replacing. He closed the access cover with a louder-than-intended clang and stood up from his kneeling position with a grunt.

"That should do it, Reggie," he said.

"Very good, sir," Reggie said, "I'll start the power-up sequence."

Nick nodded. "I'll let Max know."

"I have to say, sir, you're becoming quite adept at this."

"Thanks, Reggie."

Nick smiled at the compliment. He did feel good about what he had been able to accomplish today. He peeled off his gloves again as he made his way to the lounge, where he expected to find the rest of his compatriots. Eleanor was in there, but the little girl was fast asleep on the couch. Then, Nick heard another clang of metal on metal. Eleanor jumped slightly at the sound, but stayed asleep.

Nick closed the door to the lounge and headed toward the cockpit. He could hear Max's voice from about ten feet away.

"Charlie, are you out there?" Max asked, "Zanth, come back, are you there?"

His words were drawn out and slightly slurred.

"Charlie, do you copy?" Max asked again. When no reply came, Max cursed and slammed his mug on the console. He was flipping through the communication system frequencies and was about to try to raise his friends again when Nick spoke up.

"You okay?"

Max flinched a little, startled by Nick's sudden intrusion. His head lolled slightly as he turned toward Nick. "I thought you were workin'."

"All done," Nick said, "Reggie's about to power everything back up."

Max arched his eyebrows in surprise.

"Well, how about that? You might just be all right, kid."

Nick smiled. "Any luck raising anybody?"

Max shook his head in an exaggerated fashion. "Nobody. Nobody's home. Just me and you and a whole lot of nothing. I've known those guys forever, kid. Me and Charlie… God, I've had good times with that man, good times. He's got a bigger heart than anybody I know. Poor bastard. God damn, Sinclair. God damn, everybody. This whole shit's a mess."

Nick nodded his head. "That it is."

Max took a large gulp from his cup.

"You know, kid, I like you. You can be a little overbearing sometimes, but you've got a good heart."

Max put a heavy hand on Nick's shoulder.

"I mean that. When we get out of here, you've got to go make something of yourself. You don't want to be like me, doing the same thing day after day, going back and forth, back and forth, and back and forth."

Each time Max said back and forth, he tilted his head in exaggerated fashion from one side to the other. He squeezed Nick's shoulder, trying to regain his equilibrium. Nick said nothing, content to let Max talk.

"Been a slave to my past for so long. You don't wanna do that, kid. I was like you once. Thought I could be some hero spaceship captain, saving the galaxy from tyranny and oppression. Somewhere along the line, those dreams died away. You can't let that happen. You've gotta make something special happen. Don't be like me."

Max took another big gulp from his mug, which was now almost empty. He stared for a moment at the bottom of his cup.

"Time for another," Max said, swaying slightly as he got to his feet, "Want one?"

"No thanks," Nick said, trying to beg off.

Max wouldn't have it. "Sure you do. No man should have to drink alone on his own spaceship. Well, unless he flies solo. Then I suppose he'd have to drink alone. Anyway, that's not what I'm doin' tonight."

Nick could hear the bang of another mug on the counter. After a few moments of silence, Nick was ready to get up and check on Max. Max stumbled in, spilling about half of Nick's drink on the floor.

"Aw, now that's a damn shame," Max said, "Gotta drink for spilling."

Max took a long draft from his mug and handed Nick his. He then plopped back down in the Captain's seat and stared out the window. His eyelids drooped and Nick wondered if he was going to drift off. Max's eyes suddenly clouded up.

"You know," Max said, looking in the direction of Dust, "I was there when she was born. I looked at her hands, at her little blue eyes. She looked just like she had before. I just couldn't take it."

"I think maybe you've had enough, Max," Nick said, taking a small sip from his cup.

"You have to hold on to what you've got, kid. The worst part about getting old is all the ghosts in your head. They never stop talking to you; never let you go."

Silence hung between them for a moment.

"Christ, don't ever resurrect a ghost," Max said, "They're not the same person."

Max stood up and yawned. Nick just wrote off Max's words as the ramblings of a drunk, but this was eroding what little confidence in the plan Nick had left. Here they were on the brink of trying to conduct some kind of hare-brained rescue operation and Max seemed to be folding under the pressure.

"I need to hit the sack," Max said, "Big day tomorrow."

Max stood up and staggered off, abruptly leaving Nick alone in the cockpit holding a half-empty mug.

An hour later when Nick was sure Max had fallen asleep, Nick slid the cockpit hatch shut. He sat down in the pilot's chair and activated the console. Nick activated the communications system and entered a direct messaging code. The code was unique to an individual and would allow the message to be received by that individual, no matter where they were in the galaxy.

Once broadcast, the message would be sent to every jump beacon in proximity of the last known location of the recipient. The recipient would then be notified of the message, enter their code, and the message would be saved on whatever local terminal they were using. It was a system that had been in place for over a hundred years, ever since modern jump beacon satellites became ubiquitous.

Nick double-checked the code he had entered and then hit the audio-only record button. He then immediately stopped the recording and deleted the two second recording of nothing. He just wasn't sure this was the right thing to do. After a moment's hesitation, he saw no other option for making sure someone knew what was happening out here. He pressed the record button again.

"Hi, Mom," Nick began tentatively, "I know we haven't spoken in a while and I know I didn't exactly leave on good terms, but that's not important at the moment. If you haven't seen it already for yourself, then I'm sure you've at least heard about what happened at *Nexus Station*. The things, the creatures that attacked the station were created by Doctor Aldous Sinclair. I don't know much about him, other than he lives on Dust. His main stronghold is located at the base of Mount Aldous.

"He's well dug in there, but I'm sure that won't be much of an issue for the right people. It seems like he is getting ready to strike again. He's commandeered ships from the station and they are en route to Dust. I have no idea where he plans to strike next. I…I'm on one of the ships, a freighter called *Hannah*. We're on our way there, trying to get a few people off planet. I'm not sure what's going to happen…"

"I love you, mom. Miss you very much."

Nick stopped the recording and pushed the send button.

CHAPTER 12

"Shit," Max said.

"What now?" Nick eased into the co-pilot's seat with a fresh cup of coffee. His eyes were still slightly red-rimmed after waking up from a fresh batch of nightmares. He would give a lot for a night of dreamless, uninterrupted sleep.

"It looks like a Republic Fleet just dropped into the system," Max said, "Looks like 12, no 15, ships. God damn."

Nick sipped his coffee and focused on keeping a straight face. He was impressed by the speed of the Republic's response. He felt the urge to jump up and give Max a high five, but Max would probably just punch him in the face.

"Looks like they've got a half dozen fast attack ships," Max said, "Moving fast. They'll be at Dust in less than a day. Couple of bigger cruisers, too. Ah, this is not good."

"What's the plan, then?"

"Good question." Max rubbed his graying beard as he sat back in his chair. The communication system chirped as it received an incoming emergency broadcast.

"This is Commander Dorn of the Fifth Fleet of the Republic. All ships in the Dust system are ordered to deactivate their drive systems and prepare for boarding and inspection. This system is being placed under Martial law. Any ship that does not deactivate its drive will be fired upon.

No ships will be given clearance to leave the system until they have submitted to an inspection."

"Well, at least she's consistent in her message," Nick said.

Nick took another sip of his coffee and watched Max's reaction. Max was now leaning back with his eyes closed while the Commander's firm voice filled the cockpit. When she finished speaking, Max leaned forward, looked at the position of the Republic ships on his console, and cursed again.

"I thought we'd have more time," Max said with a shake of his head.

"On the bright-side, at least Sinclair won't be launching any more attacks," Nick said.

Max shot him an annoyed look.

"So, do we shutdown the drive or what?"

Max recoiled at the suggestion.

"Hell, no. We do what we came here to do," Max said, "Once we pick my ex and her daughter, we'll figure out where to go next. It's a big system; I'm sure we can find some place to lay low for awhile. We can get by on the ship's stores for a couple weeks if we need to."

"Come on, Max," Nick said, "What's the point in that?"

"Hard for me to explain, Nick, but you'll see in a few hours," Max said.

"Just tell me what's going on. Is this why you got drunk last night?"

"This is good," Max said, "You're prepping me for facing my wife again."

"I'm serious, Max."

"So am I."

Nick shook his head in frustration and looked out the window. Dust was getting pretty big in the window; they would be there soon. As Nick settled into his seat, a message arrived on his wrist computer.

Thanks for the tip. Look forward to catching you. - Dad

An hour later, the *Hannah* completed its orbital insertion burn. The curvature of Dust dominated their view. In the foreground, Nick and Max could see periodic thruster firings from other vehicles ahead of them. Max was monitoring their trajectory on his console and had taken control of the thrusters away from the ship's computer.

Periodically, Max fired the thrusters in short bursts in order to alter their approach. He would slow the ship down slightly and then check the alterations to the trajectory on his console. Reggie, standing just behind Max, would independently verify the course correction and provide Max with thruster fire counts. They could have preprogrammed the computer to handle all of this, but with all the other ships in the immediate vicinity, Max was worried that he would have to make some last second modifications to his plan. Besides, he liked it better this way.

He looked over at Nick, monitoring his console for any potential collisions. With each burn, the ship's computer evaluated the trajectory of any object that might cross their path. That data was then projected on Nick's display through a collection of differently colored icons with associated velocity vectors surrounded by cones of uncertainty.

"How's it look, Nick?"

"Like spaghetti."

"That's helpful."

"There are so many other ships it's almost impossible to sort out," Nick said.

"Well, if any of those cones turn red, call it out."

A beep came from the console. A link had been established with the Orbital platform they were approaching. The platform had grown from a tiny silver dot on the horizon to a large flat, spindly structure in orbit just ahead of them.

Reggie said, "They're trying to initiate communication protocols with the drone."

"Are you able to reply in kind?" Max asked.

"Yes, sir," Reggie said.

"Good," Max said, "What do they want?"

"They're feeding us orbital parameters," Reggie said, "We're also getting instructions to ensure our jump drive is off-line. And a request…"

"For what?" Max asked.

"Jump drive and power core specifications and schematics."

"Any idea what they're doing?"

"No, sir. It's not clear. We're in for quite a wait though; there are 57 ships in the queue ahead of us."

"Must be rush hour," Nick said dryly.

"Reggie, when I fire the port thrusters, feed them the thruster failure signature," Max said, "We'll burn for thirty seconds. That'll put us in a lower orbit and we should slip on by."

Max knew that Reggie didn't need to be told all this again; he just couldn't help it.

"Yes, Captain," Reggie responded, "On you order, sir."

Max nodded and monitored a countdown timer that was rapidly approaching zero. Suddenly, a yellow indicator light appeared on Nick's display.

"We've got a failure of a power transfer circuit," Nick said, "Thruster control for the port thrusters is offline. It's rerouting."

"Crap," Max said, "Might not have to lie after all, Reggie. Nick, watch that collision display."

The timer on Max's console hit zero and then started counting up.

"Reggie, are you still in contact?"

"Yes, sir," the robot responded, "They are aware of our current situation."

A collision threat turned red on Nick's display. The data was hardly necessary as an old patrol frigate was growing increasingly larger in the window. Nick's console finally beeped.

"Power's rerouted," Nick said, "You have control."

Max didn't waste any time responding; he activated the thruster and the ship canted downward just below the orbital plane of the frigate. Seconds later, the two ships passed, clearing each other by mere meters.

Nick exhaled and said, "That was close."

"I've had closer," Max said, "Reggie, are you still in contact with the platform?"

"Yes, sir. I've sent them the thruster failure signature. They've sent us updated orbital parameters if we regain control of the ship.

"We're in the clear then," Max said as he opened an intercom channel with the lounge, "Eleanor, get ready for re-entry, this could get a little bumpy."

"I copy," she responded with a hint of excitement.

Max smiled and said, "At least someone on this ship knows how to acknowledge an order."

"You're hilarious," Nick responded.

A new timer appeared on Max's console and when it struck zero, he executed a re-entry burn that put them on course to enter the airspace above Dust's main continent under the cover of darkness. Everything was going according to plan.

Within thirty minutes, the ship was a fireball in Dust's atmosphere. The sky around them was a brilliant orange-yellow fading to black as they entered the atmosphere in dusk and quickly passed into night. By the time the fire from atmospheric re-entry dissipated, the sky was fully dark. Max then adjusted their course to the north. They would be down in minutes.

"Go prep the sled, Reggie," Max ordered.

"Yes, sir," Reggie responded and then tromped out of the cockpit.

"Hope we're ready for this," Nick said.

"No turning back now," Max responded, "Just be ready to move as soon as we set down. We won't have much time."

"Think Sinclair knows we're here?"

Max shrugged. "With any luck, we won't be here long enough to find out."

Nick nodded and Max could see the concern on his face.

"Just relax, Nick," Max said, "Sinclair's not looking for us. Besides, with the Republic here, I'd say he's got bigger problems to worry about. I doubt he'll have the time to worry about one decrepit old freighter that strayed off course."

The *Hannah* set down on a small landing pad just fifty meters from the coast. It wasn't much of a facility, just a couple of solar-powered lights and a flat landing pad roughly a hundred meters square. The pad itself was nestled in a little alcove cut into the base of the sheer cliffs that dominated the landscape. Nick couldn't imagine trying to land here in a storm; it was easy to see how a ship could've crashed out here long ago.

Nick stood on the pad and listened to the roar of the ocean surf as Max opened the hold door and retrieved the cargo sled. A constant wind blew in from the ocean and with it came the smell of salt on the air. Nick breathed deep. If this had been his first taste of Dust, he would've never wanted to leave.

The alcove they were in acted as a bit of a funnel, causing the air to constantly swirl about him. The air that hit him was moist, but cool. The sounds and smells of the beach were incredibly refreshing after being cooped up in the artificial environments of the ship and the station for so long.

Standing there, staring out at the ocean, hearing the rhythmic pounding of the waves, Nick felt more relaxed and at ease than he had in weeks. There was something to be said for having your feet firmly planted on solid earth and hearing, seeing, and feeling nature all around you. Perhaps Max was right after all; maybe he wasn't cut out for living life aboard a ship.

That thought would have to wait as the cargo sled smoothly slid out of the back of the hold with Max at the controls. He waved Nick over.

"Let's get going," Max said, raising his voice slightly to be heard over the wind and surf, "I don't know if anyone will be looking for us, but I'd like to be out of here as quick as we can anyway."

"Time's a wasting, then," Nick said as he climbed on the flatbed that comprised the back half of the sled. He watched Max at the controls; Max seemed to hesitate a moment, a look of uncertainty crossing his face. "You okay?"

"Yeah," Max responded. He briefly looked out at the dark, frothy surf.

"Are you sure?"

"No," Max said with a shake of his head, "It's been a long time since I've been out here, going on about eight years now."

"Let's try to make it a short trip down memory lane," Nick said.

Max looked down at the paper-thin screen of his wrist computer.

"Nick, it's entirely possible that my wife will not give me the time of day, but we've got to get them out of here. I've got to do this. This place…well, nothing's going to be the same here again."

"Let's just get going," Nick urged.

Max carefully guided the sled along a small trail at the base of the cliffs. They slipped from side to side as the path wound ahead staying just beyond the reach of the surf which Nick hoped was at the peak of high tide. Nick felt the urge to grab onto a handrail on the side of the flatbed as the sled went around another sharp curve.

Nick looked at Max whose expression looked untroubled by their weaving route. Actually, that wasn't right; Max didn't look like he was there at all. Nick used his wrist computer to activate the sled's noise-dampening field and the sound of the pounding surf became distant.

"Are you okay, Max?"

Max blinked and nodded absent-mindedly. Nick wasn't going to let the subject go that easily.

"What's on your mind?"

Max inhaled slowly.

"Nick, have you ever wondered why the population control laws are still in affect? Why they weren't enacted with some kind of timeframe? At what point does the law get repealed?"

Nick shrugged. "I don't know. I assume somebody has that plan; I just don't know it."

"Don't you think that after 50 years of these laws being in place that we'd start to see some real results from this? Shouldn't the population be going down? Shouldn't the Republic be contracting?"

"I guess so. I mean, they've told us plenty of times that the population has started decreasing," Nick said as he stared at the waves, "Is this really what's bothering you?"

"I just think you can't outlaw something that is in our very nature. Someday, Nick, you'll have your own child. When you hold that life in your arms and see how fragile it is, you'll know what it means to feel responsible.

"That life you hold will be so fragile and innocent. When you hold them, when they're that little, you realize how special they are, how much they need to be protected. As they grow, they give you purpose; you want to build a better life for them.

"To have that ripped away. I can't explain the feeling. Some people can't live with only one opportunity. They'll do anything for another chance. Anything."

Nick was silent for a moment. A wave crashed close to the sled and Nick ducked his head to avoid getting sprayed in the face.

"Is that why your wife had another baby?"

Max nodded and they rode in silence for several moments. Nick didn't know what to say. He looked at Max and saw the pain in his expression, the tiredness around his eyes, tiredness and pain that were always there.

"When this place was first settled," Max said, breaking the silence, "They named it Point Hope. It was supposed to be the crown jewel of Dust, a picturesque settlement that would be a hub of humanity. A pilot on a routine shipping run misread the winds around the cliffs. He plowed his ship dead center into the middle of the city. The reactor core on the ship ruptured and contaminated the entire area. Killed dozens."

"So why am I not wearing hazard gear, then?" Nick asked.

"Well, the Conglomerate didn't think it was worth the money to clean it up. They settled in Windy City since it was closer to the equator and easier to reach orbit, more cost effective. Some of the colonists, though, didn't like getting off on such a bad foot here.

"Sinclair created some microorganisms that came in here and cleaned up all the radioactive material and any contaminated soil. It only took weeks. Nobody ever bothered to report to the Republic that the area had been cleaned up, so it still shows up on the charts as quarantined."

They had traveled about two kilometers from the pad when Max banked left a little suddenly, more abruptly than Nick expected. Nick had to brace himself by jamming his arm against the flatbed. They had turned onto the bank of a wide river that fed into the ocean. They were now at the base of a wide, jagged canyon, cut into the surrounding plateau through many years of running water.

It took a few moments for Nick to orient himself and figure out what he was looking at. A full moon had risen over the mountains in the distance, casting the canyon valley in a pale blue glow. With the light of the moon, Nick was able to see what looked like giant steps, eight in all, carved into the canyon walls on both sides. Strung between them at odd intervals were small, antiquated foot bridges. When viewed at a distance, the walkways, some straight across, some sloped to allow passage from one step to another, looked like the web of a giant spider.

The steps and walkways were lined with small lights for as far into the distance as Nick could see. As they got closer, Nick began to make out doors and entryways carved into the canyon wall. There was a light for every door. They traveled a kilometer inland, Nick counting lights as they moved along, hundreds upon hundreds of lights.

"Are...are all these homes?" Nick asked.

"Some are," Max responded, "Some are businesses, some are schools, some are local government offices, just like any other city."

"Any other city that's not classified as a hazardous area. If they're trying to hide, these people are doing a lousy job of it."

"Nobody's looking," Max said, "This isn't Valhalla, Nick. The skies are not filled with surveillance satellites."

The sled started slowing down and Nick could now make out numbers carved into the doors. Max then brought them to an abrupt stop. Max sat for a moment, staring at the door. The engraved number on the door read 1927.

"Come on. Let's get this done," Max said.

Max inhaled deeply and got off the sled. He walked up to the door and then checked the time on his wrist computer. It was still a reasonable hour; she should be up. Max pressed a spot on the computer screen. An icon appeared on the screen, indicating the door chime had rung. When Sharon checked her computer, assuming she had it on, it would let her know who was at the door.

Max waited. He could hear his heart beating somewhat faster than normal; his hands felt clammy. Nick stood two paces behind him and to his left, watching cautiously. The door slid open and Sharon was standing there, arms folded across her chest, glaring at him.

She was a short, trim woman with her dark hair pulled severely back into a knot behind her head. Her hair had streaks of gray in it. She was wearing a simple cream robe and nightgown, something that had been made locally.

"What do you want?" She asked very sharply. Her disdain for Max was readily evident.

"We need to talk, Sharon," Max said, "This is important."

She frowned and then took a step out of the doorway and looked to see who else was around. She noticed Nick for the first time.

"Who the hell is this?" She asked.

"A friend," Max said, "He's working for me."

She shook her head in aggravation and gestured to them to come in.

"You've got five minutes, Max."

Max closed his eyes, took a deep breath, and stepped into the house. Nick quickly scurried in behind him. Sharon looked at them icily; Max knew she would explode at either of them if given the opportunity. They entered a well lit living room, illuminated by the same vines that covered the ceiling of the residential district in Windy City. The light highlighted the elaborate ceramics that covered the walls, tables, and countertops. Everything was pleasantly cool to the touch.

Sharon closed the door behind them and marched into the small living room with her arms folded across her chest. She glared at Max.

"This had better be good," she said.

"Sharon, I need you to listen to me on this. I know we've got a lot of crap to sort through, but we don't have much time," Max said, "I need to get you two out of here."

"What are you talking about?" Sharon asked.

"Sinclair has lost it," Max responded, "He's created some…some kind of creature, an army of them. He launched an attack on Nexus. It's not safe here anymore. The Republic's already in the system. No doubt they'll be here soon. I've got to get you two out of here before that happens."

"Have you gone insane, Maxime?! After all this time, after years without a word, you show up late at night, riding in on your white horse expecting to be the hero? Christ, you're an asshole, Max," Sharon yelled.

Out of the corner of his eye, Max watched Nick shrink against the wall. Max stood his ground; he had been in too many of these arguments to get intimidated by Sharon's anger. This was not how he wanted the conversation to go, but it is what he expected.

"Sharon, will you please listen to me?" Max pleaded, his voice rising, "We don't have time for this."

"You can't show up after eight years without even a word and expect me to just walk off with you! I don't care if God himself told you to come get me! It doesn't work that way, Max! You had your chance! You abandoned us long ago!"

"Sharon, I didn't abandon you!" Max yelled back, "I couldn't…damn it, Sharon, this is not the time for this argument. We've got to get you out of here. Everyone on Dust is in danger now. Everyone! And this bullshit between us doesn't matter. You have to believe me."

"Believe you? How the hell am I supposed to do that? Am I supposed to just pull together my things and march on out the door with you? You have lost your mind if you really expect me to do that."

Max rubbed his temples and furrowed his brow, his expression especially pained. He looked plaintively at Nick, who was intensely studying the patterns in the tile.

"Do you really think I'd come here if it wasn't an emergency?"

"I think you've become completely delusional, Max."

Nick was beginning to think the same thing. He wanted no part of this conversation. Wish Max had left me on the ship for this one, he thought. Nick tried to find anything in the room to focus on other than the two of them, looking from floor to ceiling and back.

The walls were lined with projected images of Sharon and Hannah. One picture showed the two of them at the park, next at some school function, next Hannah sitting on Sharon's lap. The images showed the girl at various ages, slowly growing up. The final image was of Sharon and Hannah walking along the beach, holding hands. If Nick didn't know better, he would have said Sharon looked the same age in this photo as she did standing there. Age therapy was a wonderful thing, Nick thought.All these pictures made it seem like Hannah was still alive, as if she would walk into the room at any moment.

And in the very next moment, she did. The little girl in all the photos, a red-headed little girl of about eight, poked her head from around the corner of a hallway on the other side of the room. She was the twin of the girl in the images Max had shown him. Nick stood there, jaw agape.

"Mom," she said softly, through a sleep-induced haze.

Sharon looked at the girl, taking her exasperated stare off of Max. She walked over, put her hand on her shoulder, and knelt down so that her face was right in front of Hannah's.

Max spun on his heels as well. "Hannah…"

Sharon cut him off sharply. "Don't you dare. You gave up any right to speak to her eight years ago."

Sharon leaned in close to Hannah and said, "Go back to bed, sweet girl. I'll be back in a minute, Max, and then we'll finish this."

Then, she led the little girl back out of the room. Nick's mouth had gone dry and his face flushed. He struggled to find his voice.

"Wait," Nick said, "Who the hell was that?"

"My wife's daughter," Max said, "I told you that."

"Bullshit, Max. Tell me that's not the same little girl from the pictures on the ship," Nick said.

"It's not, Nick. My daughter, my Hannah, died ten years ago," Max said, casting his eyes to the floor.

"You had her cloned! Oh, tell me that's not true! Tell me you lied about everything else, that she never really died in the hangar, and that the girl who was just standing there is not the creation of that lunatic Doctor."

"Nick, please," Max said, clearly struggling, "I can explain."

"Don't tell me this is okay, Max," Nick said, "I don't want to hear that. It's not, Max. This is not okay."

"Christ, Nick, we don't have time for this. I'm having a helluva time getting my point across to her. I don't need to worry about your crap as well," Max said, his face growing red, "Yes, that little girl's a clone, an exact copy of my daughter who died ten years ago."

Nick was flabbergasted, unable to speak. This wasn't just having another child.

"Sinclair made her for us, for my wife," Max said.

"Is that why you defend him so much?" Nick asked with contempt, "Because he made you that thing?"

In an instant, Max grabbed Nick by his shirt and pushed him against the wall. His face was inches from Nick, his eyes bulging slightly. "She is a little girl. No different than you or I. Just because she was made differently, doesn't make her any less of a person."

"She's an abomination," Nick said. Nick couldn't move; Max had him pinned with all his strength.

"You really think that, Nick? You really think that she's not a real person just because she was grown? Guess what, she came from the same cells you did. So what if they didn't grow in her mother's womb. She's still life; she's still alive. Her heart beats the same as yours.

"Look in those images, Nick! Do those little girl's eyes look dead to you? Does she look like a creature of the damned, the spawn of the devil! She's not, Nick, she's made of the same stuff you and I are. She bleeds red, just like you and me. Just like all the other cloned kids in this valley."

Max finally let Nick go, but Nick was too stunned to notice. Nick slid down the wall slightly. He remembered their trip here, all the lights that lined the valley, hundreds, possibly thousands of them.

"Do you remember the couple at the Dry Dock?" Max asked. "The ones who ran up to Francis the night he knocked you out."

"She was the woman on the subway," Nick said, "The one who was crying."

She had been crying as she made her way to the Windy City bank. Nick remembered their joy and their relief when Francis gave them the nod to come with him.

"All of them?" Nick said weakly.

"All of them," Max said, "Every person living in this valley has had a son or daughter brought back to life through

Aldous' cloning. Welcome to Resurrection, Nick, where the dead walk the earth."

"How many are there?" Nick asked.

"Over two thousand," Max said, catching his breath.

"Holy shit."

"Yeah, well, Aldous Sinclair has basically signed them all up to a life of misery," Max said, "Once the Republic gets here and checks the ID chips of everyone here, the secret will be out. They will all be rounded up, probed, and prodded while the government decides what their fate should be.

"Some will want them destroyed, like they're animals. So many in the Republic will see everything like you just did. They will be inhuman, abominations and they will want them slaughtered. What do you think, Nick? Do you think you could take that little girl who was just in here and cut her throat? Do you think you could take her life away like that?"

Nick was silent, his mouth agape. Part of him wanted to say yes, that she should be slaughtered. It was the part of him that believed that rules should be followed, laws obeyed, and people should live righteously or suffer the consequences. However, another part of him saw what Max saw. She was just a little girl.

Nick shook his head slowly and softly said, "No."

"Well, neither could I," Max said, "And I can't let them stay here, either. That's why I need to convince Sharon that the two of them need to leave."

"And you really expected them to just come with us? After you left your daughter for eight years?" Nick asked. His mind was swimming; he felt a bit lightheaded.

"That's not my daughter," Max said quietly, "That's a copy, a clone, but she's not the same person."

"You just said that clones were just like everyone else. Made of the same stuff," Nick said somewhat agitated, "So what is she, Max? Is she your daughter or not?"

"She is a copy," Max said through clenched teeth, "She might be an exact genetic copy of my daughter, but she's not the same person. She doesn't have the same memories, she hasn't lived the same life, she hasn't had the same experiences. That little girl is not the same one that I cradled in my arms the day she died. That was my daughter. My daughter died."

Max's hands were shaking; his cheeks were flush.

"That little girl in there may look like her, she may sound like her, and she may even have the same talents as my little girl, but my little girl is gone. No amount of wishing would ever bring her back."

"So you just left them," Nick said.

"I didn't want her brought back, Nick," Max said, practically fuming, "I couldn't face her, all right. I couldn't do it. Didn't want to do it. My wife wasn't there that day, Nick. She didn't cradle her little broken body, didn't feel her skin grow cold. She didn't have her blood running between her fingers!

"You want to call me weak? Fine. Think whatever you want. I knew that I couldn't wake up every day and see that little girl's face; just thinking about it tore my heart to shreds. But I knew that Sharon needed this.

"So I did it for her. Because I loved her too. Because what the Republic denied us, another chance to get this right, wasn't fair to her."

A sense of understanding crept into Nick's expression.

"All this work for him, for this twisted son of a bitch, was to pay for this gift he gave you. You paid for it with your work for Sinclair."

Max nodded.

"Someday you'll understand, Nick. Like I said on the ride here, when you hold your own child in your arms for the first time, look in her eyes, and touch her soft skin, you'll know that it's your mission to protect her. And you damn well better succeed, because it's the only chance you'll get. You don't know what it's like to have that life ripped away."

Max sat down heavily on a small footstool in the middle of the room while Nick now sat on the floor with his head leaned back against the wall. Max stared vacantly ahead.

"Sinclair could do something that nobody else would. He could give my wife her little girl back. My wife would've paid anything for that. I couldn't deny her that chance. To Sharon, she was the same little girl. She was an opportunity for our whole family to be reborn. That day Hannah died, a piece of all of us died with her.

"Sinclair offered a chance to resurrect that piece, at least for Sharon. His price was high, well beyond what I could afford. Sinclair needed something though, something I could provide. I had no problem signing up to be Sinclair's pilot. It was a price I had to pay."

Nick could see the hurt and sorrow on Max's face as he sat heavily on the stool, shoulders slumped. Max looked defeated. Old wounds had bled out leaving a tired, old man behind. Wounds had been buried under the tedium of the daily grind, as Max had done the bidding of Sinclair every day for the past decade. Nick knew Max would never pay his debt, either the one to Sinclair or the one to his dead daughter.

Nick walked up to Max, who sat staring bleakly ahead, and placed his hand on Max's shoulder. Nick could feel the tension in Max's shoulder where knots of muscle had built up over years of grueling work. Nick couldn't think of anything to say. Max was a slave to his past, who couldn't let it go or put it behind him. Every day Max faced the consequences of that horrible tragedy.

Max exhaled through clenched teeth. He finally broke the silence and asked, "Where the hell is Sharon? We're running out of time."

As her name came out of his mouth, she came back in the room. Tears were in her eyes; she had obviously been listening.

"I'm sorry," she said. Nick watched as she tapped a spot on her wrist computer. Both men turned as they heard the front door slide open.

"What did you do?" Max asked.

"Max, I had no choice," Sharon said.

Nick crept toward the entryway. Remembering the stun gun, he immediately reached for it. Suddenly, one of Sinclair's creatures shot forward and punched Nick in the chest with a balled up talon. Nick flew backwards, hitting the back wall of the room with a thud.

Sharon screamed while Max looked around frantically for something to use as a weapon. This creature, while it looked the same as the ones on *Nexus Station*, seemed to be vastly superior to its cousins. Its movements were more precise; its reactions swift. Just as Max picked up the small stone stool he had been sitting on, the creature lashed out with its unusually long arm and backhanded him across the face.

In the next instant, the creature pounced forward and grabbed Nick by the throat. Nick clawed desperately at the demon's wrist to no avail. The creature lifted him bodily off of the floor and Nick felt its talons break the flesh of his neck. Blood trickled down his chest and his lungs began to burn as he struggled to breathe.

Max regained his footing and found the small stool again. He charged forward, ready to throw his full weight behind the swing. The creature's head swiveled quickly in Max's direction. It pounded Nick into the wall again and then delivered a swift kick into Max's midsection. Max gasped as air was forced from his lungs. He collapsed to one knee.

Nick was dazed; the blow to the back of his head caused his vision to explode with stars. The room around him seemed to wobble and he wondered if he was about to take his last breath. He locked eyes with Max; they were beaten. A fear of death passed over Nick, but he did not let that fear hold him.

The creature let loose a blood-curdling shriek, louder than anything Nick remembered hearing in their previous encounters. Deadly intent shone in the creature's eyes. It started toward Nick, when suddenly someone yelled, "Enough! Relent, Gordo!"

The creature froze. The bloodlust disappeared from its stance and it assumed an odd parade rest with its long arms folded behind its back and its head held stock still while gazing forward. Nick and Max both kneeled on the floor, Nick down on all fours. They were both gasping, bleeding from multiple cuts, with Nick trying to stay conscious.

Francis entered the room and looked at Max with a bit of surprise.

"Never expected to see you again," Francis said. His false eye zeroed in on Nick, scanning the young man.

"Go to hell, Francis," Max replied.

Francis gave a nod to Gordo and it lashed out with its foot, striking Max in the dead center of his chest. Max fell backward, hitting his head on a small table. He felt blood pooling under his shirt and trickling down the back of his head.

"Watch yourself, Max," Francis said, "Gordo doesn't appreciate your tone of voice."

Francis looked back to Nick. "Looks like your wounds aren't fatal. You should count yourself lucky, for now."

Nick didn't bother to reply; he was still blinking his eyes, trying to stop his head from spinning.

"You're quieter than I remember you, kid," Francis said. Francis waited a moment for Nick to respond; Nick just sat there refusing to be goaded. "I guess the only courage you have is found in a bottle."

Francis cackled and the two creatures that accompanied him, Gordo and the one behind Francis, started in their best approximation of a laugh. It was a chilling chittering sound. Francis backed away from Nick, slightly disappointed that the young man gave him no reply. After another moment, Francis turned his attention back to Max.

"You've made this day even more interesting, Max," Francis said, "Father will want to have a word with you."

"That's good," Max said, feeling the back of his head for any blood, "I have a few words I'd like to share with him."

Sharon had knelt behind him, helping him off the floor. She was looking at Max with a mixture of sympathy and sorrow.

"Well, you'll certainly have that chance," Francis said, "Gordo, Wally, pick them up. We need to get back."

Gordo picked a still dazed Nick off of the floor and held him in an iron grip with his arms pinned behind his back. The one called Wally did the same to Max. As they were being dragged out the door, Max looked back to Sharon, who simply watched from the middle of the room in stunned silence.

"I'm sorry," she said to Max.

Francis responded before Max could, "Don't be, ma'am. You've been a great help to us."

Francis laughed again as the two men were dragged onto a waiting sled.

CHAPTER 13

The morning sun crested over the red mountains to the west as the *Hannah* flew by overhead. Nick watched the ship disappear into the horizon as he sat on the flatbed of the industrial grade cargo sled. When the *Hannah* disappeared from view, Francis looked at Max with a sneer. Nick had the slight urge to get up and punch his disfigured face until the sneer faded away, but he knew that would only get him killed quicker.

As it was, Nick had trouble seeing how they would survive the day what with Francis at the controls and his two gruesome pets perched atop some handles that protruded from the rear of the sled. Nick's gaze hung on the creatures for a moment. They stood perfectly still in their odd parade rest stance, eyes closed and arms folded behind their backs.

These creatures looked different than the ones they encountered at the station. The silver plate on their heads was larger, more pronounced. Their faces and necks were coated with coarse, stubbly hair. Their muscles looked more defined.

Nick looked back to Max, whose swollen and bloody face was now basking in the morning sun. The center of Max's shirt was torn and stained with dried blood. Max's ragged, gray hair was flitting in the cool breeze as they zipped along atop a mountain ridge. He lifted his chin toward the orange-red horizon. The bright morning sun highlighted every crag, every scar on his weathered face. The edges of his mouth were pulled down as his face reflected the hope they had both lost.

"Max," Nick said, "I'm sorry. I'm sorry that none of this worked out the way we wanted it to."

Max gave him a rueful half-smile. "It was a foolish idea to go to Resurrection. Don't know why I ever thought that would work. I'm sorry to have dragged you into this."

"I would've probably done the same in your shoes," Nick said. He didn't know if he really believed that or not, but it was the thing to say.

"No, you wouldn't," Max said, "You would've gone to sector security right away and avoided all of this. I should've listened to you."

"You couldn't know…"

"I didn't trust you," Max said, "I thought you'd blab all this to security and I'd never have the chance to get Sharon and…and Hannah… out. Turns out that wouldn't have mattered. The Republic found this place anyway."

Nick grimaced and looked to the horizon. He closed his eyes a moment, inhaled deeply, and tried to gather strength from their surroundings.

"You were right not to trust me," Nick said.

Max didn't respond; he just looked at Nick quizzically.

Nick reluctantly brought his eyes up to meet Max's stare. "The other night when you got drunk, I sent a message to my mother. Told her where we were headed. Between the drinking and the way you've been acting around Eleanor, I just didn't think you were all there."

Max didn't get angry; his face didn't turn beet red. He simply smiled and laughed slightly.

"Well, Nick, I'd say that you and I need to work on our communication going forward but I don't think that's really going to matter."

"Good that we can agree on something."

Max smiled again and shook his head. "I sound like my wife."

"Heard from Eleanor?" Nick asked.

Max nodded and gestured to his wrist computer. "She sent me a message when they lifted off. She's okay. Reggie's been deactivated, hopefully not permanently. She's scared."

As she should be, Nick thought, as they all were. The sled passed from daylight into the shadow of a mountain and the air noticeably cooled. Off in the distance, the peak of Mount Aldous became visible.

"My father's here," Nick said, "Sent me a message yesterday just after the Republic fleet arrived."

"Well, maybe that'll be a good thing," Max said.

Nick nodded and looked to the sky. As he did, an orange fireball streaked across it, followed quickly by another and another.

"What's that?" Nick asked.

Max shrugged.

"Don't think it's a meteorite, but whatever it is, I doubt that it's good news for us."

The sled crested the far end of the large landing field that sprawled before Mount Aldous. The last time they had been here, the only thing on the pad was the ragtag group of rusted and decrepit freighters and haulers that belonged to Max and his friends. This time, a small fleet of silver, ovoid-shaped shuttle craft sat gleaming in the sunlight. The ships were neatly aligned in two columns and the sled took a course right down the middle.

"Do you recognize the model?" Nick asked.

"Never seen it before in my life," Max said, "They look brand new."

"This is crazy," Nick said. Max shook his head in agreement.

There was no movement on the pad with no robots or people milling about. There was no one doing maintenance checks, no one doing preflight inspections, and no one boarding. It all looked abandoned in place.

At the far end of the pad, just before they reached the hangar doors, the *Hannah* stood out like a sore thumb. It looked like an ancient relic next to the shimmering smoothness of the shuttle craft. Max looked over at his old ship as they whisked by it. Everything looked okay from the outside.

The sled slowed as they approached the hangar doors. Nick looked back at Francis, who was busy entering commands on his wrist computer. Wally and Gordo's eyes suddenly popped open and the two creatures shook out their wings and stretched. The joints in their talons popped as they stretched to the limit. A chill ran down Nick's spine.

They pulled into the hangar and the chill turned to unfathomable dread. There, standing en masse was the largest army Nick had ever seen assembled. Row upon row of the creatures, at least fifteen to twenty bodies deep in each row, stood waiting. They stood in silence, all staring directly ahead.

Were they wild animals, Nick would have expected them to be a writhing mass of feathers and talons, cawing and hopping about. But they stood stock still, waiting to be awakened.

"Jesus," Max said.

Nick had to suppress the urge to tell Max to whisper. But Nick couldn't bring himself to say anything; he just sat there with his jaw hanging open.

The sled stopped in the middle of the throng. Francis stepped down and motioned for everyone to follow him. There was no thought of running as Gordo and Wally were watching them carefully. Nick got up, his muscles aching from having sat on the sled for so long. He extended a hand to Max and the two men locked eyes for a moment.

There was nothing to be said at this point. The dread they both felt was painted clearly on their faces. Francis became impatient at their slow pace and signaled to his pets. Nick felt the claw of one of the things push him in the back and he stumbled forward slightly. Francis led them to a lift and moments later they emerged into a spacious control room.

Their attention was immediately drawn to a wall of monitors showing images from throughout the subterranean facility. On most of them, automated factory lines progressed at full speed. Nick caught a glimpse of one line that appeared to be making the creature's rifles while another appeared to be making the neural processors that graced the heads of Gordo and Wally. On another, he picked out a line creating casings for drones and another manufacturing something that Nick didn't recognize.

The images were a flurry of mechanical activity. The assembly lines moved at a frenetic pace. Automated cargo haulers ferried components from one line to the next. Completed items were automatically put in crates and then those crates were put on conveyers that took them to other unseen parts of the facility. The whole thing was mesmerizing.

This was why neither of them took much notice of Aldous Sinclair, as the slight old man stood with his back to the monitors. It was also why they didn't notice Aldous look at his misshapen son with an unspoken question. Francis nodded his head in Nick's direction.

Aldous brought his hands from behind his back, raised a gun, and shot Nick in the abdomen. He didn't use a modern plasma gun or even something like Max's slightly outdated atomizer. No, Sinclair used an antique and shot Nick with an actual bullet.

When the shot rang out, it was accompanied by the surprised scream of a little girl. At first, Nick's attention was drawn to Eleanor, seated at a large table at the other end of the room. Then, Nick felt a sharp bite in his midsection and he looked down at the rapidly spreading blood stain on his shirt before he fell to his knees. He was too disoriented to cry out in pain; he merely looked at the doctor with a complete lack of understanding.

"Now, we'll both be dead by the end of the day," Sinclair spat.

"Jesus Christ, Doc!" Max yelled. He rushed over and grabbed Nick. Nick was holding himself up with one hand while pushing on the wound with his other. Max pulled a rag from the pocket of his coveralls and pressed it firmly on the wound. He looked at Nick's back; no blood was present.

"It didn't go through," Max said.

"Tell me if that's good news or bad."

"What the hell is wrong with you!" Max yelled at Sinclair.

"Shut up," Sinclair said, "You're supposed to be dead anyway."

"I'm surprised you haven't shot me yet," Max said. He shook his head in disappointment. "And here I thought, that maybe, just maybe, this had all been some sort of mistake and that you hadn't really intended for those things to get loose on the station."

"I never hired you for your brains, Max," Sinclair said.

Max closed his eyes and tried to breathe deep, but the redness of his face betrayed the fury he felt.

"You son of a bitch," Max said and he took a threatening step toward Sinclair. One step was all he took before one of the creatures lashed out and sent Max flying with a thunderous blow to his flank.

Max was back on his feet quickly, his eyes filled with murderous intent.

"Stop, Max," Nick said, "Don't give him the satisfaction."

"Oh, I'm quite satisfied," Sinclair said, "I'm satisfied that you'll die a slow, painful death here on the floor of my office. It's a small price to pay for destroying my life's work."

Sinclair touched a button on his wrist computer and the images on the monitor shifted. Instead of views of the factory, they now showed views from orbit around Dust. Sinclair's orbital platforms were now burned-out, tattered wrecks drifting listlessly in their orbits. All around the platforms, fragments of obliterated ships floated about. A gleaming Republic flotilla was nestled in amidst the wreckage.

"I wasn't about to let you murder anyone else," Nick said.

"It's not murder," Sinclair retorted, "It's an awakening. Those people are slaves to the Republic and the corporations for which it stands."

"I'm sure killing them will open their eyes and make them sympathetic with your cause," Nick said. Fire seemed to be shooting through his abdomen. Nick's arm shook and threatened to give out, but Max put his hands on Nick's shoulders and eased him onto his back. Eleanor rushed over.

"What can I do?" She asked, tears streaming down her face.

"I don't know," Max said softly, "Help me keep pressure on it."

"The only thing you'll be able to do is let him die," Sinclair said.

"Christ, Doc," Max said, "I think that's enough."

"No," Sinclair said, "There will never be enough. There will never be enough blood, Max. Not until I bleed every last drop of blood out of the walking corpses that inhabit the Republic."

"Doc, what the hell is wrong with you?" Max asked. "How could you do this?"

"Because they took my son!" Sinclair thundered. "Because they took from me the one thing that mattered most and then denied me the means to make him whole again! I could have saved him, Max. I could have re-grown his damaged brain tissue, but they wouldn't let me do that. No, they hid behind their false morality and suggested I was a monster for trying to make him whole again. Just like you, I wanted my child back. My son was dead, but I didn't want a copy of him."

Sinclair walked over to Francis and looked up tenderly into the behemoth's eyes. Sinclair raised his old, fragile hand and placed it on Francis' cheek. He then ran his hand up and touched one of the misshapen nodules that dotted his son's forehead.

"My son died long ago, Max. This creature before you is a perverted facsimile of life, a bag of flesh and bones made to appear alive thanks to circuitry and programming. His emotional, physical, and mental responses are the outcomes from a series of algorithms I wrote myself.

"Francis feels what he is programmed to feel, he reacts how he is programmed to react, and he fights how he is programmed to fight. His brain was a prototype for the brain of my creations. It took me years to refine the code, until Francis' responses were indistinguishable from the average person.

"I wanted my son back and because of their meddling this was the best I could do. They took him from me. They robbed me of who he truly was and who he could have been. For that, I'll kill every single one of them."

Max looked down at Nick and swallowed hard; Nick could see the concern in his face. The pressure in Nick's abdomen seemed to be building. His stomach felt like it was about to explode.

"Don't you think I know how you feel?" Max asked Sinclair. "God damn. Every person in the damn valley knows how you feel."

"I'm not looking for empathy, Max."

A chime sounded throughout the room. Sinclair looked at his wrist computer.

"Please, just give him some regen pills, Doc," Max said.

Sinclair ignored him and received the incoming transmission. The far end of the room suddenly blurred and a three-dimensional, photorealistic projection of the bridge of a Republic flagship appeared. A tall, severe looking woman, dressed in her cleanly-pressed Republic uniform, stood in the center of the projection. The silver-haired, sharp-nosed woman took a measured step forward and stuck out her chin.

"Doctor Aldous Sinclair?"

Sinclair stepped forward and nodded his head.

"I should've known you'd get mixed up in this," Henry said.

"At least now you've finally found me," Nick said, "And you can stop with the veiled threats."

Henry sneered at him.

Nick stepped forward and stood inches from his father's projection. He stood up straight and looked down into his father's eyes.

"Even now, father, after everything that's happened, your first thought is about how you can profit from this. To hell with the people who died. You need to stake your claim."

"You're a naïve jackass," Henry responded, "A spoiled little boy who clearly was not taught enough about the realities of the galaxy."

Nick laughed slightly and that small movement of the muscles in his abdomen sent waves of pain throughout his body. He winced momentarily.

"I've learned a lot in recent weeks and I've had a lot of time to think about you. A new friend of mine asked me if I thought your greed, your wanton avarice, was unique to you or whether it was a part of your corporate culture. I think that answer is pretty clear now."

"Please forgive my son for interrupting this conversation with our little family squabble. He's a bit of a fool," Henry said, with an embarrassed shrug.

"No," Nick said, "This isn't just about you, about us. This is about what you've done to people, what your Conglomerate does."

Nick pulled the data crystal out of his pocket. He held it up in front of his father's projection.

"This is what you've been after, father," Nick said, "This is why you've been chasing me for the last few weeks. All your files are here. Records of every development project the

Conglomerate has undertaken under your leadership. Data from every test, logs full of observations, risk assessments, budget assessments, personnel files, everything. This is why you couldn't just let me walk away."

Henry's jaw was set and he stared at his son with his iron gaze. "You're right, son. This isn't about me. Those files you hold…in the wrong hands, they could damage the lives of so many. This has never been about me. It's been about the safety of the people.

"The Conglomerate works every day to better people's lives and some of the work we do, some of the things we delve into, would be extremely dangerous if exploited. I needed to get those back, not to protect me, but to protect everyone. You've got a good heart son, but there's so much you don't know."

Doubt crept into Nick's expression. He looked at the crystal, so small in his hand, and then back at his father.

"You're a liar," Nick said, "You always have been. Doctor Sinclair, do you have a crystal reader?"

Sinclair hesitated a moment and looked at Nick with a furrowed brow.

"Yes," he finally stammered, "Yes, I do."

Nick held the crystal out to him. After another moment's hesitation, Sinclair took the crystal from Nick's hand.

"Take this and broadcast its contents on an open frequency. Show the galaxy my father's actions. Let's show them what the Conglomerate is truly capable of."

"You're disgusting," Henry said, glaring, "Aiding a terrorist, a man who is responsible for the deaths of hundreds of Republic citizens. Dooming so many others to the same fate. I am ashamed to call you my son."

"Come now, father," Nick said, "You've killed thousands. If what you're saying is true, I'm merely following in your footsteps. I've read these files over and over again as I tried to digest the horrors you've perpetrated in the name of profit. I've read them so many times that I've memorized them. I recall one vividly."

Nick closed his eyes and tilted his head to the left.

"In limited trials, the serum enhances aggressive tendencies in subjects beyond the point of which they are able to control them. In subsequent combat trials, subjects lose the ability to fight with discipline and follow even the most basic of orders; instead they revert to a base instinct that drives them to destroy any perceived threat, which in this case is any other living thing.

"Those were the words of your project lead. Yet, you still gave the go ahead to do widespread human trials. Why don't you tell everyone what the results were?"

"This is preposterous," Henry said, "Commander that data crystal contains top secret information that could threaten the security of the Republic. It must not be broadcast."

Nick limped back over to his father's projection.

"You didn't answer my question, father," Nick said, "Why don't you tell everyone what the results were? Why don't you tell them how many people died?"

"I don't have to answer to you. You always were a disappointment. You never have understood that there are consequences for your actions."

"Nothing you could ever do to me would be worse than what I've been through these past two weeks. You don't scare me anymore."

Nick felt like he was supposed to be angry, but he felt strangely calm. After a moment, he looked away from his father over to Sinclair. The old man was standing over a console browsing through the files on the crystal.

"You see, Doctor Sinclair, you went about this all wrong. Attacking the Republic with violence won't get you anywhere. It only turns people against you and hides the real monsters. What you need to do is hold up a mirror and show the people who the monsters really are. Send those files out, Doctor. Send them to everyone."

Sinclair nodded and, moments later, activated the broadcast.

"Commander!" Henry yelled, "Stop that transmission!"

Commander Dorn had watched all of this with an impassive glare, but as Henry shouted orders at her, she visibly recoiled. She gestured at her communications officer and the projection faded away.

"You do not give me orders," Dorn bellowed.

Henry had a hard time taking her seriously. She seemed like too many other self-important career government flunkies. But, he needed her support here. There was too much at stake.

"I apologize, Commander," Henry said with practiced sincerity, "I overstepped. You must forgive me. My son's involvement in this has me a bit unsettled."

The Commander's expression softened slightly.

"That is understandable," she said.

"Are you familiar with Project Vanguard?" He asked.

"Should I be?"

"It is designated priority one by the Defense Department," Henry said, trying not to let his impatience show, "My son stumbled onto those files without knowing what he had found. Those files cannot be released to the public. This transmission must be stopped."

The political officer seated to the Commander's left cleared his throat.

"Excuse me a second," she said and then muted the audio link. Henry watched as Dorn and her political officer had a brief discussion. Henry tried to look both nervous and remorseful. He didn't want her to see the excitement that he was barely able to contain.

A chime sounded signaling that the audio link had been restored.

"I believe I understand the situation now, Mr. Papagous," Commander Dorn said, "We will do what is necessary to stop the transmission. And we'll do what we can to get your son out of there."

"Thank you," Henry said with a relieved smile.

"They've launched missiles," Sinclair reported.

A tactical projection appeared above the conference table. A blue, wireframe model of the entire compound hovered over the tabletop. Sinclair sent a few commands and missile batteries deployed from the tops of the towers along the perimeter of the landing field. Within seconds, intercept missiles fired.

The projection zoomed out with dizzying speed and the Republic missiles appeared as incoming red dots, streaking towards the compound. The interceptors quickly met them and the Republic missiles disappeared from existence.

Sinclair smiled and Nick let out a breath he didn't realize he was holding. When he did, pain flared in his abdomen and he dropped to one knee. Max scurried over and helped Nick into one of the chairs around the table. He looked Nick in the eye.

"You did good, kid," Max said, "I'm proud of you."

"Commander," Henry implored, "Please, time is of the essence. Perhaps you could just deactivate the jump beacon and prevent the transmission from leaving the system."

"I will not cut off my only link with the rest of the Republic," she said, "I assure you we are working to resolve this situation as quickly as possible. Now please, let me do my job."

"My apologies, Commander."

Dorn seemed satisfied and looked toward an unseen crewmember.

"Are we in range for a plasma barrage?"

"We will be in less than a minute, ma'am," the crewman responded.

"Launch when we're in range. What's our window?"

"Five minutes, ma'am."

"Rain fire on them until they go dark and if they don't, drop us down into a lower orbit and bring us around for another pass."

"What is it?" Nick asked.

Sinclair was furiously sending commands through his console. The tactical projection shifted to an image of the landing pad. Twenty-four pristine shuttles and the *Hannah* sat there. There was no movement on the pad; it might as well have been a still photo.

"Brace yourselves," Sinclair said softly.

Moments later, streaks of yellow entered the picture and the landing pad erupted in fire. Bolts of plasma rained across the pad and the surrounding mountaintops. Blossoms of fire sprang up across the hillsides. Two shuttles disappeared in a single fireball, leaving nothing but a smoking crater behind. Another bolt sliced through one of the guard towers. The floor of the control room shook slightly.

Plasma charges continued to streak down leaving craters in the landing pad and incinerating anything they touched. The mountain shook as a barrage landed somewhere above them.

Then, another plasma charge struck the back half of the *Hannah*, melting through the hull. A gaping hole opened on her backside and some of the rear landing gear crumpled. The ship canted; it's nose lifted in the air.

"No!" Max screamed. "No! Goddamn it! No!"

The barrage stopped. Max stood mouth agape, staring at the image of his wrecked ship.

"I'm sorry, Max," Nick said.

"Christ, I don't believe it," Max said as he rubbed his forehead, "What the hell am I going to do now?"

"I don't know, but I doubt you were going to do any more shipping runs out here anyway," Nick said with a wry grin.

Sinclair brought up another projection, this one of Dust from orbit. The orbit of the Republic fleet was highlighted in yellow with little red dots highlighting the position of the ships. The orbit lines suddenly shifted.

"They'll be in range again in 30 minutes," Sinclair reported.

A few red dots had broken away from the main fleet and were now on a re-entry trajectory. Sinclair looked around at his son.

"Francis," Sinclair said, "Ready your troops."

Francis nodded and left the room. Wally and Gordo shook excitedly but remained behind. Nick eyed them nervously and then doubled-over as a fresh bolt of pain seized him. His stomach let loose its contents. The room suddenly felt like it was ten degrees hotter.

Max tore his attention from the monitor.

"Doc, please," Max said, "Give him some regen pills. He doesn't need to die today."

Sinclair didn't turn from his console. He took a deep breath and then shook his head slowly.

"Why should I do that, Max? What makes you think anything has changed?"

"Doc, he just gave you all that data, the stuff you're now broadcasting to all corners of the Republic. The stuff that'll help you accomplish what you were really after."

"Max, be quiet and enjoy the time you have left to live. Expect no other gifts from me today."

Max gritted his teeth and rolled his eyes.

"Don't worry about it, Max," Nick said, "I wasn't trying to win him over."

"If I had my atomizer, I'd blast him into a million pieces right now."

Nick offered him a faint smile. "But those things are still watching."

Nick pointed at Wally and Gordo who had shifted their attention to the monitors as the feed showed Francis awakening the slumbering army of Sinclair's creations. They started bobbing from side to side and Max felt a chill run down his spine.

Eleanor tugged at his arm. Max looked away from the creatures and saw that she was pointing to the far wall. Mounted on the wall on the other end of the room next to the elevator doors was a first aid kit. Max patted her head and smiled. He leaned in close to Nick.

"You're going to be all right, kid. Just hang in there."

Two Republic troop transports swooped in and set down on the far edge of the landing field. The sides and top of each ship quickly slid open and four squads of combat drones spilled out onto the field. They immediately fanned out and started making their way forward through the twisted hulks of wreckage that now covered the landing pad.

Once all the drones had deployed, Sinclair activated an electromagnetic pulse. The drones stopped their approach. The monitor showed indicator lights on the drones' robotic heads switch from green to yellow. Within seconds, the lights switched back to green and the drones continued their approach.

"Damn," Sinclair said. He established a link with Francis. "There are 32 Howitzer-class assault drones on the pad, advancing in spread formation."

"Copy," Francis responded.

The hangar doors opened slightly and Francis dispatched three squads of the creatures. Their advance across the pad was not nearly as choreographed as the drones. Several of the creatures immediately scaled onto the tops of the few remaining transports. Six of the creatures split into groups of two and setup mortar positions.

The combat drones reached the midpoint of the pad and the creatures opened fire. The mortars fired little silver spheres that exploded into clouds of gray mist. The mist latched on to anything it came in contact with and started eating through it. A group of four drones were funneled through some wreckage and then disappeared as the cloud of nanite gobblers ate through their casings.

Another group of drones setup a firing position behind the splayed hull of a destroyed transport. They spewed forth a burst of flame that incinerated two advancing creatures.

Elsewhere on the pad a creature leapt from atop a transport onto the back of a drone. It lashed out with its talons and tore the optics from the drone's head.

The battle was engaged and Sinclair smiled at the carnage. His creations were beautiful. He smiled at the scene that unfolded until plasma charges started raining from the sky.

The Republic fleet was unleashing another wave of destruction upon the compound. Sinclair bashed a fist against the console as two of the mortar teams and the transports they were on disappeared in a gigantic explosion.

Even with explosions erupting around them, Sinclair's creatures fought without fear. They bobbed and weaved and jumped through the raging inferno and took out the drones that remained. The combat drones were relentless in their forward march, but they couldn't match the creatures' bloodlust. Before the last plasma barrage hit the pad, the last of the combat drones had been destroyed.

The console chimed.

"Give yourself up, Doctor," Commander Dorn said.

"Not until you drag my dead body out of this room," Sinclair replied.

"You can't win."

"Then I'll take as many of you as I can with me into oblivion."

"Commander, I'd ask that you send in your commando units," Henry said.

Dorn blanched again and her face briefly flashed from pale white to beet red. She didn't lash out though; she breathed deeply through flared nostrils. She calmly laced her fingers behind her back and took a step toward the camera.

When she spoke, the words were enunciated slowly and precisely.

"You do not give me orders. I am in charge of this fleet."

"Commander, I am merely observing that our combat drones are proving to be very ineffective against these creatures. It's clear their combat capabilities are superior. To beat these things and, might I remind you, to shutdown the transmission, we're going to need to send in better troops."

"I believe those drones are produced by the Conglomerate," the Commander said.

"You are correct and believe me when I say that I am disappointed in their performance. We will, of course, use this data to improve their combat algorithms. There have been very few opportunities to collect data from live engagements."

Another round of troop transports arrived at the landing field, this time accompanied by armored vehicles. Dozens of flesh and blood soldiers swarmed out on to the landing field with two hovertank units providing covering fire. Within seconds, the pad was ablaze with conflict.

Sinclair's entire army of creatures poured onto the pad, moving swiftly into combat positions. The Republic tanks opened fire with plasma barrages aimed at the hangar. A dozen creatures disappeared from existence as the rear of Sinclair's force was engulfed in flame. A plasma barrage hit the descending hangar door, denting it severely and leaving it stuck halfway open.

Recognizing that they were outgunned, Sinclair's army charged toward the advancing Republic soldiers. The creatures were a screaming, screeching, writhing mass of black feathers and razor sharp talons. When the soldiers and the creatures engaged in hand-to-hand, close quarters combat, the fighting was brutal and bloody.

Nick, Max, and Eleanor's eyes were transfixed on the monitors. Gordo and Wally nervously tittered in the background. Nick cast a nervous glance at the creatures. They were brutal killers on the battlefield as they kicked, slashed, and sliced their way through the ranks of the men.

Max turned away from the monitors; his face had paled and he looked ready to throw-up. He put his hands on Eleanor's shoulders and turned her away from the monitors. She hugged him fiercely.

Nick watched the horrifying scenes through gritted teeth. He watched as a creature jumped onto the back of an unsuspecting soldier, dug its talons into the man's back and yanked on his spine. The man died screaming. Nick couldn't stand to watch any longer.

"This is what my father is here for," Nick said as he tried once again to stand. His legs trembled from the effort and Max had to help him up. "Doctor, this is what my father wants more than anything. And he's going to take what you tried to use against the Republic and turn it into their greatest weapon."

Sinclair frowned and said, "You're talking nonsense. The Republic doesn't have the brainpower to create anything half as good as what I've done here."

"Which is precisely why they'll take it from you."

"I won't let them."

"That won't stop them," Nick said, "My father has never been shy about seizing opportunities and that's what you've presented him with here today. Think about the note I quoted earlier. He was making soldiers. That's what his experiments were about. And now, you've given him a demonstration of a soldier far more powerful than anything he was able to create."

Sinclair finally looked away from the monitors into Nick's pale, waxy expression. For the first time today, the old Doctor looked uncertain.

"They will come here, Doctor, and take everything you've worked on over the decades. They will take your data, your prototypes, and anything else that may help them. They'll go through every last little nugget of information they can glean from you. They'll take what you've done and turn it into something better. It's what they do; it's how they stay on top."

Sinclair turned back to the monitors and watched as a team of creatures swarmed onto one of the hovertanks. The tank fired off another plasma bolt before the creatures tore open the top hatch and shredded the pilots.

"What you wanted to tear down, Doctor, will only become stronger."

Nick swallowed. His mouth seemed suddenly full of saliva. He tasted a metallic tang. Sweat was running down his face in tiny rivers. His jaw was clenched tight as he fought through the pain that enveloped him.

Sinclair stood at his console with his head hung low and his eyes closed.

"I know you plan on dying today," Nick said, "Don't make things worse for everyone else just because you've given up. Don't give them what they want."

Eleanor stood still as Nick and Max continued their slow walk towards the Doctor. She looked over at Wally and Gordo; their attention was fully on the battle playing out on the monitors. Their heads grotesquely swiveled from one picture to the next. Wally's head tilted as it watched the first tank get overtaken.

Cautiously, she took a step towards the lift, towards the first aid kit. No one reacted. She looked at Nick. The rag Max had pressed against his wound was now completely red. Nick had started shivering; Max was rubbing Nick's arms in an attempt to warm him up.

She started to feel tears welling up. She couldn't just stand here anymore. Eleanor ran toward the kit.

The control room erupted in flame. Max heard a giant crack behind them as a plasma bolt from the remaining hovertank struck the observation window and sliced through the room. He felt a wave of heat slam into him. Then, he heard Eleanor scream as the bolt tore through the room and into the bank of monitors.

Max let go of Nick as he instinctively covered his head to protect against the incoming barrage of rock, glass, and metal. The bank of monitors exploded in a shower of sparks. Something slammed into him and he hit the floor hard, knocking the breath from his lungs. He laid on the floor with his eyes closed, arms covering his head, and knees tucked into his chest as the room was torn apart in the explosion.

After a few moments, Max opened his eyes as Aldous Sinclair shrieked in pain. Max looked over at where Eleanor had been; his heart dropped when he only saw a charred stump. Then, the sounds of her sobs reached his ears and he saw her crouched against the far wall. He looked back at the stump and then found the other half of one of Sinclair's creatures on the other side of the room.

He slowly got to his feet as he found Sinclair writhing in pain on the floor. The back half of the man's body was burned and riddled with broken glass and plastic.

"It's what you deserve," Max whispered.

Max turned and looked for Nick. He had landed a few feet behind him. He was face-down, unmoving. Max scrambled over to him.

"Eleanor," Max called out, "The kit!"

He gestured toward it and she found the courage to yank it off the wall and come running toward him. Sinclair's remaining creation watched as Eleanor ran but otherwise did not respond.

"Nick…come on, kid," Max said nervously. He reached down and grabbed his shoulder. Nick didn't move. He felt for a pulse but found none.

"No, kid, please."

Max gestured frantically towards Eleanor.

"Give me the defib patches!"

She opened the kit and hesitated.

Max gestured to a pair of large white patches emblazoned with a large red cross. He took them from her trembling hands and placed one on either side of Nick's chest. He didn't bother to remove Nick's coverall; it would take too much time. They weren't supposed to need direct skin contact anyway. Still, he hesitated a moment before putting his thumb to the activation pad on the center of the patch. A red light started blinking and Max pulled his hand back.

Nick's muscles contracted and his chest violently heaved upward.

Max and Eleanor waited, but nothing happened. After several moments, Max put his thumb to the activation pad again.

Nick's muscles contracted again. Five seconds passed and Nick still lay there unmoving.

Max grabbed the kit and tore it open, looking at each vial and packet and then throwing them aside.

"What are you looking for?" Eleanor asked.

"I have no idea," Max said as he went from one item to the next. He tried to read the labels, but he grew frustrated at how long it was taking to find something useful. Max turned Nick over and placed his ear to his chest. He didn't hear a sound. Tears welled up in Max's eyes.

"Christ, kid," Max said.

Max placed his hand on Nick's shoulder. He wanted to shake Nick until he opened his eyes. Eleanor held a syringe out to him. He scanned the contents - adrenalin, pain inhibitors, regen nanites - and decided this was the best he could do. He raised the syringe up when Sinclair spoke.

"Max…wait."

Sinclair screamed in pain as he tried to get to his knees. Max swung his head around; his cheeks were red with fury.

"Not now, Doc," Max said, not taking his eyes from Nick.

"Max, please…you must give me the shot."

Max looked over at Sinclair, his face flush with anger.

"Do you actually expect me to help you?" Max asked. "I wouldn't piss on you if you were on fire."

Sinclair's voice was a raspy whisper.

"I am…the only one…who can destroy this place. Your friend…is beyond help."

Max knelt there and looked at the syringe. He looked at Eleanor's tear-streaked face and then back to Nick's unmoving body. He leaned over and placed his hand on Nick's neck again; he felt nothing.

"I'm sorry, kid," Max said, "I'm so sorry."

Max reached down and lifted Nick up, wrapping his arms around him. He hugged the young man close and then gently lowered his body to the floor. Then, Max slowly stood up, watching Sinclair writhe in agony. The old Doctor's back was now exposed, the flesh charred; Max had to cover his nose from the sickly sweet smell. Bits of green and black were embedded in his skin. Max wanted the Doctor to feel every second of pain, but he knew Sinclair was right.

"Max…please."

Max held the syringe in a white knuckled grip as he knelt next to Sinclair. He looked into the old man's clouded, blood-filled eyes with pure hate. Then, he raised the syringe and plunged it into Sinclair's back. Sinclair howled in pain and then fell silent.

Max sat back when Francis burst into the room. Francis, blood-stained and covered in sweat and grime, stood in the debris strewn doorway and searched for his father. When he finally saw his father lying unconscious with the empty syringe sticking out of his back, his remaining human eye went wide and his face contorted into a mixture of disbelief and horror.

Francis charged across the room toward Max as he let out an inhuman growl. Max pushed Eleanor away and just tried to go limp as the behemoth crushed him. Air was once again knocked forcefully from his lungs. Pain exploded in his shoulder as Francis drove him into the floor.

Francis moved with blinding speed and knelt over Max, pinning him down. Francis raised his right fist when the elder Sinclair's faint voice cried out.

"Stop, Francis."

Francis was barely able to stop his swing. He whirled his head around and looked into his father's eyes. He scrambled off of Max and over to his wounded father.

"Father?"

"Help me up," Sinclair said.

Max blinked to try and clear the stars from his eyes. When Francis was at a safe distance, Eleanor ran to his side with pain pills in hand. He swallowed them dry and they went down rough and slow, scraping the walls of his throat as they went down. He was able to sit up as Sinclair was led to one of the remaining operational consoles in the room.

A chime sounded, but no holoprojection appeared.

"Commander Dorn," Sinclair said, "I surrender."

"Stop the transmission," Dorn ordered.

Sinclair pushed another button.

"Stand down your troops."

Francis looked at him questioningly and Sinclair simply nodded at him.

"In work," Sinclair reported.

"Troops will be on the ground shortly to secure the facility. If we detect any resumption of hostilities, I will grind you into dust."

The transmission was ended, but Sinclair continued to work at the console. Francis fetched Sinclair a chair to sit in and a fresh lab coat. Under normal circumstances, putting any clothing over those wounds would be pure agony, but Max knew that the shot he had just given Sinclair was inhibiting any pain. He could go over and cut the old man's finger off and he wouldn't feel a thing. He was tempted to do just that.

Max got up from the floor with a grunt and a helping hand from Eleanor.

"What now?" She asked. Max shrugged.

With the Doctor taken care of, Francis set off again. Max looked out the gaping hole that was once the observation window and saw the creatures filing in. Francis was shepherding them into their ranks and the creatures bobbed into place.

After an extra moment of uncomfortable silence, Sinclair swiveled his chair toward Max and extended his hand. Resting in his palm was Nick's data crystal.

"Take this, Max," Sinclair said with a harsh rasp, "And get off this world."

Max looked at Sinclair skeptically.

"What is it?"

"This is all of my data, all of my research, all of the results from my experiments. This is everything you need to recreate my discoveries, my inventions. This must stay out of the hands of the Republic… the Conglomerate. Your friend was right; I will not serve them."

Max slowly picked up the crystal from Sinclair's palm and held it up, looking at the light gleam off its surface.

"This is a little bit like giving a dog a spaceship, Doctor. Not sure what I can do with this."

"What you do with it is up to you. Just don't let it fall into their hands. Now, get out of here. There are two operational ships on the pad. Take one and go. You've probably only got 20 minutes or so before more troops arrive."

Max put the crystal in a pocket of his coveralls and started to turn toward the exit.

"There's one more thing, Max," Sinclair said, "My ships are…different. Once you reach orbit, enter your destination. The ship will take care of the rest."

Max nodded, took another step, and stopped again.

"Do something for me, Doc," Max said, "Send a message to Resurrection. I'll take anyone who's willing to leave, but they need to be ready to go in the next hour."

Sinclair nodded. Max hesitated and looked around the room. He opened his mouth to speak but nothing came out. He had no witty remark for this occasion. Instead, he turned his attention back to Nick. He knelt back down beside the young man and put his hand on his friend's forehead.

"I'm proud of you, Nick," he whispered, "You were a hero today. I'm sorry, though. Sorry I didn't do better by you."

He hated to leave Nick's body, but he had no choice. Max stood up, grabbed Eleanor's hand, and the two of them ran from the room. He wiped his eyes on his sleeve as he left the room.

CHAPTER 14

As Max and Eleanor ran from the open hangar door, Max skidded to a halt. Seeing the carnage on the monitors was horrifying, but seeing it in person was absolutely devastating. His knees weakened at the sight of the death and destruction that covered the once pristine landing pad. Max had to blink back more tears as he tried to figure out what to do.

He looked at his wrist computer and picked out the locations of the two operational ships. Before he took one, he had to make one last stop. Max ran to the *Hannah*, which was now a hole-ridden wreck on the pad. The cargo section had been completely pulverized with more than a dozen holes in the hull. Somewhere in the fighting, the cockpit was completely disintegrated. Max could look right down the central corridor from where he stood.

Max ran his hand along the hull; she would be missed.

The entry ramp was down and Max quickly scrambled up the ramp to his quarters. His bag was still on the floor of his room which was more or less intact. He took one last look around, grabbed his bag, and left.

Max bounded down the corridor and noticed Reggie crumpled in a heap next to his charging station. He knelt down beside the robot and pushed his thumb to the power-on control switch. Reggie's eyes immediately lit up.

"Hello, sir," Reggie said, "I didn't think I'd see you again."

"Same here," Max said, "Can you walk?"

"I believe so, sir," Reggie responded, "Though don't ask me to carry anything. The hydraulics in my arms are shot."

Max smiled. "That's okay, Reggie. But we do need to get the hell out of here."

Max helped the robot up and got blue fluid from the robot's damaged arm all over his hands. A moment later, they left the *Hannah* for the final time. Eleanor beamed at Reggie as he emerged from the ship. She ran over and gave the robot a hug, getting a coating of the leaking fluid on her arms.

"Where is Nick?" Reggie asked.

Max grimaced. "I'll fill you in on the way."

Five minutes later, Max powered up one of Sinclair's sleek shuttles and was on his way back to Resurrection. Max turned the ship to the east and headed for the coast. He checked the ship's radar and saw that the second shuttle, piloted by Reggie, had also lifted off. Max instinctively reached to his right to open a comm. channel, but of course it wasn't there.

He had to look around the displays on his console for a moment before he found the right control.

"How's the ship, Reggie?"

"Operating within parameters," the robot responded, "This ship is…interesting. I'm trying to go through some of the code now, but it is safe to say the Doctor Sinclair has designed some of these systems himself."

"Well, you can give me a rundown later," Max said, "For now, let's get in and out of Resurrection as quickly as we can."

Dust's sun was low over the horizon; night would be upon them soon.

An hour after the battalion of Republic Commandos arrived at the Sinclair stronghold, the unit captain sent a message back to the Republic flagship. The facility was secure. The creatures were sitting dormant inside the hangar facility; their cybernetic brains had been powered down. They still made the troops nervous though and two squads stood watch over the creatures.

Sinclair didn't blame them. If he had his druthers, he would have reactivated them here and now and then let the creatures feast on these men. But Sinclair knew he would be dead before his hand left the face of his wrist computer. Then the Republic would seize everything he had ever developed and hand it over to the Conglomerate.

So Sinclair lay patiently on his stomach in a makeshift medical tent while a medic tended to his wounds. He listened as reports from soldiers flooded back to the captain. Their scans revealed no activity, no fail-safes ready to engage.

Sinclair listened as this was radioed in to the flagship and then he heard the report that the Conglomerate shuttle had been dispatched. Henry Papagous would be on-station soon. He and his team were to have full access to the facility.

Henry's small shuttle touched down on the pad and Sinclair watched as the overconfident ass puffed his chest out and marched down the entry ramp like a conquering hero. Sinclair tried to sit up, but the Republic medic refused to let him.

"Doctor," Henry said with a smile and a nod, "Thank you for being reasonable about this. I think we can make this situation beneficial for both of us."

Sinclair simply nodded. Henry looked over at Francis and recoiled ever-so-slightly at his gray, waxy complexion and wandering, robotic eye. Francis sneered. Henry's confident expression wavered and he quickly looked back to Sinclair.

"Your son fought well today."

"Yes, my son," Aldous said, "As did yours."

Henry nodded. "And where is he?"

"He is dead," Sinclair said, "His body is in my control room off the main hangar. If you need to visit with him…"

Henry waved him off and said, "No, that's okay. My son and I have had our issues as you could tell. He died to me long ago."

Sinclair's lip twitched slightly. He looked over at Francis, who was looking back at him with great concern.

"My son also died long ago, Henry, but I loved him more than anything in the galaxy. I didn't want to let him die."

Henry smiled politely. "Yes, well…"

"I wonder, Henry, if my wife and I had had another child, would I have felt the need to do this. No child can replace another, but we would have still had our sense of family."

"It is an interesting philosophical debate," Henry said. His impatience was palpable.

"I think, Henry," Aldous said, "That you deserve this more than I do. Francis, end protocol."

At the command, Francis' eyes closed. A moment later, an electronic squeal erupted around the facility. The Republic troops brought their weapons to bear. Henry started looking around in a panic. A second later, the ground beneath them softened, turning from a hard, black surface to an oily ooze in which they all - Sinclair, Henry, Francis, the Republic Commandos, and all of Aldous's creations - started to sink.

Sinclair looked up again at Francis and said, "I love you, son."

Henry tried to take a step back towards his shuttle and noticed that the bottom of his boot had liquefied. A second later, Henry felt an excruciating burning sensation on the bottoms of his feet. Then he heard a loud metallic shriek as the foot of the landing strut for his craft was eaten off and the ship tilted backward.

Henry screamed shrilly as nanites ate through his feet. The screams of the other men joined him. Moments later, the screech of collapsing metal was heard as the structural integrity of the hangar was compromised. The screech of metal was soon eclipsed by the roar of a landslide as the mountain collapsed on top of them.

Max sat at the console in his new shuttle, poring over data. He had already calculated the exact moment in time that they needed to lift off in order to give them the best chance of escape. Reggie had been able to extract orbital data on the Republic fleet from Sinclair's remaining satellites. They needed any advantage they could get to give them the best chance of reaching orbit and heading to freedom without Republic interference.

In the reflection off the white glass top of his console, he could see Sharon standing in the hatchway. She stood there silently for a moment, arms folded across her chest, while he continued to work. She looked at him with cautious, weary gratefulness.

Sharon and Hannah had been at the front of the crowd when he landed in the little alcove on the coast. Doctor Sinclair had followed through on Max's last request; he sent the evacuation alarm to Resurrection, initiating a decades old protocol that hadn't been practiced in years. The message was simple - the Republic was invading, get out while you can.

Max was originally worried that he would have to turn thousands of people away, but much to his disappointment, there were maybe a hundred people ready to leave.

"They don't want to go," Mayor Andrews had said, "They'd rather take their chances with the Republic."

Max had looked back at the path leading to Resurrection. He felt the urge to run through the town, to knock on doors, and pull people out of their homes. But Max knew better, some people were happy in their little world and would only be dragged from it kicking and screaming.

He looked back at Sharon, who gave him a tentative smile. There was no hug when she saw him at the pad, no moment where she leaped into his arms. She just looked at him with a mixture of guilt and remorse.

"I'm sorry," she said, "I'm sorry I didn't believe you."

Max nodded his head in response. His emotions were raw; the pain of this ordeal was too fresh in his mind.

"Where's your friend?" She asked.

"His name was Nick," Max said, "He didn't make it."

She didn't say anything for a moment; there wasn't much she could say. She hadn't known Nick, hadn't known what they'd been through. She barely knew Max anymore, but she knew that he was hurting. She had seen the hollow look in his eyes many years before.

"I'm sorry," she said again.

Max nodded in return and turned back to his console. Sharon's reflection slipped away. Max's gaze lingered momentarily on the spot where Sharon had been before he glanced over at Eleanor, sitting next to him in the co-pilot's seat.

"Eleanor," Max said, "I'm sorry, but we're going to need to make another stop before I take you home."

"I understand," she said.

The only question that remained was where to go. The families that were getting settled on to the shuttles would need to go somewhere out of the Republic eye. Chances were that this scandal, once it became public knowledge, would trigger a momentary high degree of vigilance from the government. They couldn't count on taking refuge in a backwater world. People's eyes would be open.

They had to go somewhere else. Max really only saw one option.

"I don't know how we're going to get past this fleet," Max said.

"After reviewing the navigational code, sir," Reggie said, "I don't think that's going to be a problem."

"What do you mean?"

"It's complicated, but Doctor Sinclair has made some radical improvements to the jump drive. I don't think we need the beacon to jump."

Max whistled.

Sharon appeared again behind him and cleared her throat to get his attention.

Max arched his eyebrows questioningly.

"Everyone's aboard and as secure as they're going to get," she said.

"Very good," Max said, "We leave in ten minutes, that'll be the next window. Have everyone sit tight. We'll take any stragglers that come along if they can get aboard in time. How many are there?"

"86."

Max scratched the back of his head. Thousands of people were going to be left behind.

"Best we could hope for, I suppose," Max said.

"What about Windy City or Fracture?" she asked.

"I've sent an emergency broadcast to all the settlements. Told them to get out while they can," Max replied, "I don't think it'll do much good."

Sharon nodded.

"Thank you," she said and then walked slowly away.

The shuttle took off smoothly, save for a slight shimmy on the right side during liftoff. Max made a mental note to have Reggie check out the vector control nozzles on the starboard side thruster array. An indicator light on his console told Max that Reggie had a solid link with his flight computer; Max still preferred to confirm that himself.

"How are you doing, Reggie?" Max asked.

"Good, Captain," Reggie responded, "We'll be able to make the jump in approximately eight minutes."

The time matched the countdown clock on Max's console. Max turned his attention to the trajectory display. Their flight path remained clear. If the calculations were correct, the Republic fleet would be on the other side of the planet at this point.

The cockpit door opened and Eleanor took a tentative step in. Max glanced back and frowned.

"You should be strapped in during liftoff and ascent," Max said, fairly sternly.

"There's too many people back there," Eleanor said, "Mind if I sit up here?"

Max thought about sending her back; this was no place for a little girl. The cockpit could erupt into chaos at any moment. A failed thruster here, a reactor overload there, and the whole operation could turn into one giant flail in a heartbeat. Of course, with everything else that she'd been through these past few days, any of those problems would seem like nothing.

"Hurry up and strap in," Max said, "If you're going to spend time on a spaceship, you have to remember the rules, young woman. You never wander around when the ship is in powered flight, it's just not safe."

Eleanor smiled and hopped into the co-pilot's seat, taking Max's lecture in stride.

"I'm not going to be a pilot," she said, straining to look out the window, "I'm going to build robots, remember?"

"Right," Max said with a smile. He watched her out of the corner of his eye as they thundered through Dust's atmosphere and entered orbit. Her face lit up with wondrous awe as the space around them faded from blue to black. Dust's primary star dawned on the western horizon, its brilliant light reflecting off the planet's thin atmosphere.

"It's beautiful," she said softly.

Max's proximity display beeped; chunks of debris littered their orbital path. Then Max noticed something else; another ship, one of the fast attack interceptors, was in a trailing orbit. An alert for an incoming message flashed on his console. Eleanor stared at Max as he thought about what to do. He silenced the alert and ignored it. Four more minutes until the jump.

The drives for the two small shuttles kept firing, pushing them beyond low Dust orbit and farther into space. The planet was receding into the background and soon would not be visible from the cockpit. Max couldn't help but stare for a minute.

Dust had been his home for ten years. He had been carrying the burden of his daughter's death with him on every journey back and forth to this planet. With every garnished payday, he was reminded of his indentured servitude to the Doctor. He had essentially resigned himself to living out the rest of his life ferrying goods back and forth to Sinclair's stronghold.

Now, that was done. He was free, free to live whatever life he chose.

The countdown clock was at thirty seconds. The Republic ship chasing them was still in pursuit, but was no real threat. The clock hit twenty seconds and Max looked over at Eleanor to make sure she was fastened in appropriately. At ten seconds, his eyes welled up as he realized he would never be back here again.

The clock hit zero and the two ships jumped.

EPILOGUE

Max sat in the cockpit of the shuttle, listening to the eerie sound of silence around him. The ship was empty, save for Reggie who was off in the rear of the ship inspecting the power core containment system. Eleanor had finally been returned to her father that morning, leaving Max all alone.

Her father was disappointed with Max's insistence that he did not want a hero's welcome. Max refused when he asked to have media coverage for the moment of landing. He just wanted to get Eleanor home, back with what family she had left.

Eleanor's face had lit up when she stepped on the bottom of the boarding ramp and saw her father standing there. It warmed Max's heart to see her run up to him and wrap her arms around him enthusiastically. They had asked him to stay that night, to at least enjoy a meal with them in thanks. Max refused. He had to get going; people were counting on him.

The little makeshift colony he and the other refugees from Dust had established on Maisha needed help to survive. They needed food, medicine, materials, clothes, and other staples of life. Max was back in business. He was once again shuttling between the stars, this time of his own choosing, which made all the difference in the world to him.

Maisha, Max thought, had been Nick's idea. It's a beautiful world, Nick; you would have loved the place.

Max shook her father's hand and started to turn back toward the ship, when Eleanor rushed up and enveloped him in the same hug she gave her father. She wished him and all the others good luck. That little girl was the only person in the galaxy who knew where they took refuge. It was a big secret for her, but Max knew she would do right by them.

He patted her on the back, gave her one last smile and wave, before disappearing up the ramp. Now all Max was left with were the ghosts of the memories in his head, the sound of Nick's boots stomping up and down the corridor or the sounds of Eleanor playing with Reggie. A wave of sadness washed over him. He finally broke the silence by turning on an updated news report.

A perky, blonde-haired reporter sat next to a projection of Dust. Max turned up the volume.

"Scandal rocks the Republic as more details emerge on the recently uncovered human cloning farm on the colony of Dust," she stated, "Over 500 cloned children have been positively identified. Turmoil gripped the Senate as they struggled to determine how to deal with this crisis."

The image shifted to that of a gray-haired, withered Senator who looked to have foregone any rejuvenation treatments, "These children are not children of God; they are children of men. As such they do not have the rights afforded to decent individuals of the Republic. Their continued existence is a mockery of all that is good in this universe.

"We uncovered over a hundred violations of Republic law at this colony from multiple child births to unlawful modification of the native environment. Clearly, we need to police these fringe colonies better. We can no longer tolerate these cesspools of crime along the frontier."

The image shifted again to another Senator, a white-haired woman, who stood tall before a gathered throng of reporters, "These are living, breathing children. We can't just slaughter them like animals. My colleagues continue to push the agenda of their corporate sponsors. Just because some don't want these children to exist, doesn't mean they shouldn't be allowed to live their lives."

"Senator," an off screen reporter questioned, "Shouldn't the parents be held responsible for bringing these children into the world illegally?"

The Senator thought for a moment before responding, "Sometimes, unjust laws are created in response to unjust times. Sometimes, we need to reconsider those laws and decide if they're for the greater good or not. I think this is one of those times."

The image shifted again to a tan-skinned middle-aged man with slicked-back dark hair. He stood at a dais in the Senate floor, addressing his colleagues.

"These children have no soul. They have no right to live. They are the product of a madman who set out to kill innocent members of our society. For all we know, each one of these children is a programmed automaton, ready to unleash an attack on the Republic at a moment's notice. They should all be destroyed.

"The entire colony should be destroyed. The cities of Dust should be razed and human life should never again walk on its surface. It is our duty as representatives of this Republic to make sure that happens.

"They may look like us, they make act like us, but they are not us. They are the grotesque results of man playing God."

The image shifted back to the reporter now with an image of the Marshall Conglomerate logo over her shoulder.

"The President of the Marshall Conglomerate released a statement today on the leaked internal documents that allegedly implicate some high ranking officials in the company in the deaths of thousands of human test subjects. In his prepared statement, he stated that the company is cooperating fully with authorities in the investigation of the incident, but that he is sure the company will be cleared of any wrong-doing."

Max shut off the report; he could no longer listen to the rhetoric. He turned back to his console and started running through some maintenance routines.

END

ABOUT THE AUTHOR

Jason T. Hutt is the author of two books and various pieces of short fiction. He resides in Houston, Texas with his wife, three daughters, 3 rescue dogs and a rescue cat. He grew up in Philadelphia and is an ardent supporter of the Philadelphia Eagles and Flyers despite the constant heartbreak and disappointment they routinely offer up.

He has worked in human spaceflight for almost two decades at NASA Johnson Space Center over which time he has supported the International Space Station operations and training and is currently working on the Orion program.

If he's not in meetings or behind a computer screen, you'll most likely find him hiking in the mountains or pulled over to the side of the road, waiting for roadside assistance.

Connect with me online:
Twitter: http://twitter.com/jhutt75
Facebook: http://fb.me/jasonthutt
Amazon: http://amazon.com/author/jasonhutt